JON DOBBIN

JON DOBBIN

BOOKS

Published in Canada by Engen Books, St. John's, NL.

Library and Archives Canada Cataloguing in Publication

Title: The risen / Jon Dobbin.
Names: Dobbin, Jon, 1982- author.
Identifiers: Canadiana (print) 2021024383X | Canadiana (ebook) 20210243910 |
ISBN 9781774780534
    (softcover) | ISBN 9781774780541 (PDF)
Classification: LCC PS8607.O215 R57 2021 | DDC C813/.6—dc23

Distributed by:
Engen Books
www.engenbooks.com
submissions@engenbooks.com

First mass market paperback printing: June 2021

Cover Image: Jon Mercer

For Thomas, Brianna, and Conan.
My pride, joy, and contentment.

CHAPTER ONE

I

A lone rider crossed the open plain on a horse about to die. Bill Weston leaned forward. His tongue darted across dry, chapped lips and whispered something into the horse's fluttering ear. He patted its solid neck.

Weston removed his hat and ran his hand through greasy, brown hair. He looked up at the relentless sun, felt the blistering heat on his face, and sighed. The canteens were dry, had been for some time, and he was far from any towns—those that he was aware of anyway.

He brought the horse to a stop and dismounted. He rubbed at his legs, feeling an ache in his muscles. It was slow going. The horse whinnied and grunted behind him, pulling at the reins in Weston's hand. Thick strings of saliva hung from around its bridle, its teeth.

When it finally collapsed to its side, its breath coming in large gulps, Weston slumped down next to it.

"Figures," he said into the empty air, and caressed the dying horse's snout and neck with one large, shaking hand. After a few minutes he pulled one of his guns and put it out of its misery.

It took all his remaining will to force himself to continue, but he did. He took to his aching feet, slid his large Colt six shooter back into its holster and walked on. He hesitated a moment over the horse's corpse, wondering if he should reclaim anything from the saddlebags, but the few clothes and doodads he had kept there would be of little value to him now, circumstances as they were.

The plain he crossed was rocky. Sand and dirt crusted over any grass that may have spotted the landscape before travelers and caravans had taken it as a viable path. And that was before the railway. Before the country had really become an open door for those of the north, south, east, and west. No one would have travelled by this path in years. Except for those that didn't want to be found.

Weston coughed. It was dry and painful, his throat raw from lack of water. He shook his head and rubbed at his shoulder and chest. The heat seemed to draw out the dull pain from the bloated, purple scars that he found there. A wound that hadn't healed quite right, that he feared might never heal.

The sun was high in the sky when he collapsed to his knees. He was lightheaded and tired, his eyes heavy. Weston's body screamed at him for rest, for nourishment, for water. None of which he could provide. He crawled on his hands and knees. He didn't have hope for survival, or that he would stumble upon a town, a well, any water source. He didn't hope for anything. Despite this, Weston forced himself forward, ignoring the cramps and the urge to vomit. He ignored the harsh, labored attempts at sucking air, and the creeping darkness at the edge of his vision.

He crawled forward, his hands and knees pierced by sharp pebbles and rocks that littered his path. Like his horse before him, he collapsed to his side. He could feel his body spasm under the hot sun. His eyes finally closed, and his mind succumbed to the darkness.

II

It was a slow crawl out of the shadows. In the darkness, he'd become aware of someone moving about him; the rush of fabric as it passed his displayed skin, the dull click of heels on wooden floors, a low humming in the distance and at his side. Weston's eyes fluttered open, his sight hindered by the bright light that poured over him.

He was in a bed. The sheets were clean, crisp, and had been drawn taut over his shirtless frame. They were cool, soothing on his aching muscles. The room around him was open and bright, the smell of the aging cedar hanging in the air. To his right was an open window, the sheer curtain blowing in long, lazy billows, like a loosely draped arm reaching to caress but falling short. To his left was an open door and a hallway. The humming continued, a pleasant sound that soothed his worries. A sound that reminded him of home.

Weston's arms were weak. Wiggling them free from the blankets was chore enough, and he found himself tired and sucking air from just the attempt. He fingered the bulbous scar on his chest, giving himself a moment to rest before his next attempt to sit up. The wound had healed ugly. An evil wound, that carried evil in it. It stung to prod at the scar, and it made it itch. At times it would bleed a dark maroon ichor that reminded him of…

"Don't poke at it," a raspy voice with a thick Mexican accent said from the doorway and drew Weston's eyes. He dropped his hand from the scar.

"Necesita una cataplasma." A black habit cascaded over the woman's head and back, concealing any hair she may have had. The white band that sat on her creased forehead accentuated her dark skin and her hazel eyes.

"Who..." Weston's voice croaked and died in his throat. It hurt to speak; a headache pounded at his temples.

"Sister Mejia," the old nun said, rolling her sleeves over her thin forearms. "Now, hush." She placed one of her craggy hands on his chest and looked him in the eye. Her hands were warm — strong and calloused from hard work. Weston relaxed some. The tension in his shoulders eased as the old woman examined him.

"You were in the desert for some time." Sister Mejia's voice was soft. Her eyes followed her hands as she probed for injuries. "When I found you, the dust had already started to cover you. It was a miracle I found you at all. Lucky for us both, I work in miracles." She tapped a crucifix that hung about her neck and a grin wrinkled her face pleasantly.

Weston nodded. His throat, still raw and dry, wouldn't let words escape his lips even if he had tried. His eyes wandered as Sister Mejia did her examination. The open room was bare save for the bed and a solitary chair that took up residence beside it. The only decor was a cross nailed to the wall directly above his head. He frowned.

"Esto es nuevo," the sister said, her hand moved in a claw like motion above his shoulder scars. Weston flinched away from her, gasping. The old nun stepped back, her eyebrows furrowed, and crossed herself, muttering a prayer under her breath.

Their eyes met for a moment, neither wavering. It was a measuring stare that Weston had to relinquish; his body and mind were exhausted. He wasn't sure what that would mean to the nun whose expression darkened as he fell back onto the bed.

"I'll go make up a poultice. You rest," she said, then

left the room. Silence engulfed him, and he wandered around in the bizarre memories of his life. He couldn't block it out anymore. He was too weak, too tired. Mary's lopsided smile and heart shaped face floated before him as he fell into the darkness once more.

Knock Knock

Weston's eyes crept open. Pain stabbed into his brain, an ice pick clearing out space.

He pushed himself up to his elbows and flung the crisp sheets from him, ignoring the lingering soreness of days gone by. He sat on the edge of his sickbed, wrapped his arms around his stomach, and watched the curtain blow in the soft breeze.

His breath was labored already, his back and chest rising and falling in a rapid staccato. There was a rough gurgle in his chest that he didn't like the sound of, but he was up. He was moving.

The breeze from the open window was warm. Running over his bare chest and legs, the sensation made a shiver run up his spine. He clutched at his scarred shoulder and gripped the bandage and soft poultice that the nun had applied earlier in the morning. Had it been the morning? Weston shook his head. A flash of white-hot pain answered him.

Knock Knock

He stumbled around the room on his heavy legs. One arm braced him as he moved from the bed. His gait was stuttered, and he was stooped over when he finally cleared the bed. His balance was good, but he was tired. So tired. Each step was a chore, and it frightened him. Weston had relied only on himself since he was a boy, his senses were honed to survive, his body the tool for that survival. It had never failed him. Until now.

His hand slapped the door frame as he moved through it, taking a moment to rest before he pushed on. The hallway was narrow. Each of the two doors on either side were closed. The rooms emitted no noise. He passed on with a grunt.

He could feel the sweat building on his brow, running down the small of his back. His lungs burned; his breath became more labored. The horrible wheezing and gurgle echoed from his chest louder now. A cough bubbled on his chapped lips as he reached the end of the hallway.

The kitchen before him was a modest affair. A washtub stood to the side, a stove in the center with wood piled neatly next to it in separate piles: splits and logs. The fire had died to embers, though a pan was laid upon the iron surface with the remnants of breakfast still scattered across it. The heavy, dark oak door stood just beyond the stove; a cross-shaped window of stained glass sat near its top. The image of an angel was depicted in the window, its wings extended with beams of light or power emanating from it. Around its head was a wreath of fire, and it held a club in one hand. Its blue eyes stared out upon those who approached the door, or perhaps it stared at those within.

Knock Knock

"Sí, sí. Paciencia," the Nun said, wiping her hands on a cloth that hung from her waist. "I'm coming."

Weston pressed himself to one side, letting the cool wall sooth his bare skin. With the door open, a warm breeze snuck in around Mejia, and ran over his sweaty frame. Weston shivered.

On the other side of the door, two large men looked down upon Mejia. The nun stepped aside to grant them passage, and Weston became suddenly aware of how diminutive Mejia was in stature. Looking up at her from his bed she seemed a giant.

"Dermot," Mejia nodded. "Ambrose."

"Sister," Dermot said and removed his hat. He was the older of the two. Gray touched his temples, and laugh lines bunched together on the outset of his eyes. His broad shoulders spoke of hard work, a farmer or the like, but the bulging stomach that protested against the tight buckskin jacket said those days were likely behind him.

"How've you been, Mejia?" Ambrose said and gave the nun a hug. He had the same wide jaw and bright blue eyes as Dermot but lacked any of the age. His own buckskin jacket was wrapped around his shoulders. Slimmer than the older man, he had a broad smile that creased his freckled cheeks.

"What are you boys doing out this way," Mejia said and gestured towards the chairs in the sitting room. "I thought you'd be helping setup for the mayor's triumphant return."

"Sister, it's happened again," Dermot said. Weston could see him nervously kneading the brim of his hat, twisting it in circles with his thick fingers.

"Again?" Mejia took a step back. "Who?"

"Horace Puddicombe and Percy Gulliver."

The old nun put a hand to her mouth either to stifle a gasp or rub her chin in thought. Weston couldn't tell.

"You boys get back to town," Mejia said, her shoulders slumped as she looked back towards Weston's room. He could feel her eyes slide over him. "I have to get some things together, and then I'll be on my way."

"Found yourself another stray, Sister?" Ambrose's smile grew as he followed her gaze.

"Something like that."

III

The ride into Millwood was quiet. Weston took the time to rest. He leaned his large frame into the wagon and closed his eyes against the steady sun. Mejia had the reins and directed her horse, Javier, at a slow pace over the rocky and dusty trail.

"You're shaking," Mejia said at last, a warm hand on his head. "No fever. Are you having much pain?"

"Some. It ain't so bad anymore." That was the truth. Before they had left, Mejia provided him with some fresh clothes and helped him into them. It may not have eased the pain much, but the feeling of clean clothes did a body some good.

"I see," she leaned closer to him, her head nearly to his chest. "Breathe."

It hurt to breathe in, hurt to breathe out.

"I don't like the sound of that." Mejia gave him another look before she flicked the reins once more. "Pero lo estás haciendo bien. Strong, hmm?"

"Stronger anyway," Weston nodded.

"Good. I wasn't sure you'd make it when I first found you. Where was it you thought you were heading?" the nun said and raised one thin eyebrow.

"That's a pretty fancy picture you had on your door back there." Weston turned on the bench to face the nun.

Mejia smiled. "Yes. Saint Jude. He's my favorite apostle."

"I didn't think you were supposed to have favorites. They're all equally holy, right?"

"Bah. A girl is allowed to have favorites." She waved a hand at him, her smile growing. "Even when she's a long way past girl." She chuckled warmly.

"Why?"

"Such a little question, yet it can mean so much." She paused. "He's the patron saint of lost causes. I like that."

"I suppose that's how you see me." Weston gave her a side-eyed glance, hair dangling in his eyes.

"Or it's how I see myself." She gave him a curt nod, her gentle face stern once more. A mother chastising her child. "La puerta was a present from my former convent."

"That's awfully generous."

Mejia pursed her lips and nodded. "Not as much as you would think. I heard they were renovating and wrote to them for it," she shrugged. "Nice enough I suppose."

A chuckle surprised Weston as it passed through his lips. "I bet your fellow nuns really enjoy it."

Mejia sat back. "You noticed that, huh?"

Weston nodded. He hadn't been up and about much, but the house was too damn quiet for a whole herd of people living there, nuns or otherwise.

"There were a few of us at first. It was a noble cause, setting out to tame the wilderness with love and compassion. Hired some men from Millwood to come over and build our houses, but then the drought came. Scared my fellow nuns away. Ran out of money so the builders had to leave. Left me with my humble surroundings."

They fell into an awkward silence.

"Have you been around death before, Mr. Weston?" the nun asked and cleared her throat.

Weston nodded and crossed his arms.

"Maybe you'd find it hard to believe, but this old nun has seen more than her fair share." Her voice was low, rumbling in tune with the bouncing wagon wheels.

"It's a hard-old world, Sister. Death is just another part of it."

"But not all death is the same." Mejia snapped the reins and pushed Javier to move faster. "Some are lucky enough to pass peacefully. Their end comes over them naturally. God welcomes them into His garden with open arms."

Weston turned his eyes on the nun. She was staring off into the horizon, into the cloud of dust left behind by Dermot and Ambrose.

"Others, Mr. Weston," she took a shaking breath. "Well, others don't pass so sweetly. Others meet violent ends. Those people in the war." She shot a quick glance at Weston. "Those men died violently. Nada de eso fue agradable."

Weston nodded. He'd seen the results of the war first-hand, had seen friends mutilated and killed. He'd swum through a sea of his countryman's blood and gore.

"Even that is better than what is happening in Millwood right now." Mejia met his gaze, held it. "When a man kills another man, it is terrible, make no mistake. Families, friends mourn but it *can* be accepted. Not always, but with time most can accept what happened and move on. Some are even able forgive those who did it. Only by the grace of God, no doubt." She took a long, shaking breath. "When a man dies by something else's hand, however, it leaves something behind. Algo duradero. A stain." Mejia's eyes were hard now, tears crept into their corners. "This is what we are going to see at Millwood, Mr. Weston. I don't deal with the bodies left behind, I deal with the stain and what made it."

Weston squeezed his shoulder, feeling the scars through his shirt. A stain.

By the time they got to town the sun was sliding out of sight behind them. A wine-coloured sky cast a dubious light on their path, making their shadows long and distorted. Every subtle movement seemed malignant. Weston covered Sister Mejia with a riding blanket; she welcomed it with a short grunt. He hung a spare poncho over his ruined shoulder, trying to keep the cold away from it.

Millwood was a sprawling town, dominated by a mountain and a forest on its far side. The black outline of the buildings stretched out from them like jagged, craggy fingers. Lights flickered in windows, smoke rose into the sky, and the harsh echo of a train whistle cracked the silence around them.

Ambrose met them at the entrance into town, sitting cross-legged and chewing on a strand of grass under a sign that proclaimed the town's name. He wasn't alone. Sitting next to him was a tan skinned boy, his eyes obscured by shadows. The boy couldn't have been more than ten, but there were premature worry lines that crisscrossed under his eyes, on his cheeks.

"Evening, Sister," Ambrose said, one skinny arm raised in greeting.

"Ambrose," Mejia said with a curt nod before turning to the boy, "Alberto."

The boy nodded in return, stifling a grin.

"I see you brought along your stray," Ambrose said and fed grass to Javier, who took it obediently.

"And you brought your boss," Mejia said sparing a broad smile to the child.

"Derm wanted me to wait it out for you, wanted me to show you the way," Ambrose said. "This old boy thought he'd do me a favour and wait alongside me." He nudged the boy with his elbow.

"I'm more than capable of navigating this town," Mejia said and jerked her thumb over one shoulder. Ambrose hopped into the carriage. "You coming too, chico?"

"Head over yonder, towards the woods there," Ambrose said after he helped Alberto into the wagon. He pointed one long finger between Weston and Mejia in the direction ahead.

The cluttered streets made way for the wagon as it rolled between the main stretch of buildings. Some of the townsfolk nodded or waved to them, and Ambrose struck up a short conversation with more than a dozen or so people on the way through the town. His laugh was high and contagious, and he shared it with anyone who tipped him a greeting. Sister Mejia, for her own part, gave a warm smile to those that recognized her. The boy remained quiet. Weston focused on two boys that ran abreast the wagon, lighting lamps along the road with their long pole wicks.

"All gas lamps?" Weston pointed to the poles astride the road and the lamplighters making their rounds.

"Yep," Ambrose stuck his head out from the wagon. "Mayor Winter proposed that—what do you think, Bert—three years ago?" Ambrose nudged the boy. "Plenty of people put up a stink about it. Didn't like change if you ask me. But they had a vote on it in town council and it was passed through. People were still unhappy, course, but they can't argue with the results."

"That's a heavy undertaking." Weston said, his eyes still watching the lights ignite on either side of them. "Running gas lines like that."

"Oh sure, it took some time. Only really got up and running this year. But, like Mayor Winter says, 'to be a city, you have to *be* a city.' Can't do that without the fancy things, right?"

Ambrose settled back into the wagon and started shouting and laughing with another of the throng of people that they passed.

"A city?" Weston turned to Sister Mejia.

"Oh yes, the mayor has some big ideas and lofty ambitions. He wants Millwood to be the next Boston or New York." She waved a dismissive hand.

"That's right. New York City," Ambrose whistled from behind them. "New Millwood City!" he yelled then stood, stretching his arms to the sky. Laughter and hoots and hollers came back in reply. Sister Mejia rolled her eyes and clucked her tongue. Javier picked up his pace.

"Hey," Ambrose laughed as he fell into the wagon.

Weston turned his gaze back to the lamplighters as they ran along the side street. Not much older than the boy in their wagon, Bert. Sister Mejia was outpacing them now, just so. One of the boys had missed a light and had to run back for it, while the other was waiting, his foot tapping. They'd catch up soon enough, Weston thought. Give them another year and they'd surpass the wagon with ease.

"Not everyone keen on the mayor's vision?" Weston asked pointing to a sign nailed to one of the lamp poles:

Vote

Horace Puddicombe

Mayor

Of Millwood Township

"No," Mejia whispered, "the election was supposed to be in a couple of weeks. No one's gone up against Frank Winter, not since he first came into office. Horace was the first to try."

"So, he either had a pile of guts or shit for brains."

"Horace Puddicombe wasn't a stupid man, but he wasn't your average resident either." Mejia cleared her throat.

"And he was killed?" Weston said.

"Yes, and one of his employees. "

"Ole Percy. I played cards with him every now and again," Ambrose said, sticking his face between Weston and Mejia. "Good fella. Hard worker."

"They say Horace struck gold, spent nearly all of his fortune on some worldwide adventure before he settled down here in Millwood." Mejia eased Javier to a stop.

"This is your stop, mijo," Mejia reached back and ruffled Bert's hair. "Be careful, and if you need anything you just come find me, Dermot, or Ambrose. Si?"

"Okay," Bert said around a strained smile and ran across the road into a building.

"It really burns you that Bert is working there don't it, Sister?" Ambrose asked.

"Why, what's that place?" Weston tried to see the building better, but Mejia had already started the wagon moving again.

"That's the Last Chance Saloon, finest drinking establishment in Millwood," Ambrose said over the derisive grunt of Mejia. "Our fair Sister here doesn't like it much because they sell as much flesh as they do booze. That and Etta Dumond." Ambrose had taken a seat in the back of the wagon again, but Weston could feel the smile on his words.

"Who's Etta Dumond?"

"Enough talk for now, we're almost there," Mejia said and clicked her tongue. Javier moved forward approaching the far edge of town.

CHAPTER TWO

I

They broke through the maze of buildings and houses to find more people milling about in front of a thick layer of trees. Some men were walking at the tree line with oil lamps, others with rifles drawn or resting on their shoulders. Many were standing in a small clearing just outside of town, and from the sounds of it they were engaged in a lengthy and heated argument. Above it all the shrill whistle of a train screamed.

"Over yonder, Sister, that's Dermot over there." Ambrose jumped out of the wagon and made his way toward those having the argument. He looked back over his shoulder from time to time to ensure the wagon was still following him, but he kept his distance from it.

None gathered paid much attention to them as they maneuvered around the small groupings. Ambrose certainly wasn't as talkative with this bunch as he had been with those he'd passed in town. Perhaps for good reason. Most of these men looked grave or nervous. one of them had the time for Ambrose's foolishness now; work was to be done. Weston approved.

"Father, I appreciate your position, but I'm the Sheriff here and this is *my* God damn job." It was a deep and thunderous voice, which rose above the other chatter. As was habit, it tended to draw everyone else to the conversation at hand, Weston and Sister Mejia included.

"Sheriff Johnson, Port, please, it was one of my parishioners. I need to perform Last Rites." Father Mason had a much softer voice, but it rang clear through the night. The father was a small man to match his voice. Wisps of white hair covered his mostly bald pate, and sagging bags underscored his luminous blue eyes. His collar was a bright white that almost glowed in the growing darkness above his black vestments, and he held a small Bible in both hands in front of his chest, a shield toward the thorny Sheriff.

"Last Rites? Father, you're the only preacher that I know who's willing to give Last Rites to a fucking dead man." Sheriff Johnson towered over the priest, his big hat pushed back high on his forehead and hands on his hips. Scars crisscrossed the man's face, the most obvious so thick that it crossed his two lips from cheek to chin. He wore his long coat open, and Weston could see a smart pair of silver guns glinting at his hips.

"It's better than nothing, Porter," the priest said, looking around him to see if there were any other objectors. None met his gaze. "Port, there have been two men killed and I wasn't able to do anything for them. I stand there on Sundays and tell people not to worry. I stand there and tell them that God will protect them. Words, Port. That's all I have. They don't always help, but this," he jabbed a finger towards the trees, "this could. Let me use my words this time."

Johnson gave the priest a strange look, his scarred mouth moved slowly as he chewed on his own mustache. His dark eyes considering the value of the man before him.

"I can go with him," Sister Mejia lowered herself to the ground and made her way to the circle of men. Weston followed.

"The fucking nun now?" Johnson spun and threw his thick hands up in frustration.

"I don't get sick at the sight of death. I can help him do the Rites." Mejia lay one reassuring hand on Father Mason's arm and gave him a small nod. The priest smiled in return.

"Just let them go, Port," Dermot stepped forward and waved a hand at the nun and priest. "It ain't gonna harm nothing."

Johnson shot a baleful glance at Dermot but let out a loud and drawn-out sigh. "Fine, go and do your damned Last Rites. Be quick about it." He turned toward Derm. "You and Ambrose go with them. Make sure the preacher here doesn't get sick all over the bodies."

Dermot gave him a nod and motioned for Mejia and the priest to follow him. Ambrose came up behind him from the crowd, a quivering smile aching to explode onto his face. Weston followed the sister, moving his way through the gathering as quietly as he could. A rough hand grabbed him by the bicep and spun him around.

"Whoa, whoa, whoa." Johnson looked furious, his facial scars whitened against his drawn and angry face. "Who the fuck is this?"

Weston pulled away from the Sheriff, careful not to back up. He knew Johnson's type: hard men who had grown accustomed to throwing their weight around, their strength. Men like that expected everyone to kowtow to them, to bow away or slink off once voices were raised. He met more than a few of them in the war, big mouths and bullies. The thing about hard men, Weston knew, is that they can break. He stared the sheriff in the eyes.

"He's with me," Sister Mejia pushed her way between the two men and looked up at the sheriff. "He can help with the Rites."

The Sheriff didn't take his eyes off Weston's. "Oh no he can't. I ain't letting no stranger scurry about in there. Hell, maybe he's the one that done it."

There was a murmur amongst the men gathered. Some came closer, tightening the circle around Weston and Mejia. Weston's hands dropped to his hips and found nothing but his belt. He cursed himself.

"Now come on, Sheriff," Ambrose said from his place by the tree line. "Does he look like the type who could do this sort of thing? He ain't got the right tools for one. Hell, he can barely stand."

The Sheriff wavered some at that. "Fine. Maybe he didn't do it, but he sure as hell ain't going in them woods tonight." The Sheriff stepped away from the sister and Weston.

Sister Mejia turned to Weston, her eyes pleading.

"It's fine. I'll stay with the wagon. Got to rest anyway, right?"

"Thank you." She moved off to join the priest and, with Ambrose and Dermot in tow, entered the thick line of trees.

Hard stares still fell upon Weston, but he met each one in turn, not flinching for any man. He settled himself in the wagon and stared into the now dark sky. Something didn't feel right here. What did Ambrose mean by not having the right tools? Guns, probably. Or was it something else?

As much of an ass as the Sheriff surely was, he had a good point. What business was it of a priest or a nun performing Last Rites on a dead man? And why were they so adamant about doing so where the body was found.

I deal with what was left behind, the sister had said on their way into town.

Weston thought that over, staring into the sky. The moon emitted its ethereal glow, interrupted by the harsh orange light of the lamps that the men carried with them. The city beyond was a beacon of light itself, the lamplighters having done their job. The noise of the city rose and mingled with that of the men around him, and it was the first time Weston was aware that he could not hear wildlife, just men and women and their own distractions.

The glint of light off something wet and viscous drew Weston back to the wagon. "Thought you were supposed to be working," he said and sat up. Bert's green eyes peered at him in the near darkness.

"Ms. Dumond didn't need me," the boy said.

"Hoping to get a glimpse of a dead body?" He was a small child, his arms little more than the thin branches of saplings, and his wet, green eyes betrayed a boy who'd seen more than he should've. Still, he *was* a boy. Interested in life and death and things he wasn't allowed to see. Weston tried to give him a small smile. Bert shrugged, his whole-body sagging.

"Did you know this Puddicombe fella?" Weston massaged his bad shoulder.

"I saw him sometimes. He was nice. So was Mr. Percy."

"Did they ever rub anyone the wrong way? Have any squabbles around town?"

Bert thought for a moment, his eyes wandering. "Maybe Delbert Cornish. Mr. Puddicombe always said that Mr. Cornish was gouging his customers with his prices."

"I guess Mr. Cornish didn't like that much?"

"No, sir. He banned Mr. Puddicombe from his store, so Mr. Puddicombe had to order all his supplies to be delivered by train," Bert said, more animated now, a smile on his face.

"Thanks, kid. You got anymore town gossip to share?" Weston tried on a smile but wasn't sure it fit.

Bert shrugged.

"Well, I don't think you'll see any dead bodies tonight, boy. The sheriff's in quite a mood. I wouldn't risk it if I were you. Head on back to town now, before you get in trouble."

Weston watched the boy walk away. When he was sure Bert was gone, he slid away from the back of the wagon, careful not to garner any more attention than he already had, and made for the forest, hoping to see what Mejia and the priest were attempting to do.

II

Weston kept low to the ground and moved through the open field. He let the dark aide him, sticking close to the shadows, away from the light. He was quiet; a childhood of hunting animals taught him well. Still, the sheriff's men weren't amateurs. Two men walked in shifts back and forth past the tree line. When they met in the middle they turned around and walked back. That was Weston's best chance, the few moments when they had their back turned to one another. Even then he had to contend with the other men that were floating around, pacing like dogs waiting for food.

The sister and priest had entered the trees though a makeshift path, unmarked but showing signs of use. Most of the men gathered had their eyes pasted on that little country path, including the sheriff himself, waiting for the holy interlopers to exit. Weston aimed to steer clear of it.

Crouched next to a wayward bush, Weston timed the patrol as they moved. He caught himself in two false starts. Each time a straggler walked into his path or the patrol-man stopped to talk with one of his colleagues. When his time came, he kept low and moved as slowly as he could. His body ached, his limbs shook, but he wouldn't stop.

When he hit the trees, the patrollers were on the back half of their chore and facing opposite directions. The un-bidden crack of branches had likely caught their attention, but Weston didn't bother to stick around to find out. He was in the forest and moving fast.

No stranger to hunting and tracking, Weston had spent most of his life navigating the dark forests of Col-orado and Utah, many of his formative years crawling through the wilderness after his reverend father and his traveling band of followers. No matter the age of the tree or thickness of the brush, Weston figured he'd have no is-sue finding his way. The forest of Millwood proved him wrong. Light died there. The moon and starlight blotted out by the tree canopy above, the orange glow from the town disappeared behind him. The lamplight of the nun's group was nowhere in sight.

The air was thick and felt as heavy as it was quiet. Weston could no longer hear the somber conversations of the sheriff and his men. Even the incessant noise of the lively town had finally quieted. He had been swallowed by the silence.

He pushed through the wilderness ahead of him, ig-noring the unrelenting muscle pain while trying to keep his balance and footing. Still, with every step the heavy brush and clutching roots snaked from the ground to entangle his feet. It slowed him, but he got into a steady pace.

As a child, Weston stumbled into the forest around his little hometown in hopes that he'd find some treasure—a long-forgotten stash left by early settlers, a cache of Native wares, or a dead outlaw's lost stockpile. The closest he'd come was a rusted-out shovel blade. Still, he kept it up. His father scolded him for it, cursed him as a dreamer when he should be doing chores. Weston got the strap often, but he always returned to those trees, his hands and eyes probing for something as of yet unfound, unseen. It only stopped the day he ran into a pack of wild dogs. Their emaciated frames heaving with strained breath, their brown eyes nearly red as they stared him down, mouths frothing with saliva. The alpha was big, some sort of Sheppard mutt with teeth the size of his fingers. When they came after him, their mouths grew into sharp-edged caverns, and he could do little but watch their curled lips and bared teeth.

Snap

In the dark, Weston turned at the noise and flailed into a tree. His bad shoulder struck its thick trunk, and its bricklike bark spun him to his knees. Eyes wild, he scanned the area for dogs, sweat dripping down his forehead, stinging his eyes.

Nothing. He was alone.

The pulsating began then, reaching out from his scarred shoulder to his chest and neck, crawling over his spine and tingled his legs. Weston continued as best he could, but the pulsing turned into an agony that made him grit his teeth and grasp his shoulder tight. Something bad happened in this forest, something Weston wasn't sure he wanted to get tangled up with.

In anguish, he crawled across the forest floor. His hands and knees scraped across rocks and roots, branches and twigs. It reminded him of his last moments in the desert, before he had fainted and before Sister Mejia had found him. Thoughts of giving up, of turning back and taking his chances with the sheriff and his men clouded his mind.

Then he saw it.

It was faint at first, an orange dot that bounced in the distance. It hid behind trees and danced between them, taunting him. Two more appeared to join the first and then another. Though the latter wasn't as strong as the first three, they were there all the same. Lanterns.

A sigh rolled from his chest. Relief swept through him and gave him the strength to stand. The pulsating died down in his shoulder, replaced by the numbness of the bulbous scars. How long had he been accustomed to that numbness, he wondered? How long would he be able to ignore it, and how long would it allow itself to be ignored?

The lights had stopped moving and Weston was able to catch up to them. Keeping his distance, he had no trouble making a nest for himself in the wake of a giant oak tree. From his vantage point, he could see the priest and Sister Mejia huddled around something on the ground: bodies. Ambrose and Dermot kept their distance but held their lanterns high to extend the range of their light. Neither man seemed comfortable with what was taking place. In a moment the priest joined them, clutching his Bible to his chest, his face grey and sickly. Only Mejia stayed near the dead men.

The nun paced around the bodies three times, each time stopping to bless herself, raise her hands to the sky, and then say something aloud that Weston couldn't hear. After this she removed something from her bag and placed it next to the remains. Weston couldn't make it out, a picture of some sort, or a carving? Whatever it was, Mejia placed it, blessed herself once more and kissed her fingertips before touching them to the image. She retrieved two candles, one green and one black, and placed them, already lit, next to the image. Again, she spoke aloud, but it didn't carry to Weston.

The nun began to walk around the body again, and Weston got a good look at Ambrose and Dermot. They were scared. The priest remained turned away, hugging into his Bible.

Sister Mejia halted her pacing and looked out into the forest. For one chilling moment Weston believed her gaze fell upon him. A curse on his lips, his breath hitched in his chest. There was something happening here, something that was a far way from Last Rites.

The dogs hadn't managed to sink their teeth into him. As they launched themselves at him, Weston stumbled back to the edge of the woods, his heart racing, adrenaline pumping tears down his cheeks in rivulets. He would've been a meal for them on their second assault had it not been for his father. The old reverend stepped into the trees, a junk of wood in one hand, heaving obscenities at the dogs as they snapped and growled. It wasn't until Weston's father bludgeoned a too brave mutt and sent it flying into the underbrush with a yelp that the pack broke off.

The reverend wasn't a man for coddling, nor was he a man of tenderness or any kind of emotion outside his fiery sermons. Weston never really loved the man, couldn't find it in himself to do so, but that day—the dogs fleeing, Weston's tears still fresh—he hugged into his father's leg. The reverend stiffened, placed one large hand on Weston's back and let him cry. The reverend was a hard man to live with, a hard man to love, even after that momentary truce in their father and son antagonisms. But that one moment with the reverend, taught Weston that sometimes you needed to protect others even when they didn't know they needed it.

Weston stood, pushed the pain and nausea down, and made to approach the nun and her cadre, but he wasn't given the chance. Mejia looked up to the sky once more, her hands held before her as if for prayer, then she turned and began to gather up her belongings. Storing them gently back in her bag. They were on their way back to the clearing.

Weston turned and sighed into the stretch of black forest that stood before him. He contemplated following the sister back but didn't want to arise suspicion with the sheriff's men. That and he couldn't say if Mejia knew he had been snooping on her—if that gaze had really pierced the dark and found him amongst the trees. Weston hoped against it. He wasn't prepared for that just yet. He needed time to think over what he had seen. Whatever it was, it wasn't like any Last Rites he had ever seen before. With another curse he set off into the trees.

It was a shorter trip back than he had remembered, though Weston wasn't sure that it was the same path as he managed on his way in. All he knew was that he wasn't sharing the well-worn path with the others and the field seemed to be on the other side of the trees before him. The noise had returned gradually as he approached, and now that he was close enough to stick his nose through the brush, light began to seep through. He was in a bad spot. There was no way that he could know the position of anyone out there, which he hadn't considered before running off. He couldn't stick his head out to get a better view without being seen, and Weston was sure the sheriff wouldn't be overly pleased with his deceptions. His only option, if it came down to it, would be to just jump out and hope for the best. That was a fool's errand though, and he wanted to avoid it at all costs. Weston looked to his right and could see the line of lights coming up the path. He'd have to time it right, but if he could leave the forest at the same time the sister and priest did, he'd have a chance.

Patience came easy to Weston, learned in earnest while waiting for his father's travelling congregation to do anything, but waiting for the sister and her companions in the near dark of the forest played on him. His arm hurt again; the pulsing traded up for stabbing jabs into each scar as if he'd fallen into a patch of thorns. As the lights approached, he could barely contain himself. His hands clenched into fists, his neck strained, and his legs went weak. When the sister moved through the opening, Weston was able to force himself through the brush, letting the low-hanging branches slash at his face.

He stumbled forward, the last residue of the forest drained from him, and the pain slipped away as quickly as it had come on. He'd left it back in the forest. While the patrolmen were still taking part in their slow patrol of the tree perimeter, the others were busy confronting Sister Mejia and her priest friend; he was in the clear. There was a hole in the brush from his exit, twigs and leaves littered the earth where he'd broke through. The patrolmen may notice that, or they may not. Weston cared little now. He gave the forest one last look, staring into the opening he had left. The pain was still in there, he knew that. He'd left it in there when he left the forest, but it would be waiting for him.

It had only been a few minutes since his return to the wagon that Sister Mejia jumped up on the seat and, cooing to Javier at the reins, got the wagon moving.

"All done here, Sister?" Weston sat up. With his back to the wagon's boards, he brought his knees to his chest and wrapped his arms around them.

"Done as much as we could do with Porter Johnson and his cronies slack jawing about." Her raspy voice was dry, strained.

"He does seem like a pleasant fellow." Weston looked out the back of the wagon as they left and kept his eye on the tall sheriff. He was sure the sheriff had his eye on him in return.

"Don't get me started on that no-good piece of dung."

"Harsh language for a woman of God."

"Some deserve it."

Weston could tell that the nun was in no mood for his jokes. He took the hint and let the road and wind do the talking as he stared out at the world around him. The town that would be a city welcomed them back with open arms. The town didn't rest, there were people walking the streets, music played from saloons and hotels, and the smell of cigars and booze was in the air. Mejia guided them with a natural ease, and, like before, the crowd seemed to split and open the way for them. Mejia was getting less hellos than earlier, but when someone ventured to greet her, she responded in kind.

"We'll have to stay here for the night." They had pulled up in front of a small church, its white clapboard still shining from a fresh coat of pain. "I'd rather not make the journey back home in the dark. We'll do that first thing in the morning."

"Not a fan of sticking around, Sister Mejia?" Weston stood and stretched some, feeling his knees pop in the effort.

"Not usually, no. This town is no place for an old nun like me." She hopped down and began to remove the bridle from Javier.

Weston hopped out of the wagon, rotated his shoulder, and took up the nun's bag and slung it over his chest.

They walked up the small pathway, Sister Mejia grumbling to herself. Weston followed her a few paces back, careful that she wouldn't turn back toward him. He slipped one hand into the bag, unable to see inside of it from this angle, and felt around. His fingers fell on the candles, the thick wax still warm to the touch. He kept searching. Clothes or the like crowded the bag. He hurried to displace it but was delayed by his caution and fear of making too much noise. He kept his eyes on the sister's back, her shoulders stooped now, her black habit pooling more easily around her feet. Whatever they had done in the woods took a lot out of her.

Weston's fingers finally fell on something solid. The edges were sharp and pressed into the calluses on his well-worked hands. It was a carving or picture of some sort, about four inches long, two inches wide. It was solid with something protruding from the center, a shape that Weston couldn't identify. The nun had just reached the door. He had a chance, if he were quick, to draw it from the bag and get a look at it.

"Sister Mejia," a low purr drew Weston's attention. He dropped his quarry; he'd have to try again later. The woman that stood in their path was beautiful. Her blond hair, with just the hint of grey, was pinned back under a purple and beflowered hat that accentuated her high cheek bones.

"Ms. Dumond," Mejia said. "I didn't expect to see you here."

"Oh, sister, you know I have to support my community," Dumond said withdrawing and folding her hands atop of one another. "I heard poor Horace Puddicombe had been killed. It can't be true is it?" Dumond's scarlet lips fell into a pout.

"I think you already know," Mejia said and made to move past the other woman.

"And who is this, Sister Mejia?" Dumond said, spotting Weston.

The nun looked around at Weston and grunted. "That's my man servant, can't you tell? He's carrying my bag."

"I'm just a stray ma'am."

"You have a lot of friends around her, sister," Weston said after Dumond had left and threw Mejia's bag to the floor. A loud bang resonated throughout the church and its lofty ceilings. It was deceptively big on the inside, and it reminded him of the little poem he'd learned as a child, illustrated with his hands and fingers. *Here's the church and there's the steeple. Open the door and see all the people.* The ten pews were a light oak lacquered with waxy varnish that Weston could feel under his fingernail as he ran them over the near flawless workmanship. An altar stood at the head of the church with a large crucifix hanging behind it. A large Bible was open on the pulpit, ready for the next sermon, next reading, next lesson. The walls were lined with stained glass windows, each one depicting a different station of the cross. Christ being laid to rest.

"They've come to know me, that's for certain." Sister Mejia said as she sauntered up the aisle. Weston continued to follow her and planked himself down in a pew directly behind her when she blessed herself and knelt before the altar. The church was empty, save for them, but it was a warm night and that didn't make it seem so lonely. The candles flickered about the altar, but there were gas lamps installed along the walls to keep the church bright.

Weston contemplated praying, thought about bending his head to his entwined hands and asking the good Lord, *what's next?* But, then again, there was no good Lord up above. There was no devil below. There were only people here and now, good and bad. When the bad turned to evil then it would twist and change and eat away at the person. It would make them a monster, a devil. He'd seen that happen in person.

The bang of the church door brought him out of his doldrums. Father Mason had returned, his face red and his breath labored.

"Father," Sister Mejia said, rising. "What did the good sheriff have to say?"

The priest shook his head and thumped his Bible on his thigh. "Porter Johnson is a bullheaded and unscrupulous man. He does nothing past what he has to do."

"So, what is it this time?"

"Bear attack."

Weston raised his eyebrows. He hadn't seen much of

the body, or the scene, but there was no doubt that a bear could have done that kind of damage. Catch a bear on a bad day, and you won't be walking home. But to do that to two men who were likely armed? Possible, but that wasn't what his gut was telling him.

"And with that the death of another citizen of Mill-wood is swept under the rug like so much filth," Mejia said.

The priest patted Mejia on the shoulder. "Let's hope what you..." The nun cleared her throat and motioned toward Weston, stifling whatever he was about to say.

"Yes, well. How about we get you two sorted for the night." Father Mason motioned to Weston to follow and all three left the church.

CHAPTER THREE

I

"What does a priest and a nun have to do with a dead man anyway," Weston said, "aside from saying a prayer while they stick him six feet in the dirt."

Sister Mejia was good to her word and they had left just after sunrise. Weston's condition hadn't improved with the few winks of sleep he'd gotten on Father Mason's lumpy couch. His eyes burned and his head ached, and the perpetual motion of the wagon made his stomach ill. None of this boded well for the nun on their trek back to her house.

"Well, Mr. Weston, we have to perform..."

"Last Rites. Which is not done on someone who is already dead." Weston turned to face the nun, who stuck her chin out and held onto the reins. Javier whinnied in front of them.

"Fine, fine." Weston threw up his hands. "But tell me this. I know you and Father Mason don't believe the shit the sheriff is pushing. So, what is it you believe happened?" He covered his eyes to keep away the sun and waited for her reply.

"I think that men were killed," she said, considering her words carefully. "But I know that it wasn't a bear, or any other such nonsense Porter Johnson says."

"Why? Why not a bear?" Weston asked, his hands clenched.

"We've seen this kind of killing before, the father and me. It's not what the killing looks like, es la mancha. It's what is left behind."

"You said that before. Do you mean there was too much meat left? That if it were a bear attack the body wouldn't have been left as it was?"

"You have some experience in this sort of thing, Mr. Weston?" Mejia asked, a half-smile cracked her old face. "To answer your question, yes and no. The body didn't look like it had been eaten at all. It was most certainly done by another man, though what kind of man could do that sort of damage, I can't say. It was horrific, Mr. Weston. Horrific." She guided Javier along the worn dirt path, clucking her tongue.

"And you said you've seen this before?" Weston was clutching at straws. He wanted to keep her talking.

"Oh yes. Same kind of death, same kind of killer."

"I assume the sheriff is aware, so why wouldn't he investigate?"

"This was before Porter Johnson's time, but let me be clear about one thing: Sheriff Johnson is either very incompetent or he knows something he isn't telling."

"I suppose we've come full circle then. What did you have to do in the forest then?"

Sister Mejia turned her eyes on him. She was tired— bags folded under her eyes between creased skin.

"It's not your concern, Mr. Weston. It is best that you stay as clear as you can." Her haphazard frown had returned. Weston opened his mouth to say more, to argue, to plead, to question. But there wasn't much more he could do.

Maybe the old nun is right, Weston thought, his eyes wandering to the barren land all around them, watching tufts of dirt work themselves up into tiny cyclones. Why had he come this far if not to escape from a whole heap of trouble, of pain? The last time he tried to help it went to shit; people died, his friends died. The best thing for him to do was hop a train out of town, do everyone a favour, and leave the town behind him. Trouble was, could he let himself do that? Weston shrugged his shoulder. Mejia was right on at least one account: evil like that leaves its mark.

They both settled into a strained silence. Weston shaded his eyes to the sun, and Sister Mejia set her eyes on her home somewhere ahead in the dusty expanse.

Once they returned to Mejia's property, the cold eyes of St. Jude looking out on them, they set about business as usual, doing Sister Mejia's chores, and taking on some repairs that she hadn't been able to get to by herself: the barn door chief amongst them. Weston figured he owed her as much.

The property was small. Just beyond the house was a modest garden that was a healthy, vibrant green. Mejia took some time to point out the vegetables she was growing: asparagus, cabbage, tomatoes, sweet potatoes, and a small patch of rhubarb. She pointed out a small tree that seemed stunted and dry.

"Apple tree." She put her fists on her hips. "Not doing well I'm afraid. I pray it can make it out of the summer."

"St. Jude." Weston forced a smile and leaned on the small wooden fence that surrounded the garden. His back was aching now. Strained and tired. Overworked.

"Si, algo como eso." Mejia offered a brief smile and took him to the small barn where she kept Javier and his wagon. The horse whinnied in their presence.

"Your sisters, they won't come back?" Weston asked. The small bit of land was more than enough work for anyone. It wouldn't be easy for Mejia to keep it up. *How long has she been alone?* he thought.

"No. Ellas no regresaran."

The next few days were more of the same. They talked very little. Weston could feel the subtle tension in the air when they were sitting down to a meal or taking a break from the housework. They each had their own way of dealing with it. Sister Mejia would take some time to say her prayers, Weston would go for a walk. Weston figured they were both doing the same thing: thinking. There was a lot of that to do after what he saw back in the outskirts of Millwood. He was sure she was thinking about it as well. Seeing death up close like that was a hard thing to push away.

It was Millwood that brought them together more than anything, saving them from the silence that had become their lives. Weston would ask questions about it, or the sister would relay some story about the people she met there.

If what the nun had said were true, Millwood started out as a small logging town. As the loggers found success (and they had more than their fair share in the thick forest Weston saw) they brought in their families. Things happened, as things are wont to do, and the families grew, intermingled and the town grew to fit. Soon after that, the loggers, and the rest of the United States, realized that

Millwood was right on a proper trade route. Caravans began to pass through. In some cases, the caravans lost a person or two to Millwood and so it grew more.

Now that trains took over the country, Millwood became one of the stops. Mostly for commerce and transportation of logs, but also because Millwood was a growing, lively town. The right person, with the right ideas, could do a lot in a place like that. Knowing all of this, it wasn't as much of a shock to Weston that the mayor was hoping to build it into a city before too long. After all, it had happened before with other towns and cities. Why not Millwood?

What Sister Mejia was passionate about was the people of Millwood. From the little children all the way up to the businessmen and their doting wives, and the mayor all by his lonesome in his large manor. Father Mason was her anchor in town, however. Aside from calling her to be his assistant for the grislier parts of his job, Mason included her in all the essential church services and had Mejia help with community activities and efforts. The father was a progressive priest. Least ways, that's how Mejia came to know the people of Millwood, some of them anyhow. She didn't get into specifics much, never mentioned what drove her dislike of Etta Dumond, but that wasn't important.

On his last night in the nun's humble abode, the tension had started to eat away at the remaining good feelings between the two. Even talk of Millwood, its people, didn't bring them about. Weston knew his time with the Sister Mejia was at an end.

Leaning his big shoulder on the door frame leading into the kitchen, Weston watched her scurry about preparing supper. She was a good cook, he noticed in an absent sort of way. Her food managed to keep him full and comfortable, at home. He'd miss that.

"Are we going to talk about what happened the other night?" He kept his voice low, and his cold eyes on her face.

"Do we need to?" Sister Mejia kept her stride and drained a pot into the washtub. She didn't look towards him.

"Whether we need to or don't, I think words need to be said."

"Very well," she placed the pot on the table, her arms extended and clutching the handles with cloth protecting her hands. "Father Mason and I performed Last Rites. Now, I know you don't want to hear that, and I know you don't believe it, but until you're ready for the truth that's all I have to say. If you don't believe it, go ask Ambrose and Dermot. They'll tell you the same."

"I have no doubt, but I can't figure why y'all would lie about the same thing."

Their eyes met then, just for the briefest of moments, and they both knew it was finished. Mejia went back to her cooking.

"I'm aiming to head out tomorrow," Weston said sitting at the table.

"Oh? And how are you planning on doing that?"

Weston watched her old back move with her cooking, still strong despite her age.

"I was hoping you might let me take Javier into town. I'm sure Ambrose and Dermot could see that he got back to you."

Mejia nodded. "Si. That may be for the best. Te vas a quedar en la ciudad, or will you move on?"

"Haven't got that figured yet. I'll see where the wind

blows me."

"And you'll be wanting your things?" Mejia looked at him over her nose, studying his face and eyes.

"Just the clothes on my back," Weston said and forced a crooked smile.

They ate in silence.

II

A beaten old satchel sat at the foot of his bed when Weston woke the next day. The cracked brown leather was soft to the touch and moved with ease when he flipped the cover back to poke inside. Clothes mostly, some grub for the ride, and a canteen filled with water. He smiled despite himself. Weston's hands fell on the cold iron of his guns, huddled to the side of the bag. A sigh escaped his broad chest. He dressed quickly.

Weston knew that Sister Mejia was gone when he walked into the kitchen and it was sparkling clean. He didn't realize how much noise the old woman made when she was stomped around the small house doing chores, cooking up a meal, singing to herself. Now the only noise Weston heard was the wind whistling across the plains. He found Javier saddled up and waiting for him inside the barn. He gave the horse a good pat on the neck and brought him out into the open. As he closed the doors, movement caught his eye. A crucifix dangled there, its silver sheen sparkling some in the sun's rays, which broke through the cracks in the door. Weston rescued it from the rusty nail it hung from. Twisting the necklace around his hand, he stared at the cross. Jesus with his head down, dead or dying, a wound in his side and nailed to a piece of board.

"Poor bastard," he said aloud and stowed it in the

satchel.

He took one more look around the house, took a detour through the garden and around back. No sign of the sister. He took another look around the barn. It was a sturdy enough piece of work, didn't let much weather in, and Javier seemed to like it well enough. As with everything else, however, if something wanted to get in, it would find a way. At the back of the barn, he found what he was looking for. A small hole had been chipped away from the barn's walls. Dirt was dug away to make room from something to slither or crawl in and out. By the looks of things, whatever had made the hole hadn't been around in some time.

With the back of his boot, he kicked in the hole some more, the cracking sound echoing through the plain. He almost expected Mejia to pop out of wherever she was hiding and give him a tongue lashing for beating up her barn. She didn't. The only response he got was Javier whinnying from the front of the house. He opened the satchel once more, feeling the scars of age in the old leather, and pulled out his gun belt and guns. A cold feeling ran up his ruined shoulder and made him shudder. As quickly as he could, he shoved the guns into the hole. With that done he found some scrap wood lying about from their last few days of chores and concealed the hole with it. Mejia may find it, but he'd be long gone by then. Guns were just an excuse to act, and Weston didn't need that kind of action, not anymore.

He took another look in the house, craning his neck to look through the window of his former sickbed. It was just as he had left it.

"The old bird really didn't want to say goodbye," he said to Javier as he slid into the saddle. Their last conversation hadn't been the most pleasant, but nothing hurtful was said. Then again, he thought, it's what went unsaid that really mattered. Regardless, it had to be done. Lies beget more lies. Weston had had enough of that in his lifetime; he wouldn't suffer through any more of it.

He flicked the reins and gave the horse a little thump with the heels of his boots and put

Sister Mejia and her house in his dust.

The ride to town was long and exhausting. Weston's old wounds began to act up on him as Javier jostled him during the ride. His ribs in particular caused him grief, and, before the end of the trip, he had one arm wrapped about them trying to allay the pain.

He walked into town near midday dragging Javier behind him. Millwood was a different beast in the daylight. The streets were practically crawling with people, though they seemed slightly more driven than they had on the previous night that he had spent here. There were less drunkards scuttling about anyway. Just a few days after one of their own had been murdered, and everything was back to normal. Millwood, it seemed, didn't have the time to mourn.

Millwood may have been determined to become a city, but it certainly didn't look much different than any other small town Weston had blown through. There was one main throughfare with some side streets that branched out from it, curving and uneven. Not too far ahead of him he could see the saloon they'd passed upon his previous visit. Further in the distance he could see the church, and the mountains stood in solemn guard even further off.

Hitching Javier to a post near a trough, Weston set out

to explore. The first building he sought out was the train station, looking to keep his options for travel open beyond horse after his near disastrous trip with Javier.

It was a quaint little building, just off the main through-fare of the town in a beatdown area of dirt and mud. No train was pulled up in front of station, but there were still people milling about, crowding the entrance and plat-form. Most that were there were decorating: men were hanging banners and streamers, women were setting up tables along the tracks, and games were being erected in the courtyard just beyond. Weston pushed forward try-ing to get a good look at the schedule, a small chalkboard hung near the main entrance of the station. There weren't many trains coming or going in the next few days, though a train from Denver was coming in two days' time, look-ing to loop around and return to Denver just after that. Weston considered it. Denver was far enough away, and it was as good a place as any to get where he was going. He still didn't know where that was, but he could probably get there from Denver. Perhaps he'd head down south, make a trip through California, and go into Mexico. He shrugged and walked to the ticket office to purchase his tickets.

"No, sir, no trains."

"What kind of a train station offers no train service?" Weston said and hammered his fist down of the little coun-ter. The station was little more than a small room with a ticket desk that faced the only entrance. The only employ-ee, the ticket vendor, was behind the ticket desk, a barred window separating him from the rest of the room—the rest of the world.

"Listen, fella," the old employee said, his tight face pulled tighter by a growing frown that now hung under his long, white moustache. "We ain't got no trains. Now you can have a fit about it all you want, but that ain't gonna change nothing."

"What about the sign out front?" Weston hitched a thumb towards the front door. "Says out there that you have a train coming in from Denver."

"Yes, sir, that's the train carrying the Mayor and the Governor."

"So, let me hop aboard that one," Weston said, mollified some. "I'll take anything."

"I feel for you, son, I do, but after arrival that train won't be going nowhere."

"What the hell is wrong with you?" Weston slammed an open hand into the barred window, the vibration of which echoed through his arm and took some of the bite from his words.

"Listen, boy, I'll explain it slow so you can understand. The track is out of order. Some half-wit train robber blew the thing to shit. So, anyone going south of here, like all trains do, are just out of luck. Now, if you want to buy tickets, I assure you they will be honored when the train is up and running. Otherwise, get the hell out of my station."

Weston took a deep breath, rubbed his thumb of the thick scars on his shoulder. His ribs still pained, his legs too, but he could deal with it. "You know of any horse dealers around here?" He said after a short time under the scrutiny of the old train man's pouched blue eyes.

"I do, sure. Livery is just up the road, and you might find Ezra Hames with an overabundance of horses he'd like to get rid of. He's out by Puddicombe's place. I should say, boy, that I wouldn't advise a horse ride out of this here town. To the east is all but a desert for miles, and to the west, well that's mountain land. Mountain weather is rarely predictable, and you may run in to some snow. Snow that no horse could make it through."

Weston sucked on his teeth. "I'll take a ticket for the next train."

Bert hadn't noticed the man until he almost bowled him over. Bert bounced off Weston's stomach. He would've fallen over if the man's rough hands hadn't grabbed his shoulders to keep him upright.

"Take it easy, kid," Weston said behind a frown. "You all right?"

Bert remembered Weston from a few nights ago, the same night Mr. Puddicombe and Percy had been found, the night that he skipped work to try to see the dead men. Mr. Weston didn't look too pleased.

Under the big man's scrutiny, Bert's eyes crowded with tears, his face felt warm, and sweat trickled down his cheeks and back. He nodded, averting his own gaze from Weston. He didn't want to be seen crying.

"What's the rush, Bert? It is Bert, right?" Weston took a knee, squeezed Bert's shoulder.

"I'm just trying to do my job," Bert said, his head still down. He knew that Ms. Dumond would have a punishment in mind for skipping work, but, as always, she kept it to herself. One of the working girls, Anita, said that it was because Ms. Dumond liked drawing it out. "Really twisting the knife," was how she put it, her light hand rubbing his back.

Bert knew what she meant. Ms. Dumond liked to torture those who went against her. She liked to hurt them as much as possible. Ms. Dumond was usually fair with him, and he had a living wage. Still, the few times her maliciousness touched Bert, he longed for the days he spent with Sister Mejia in the quiet of her garden.

Bert's punishment this time was to bring an order to Delbert Cornish. Anita said that if any man were a representative of Millwood, it would be Mr. Cornish. He had been a part of the town from the beginning and was as physically deranged as any of the patrons who frequented the Last Chance. He was a proper miser and any attempt to talk his prices down were met with anything from berating remarks to physical violence.

"Job for the saloon?" Weston asked. "What happened?" He tried to lift Bert's eyes to meet his own, but Bert shook him off.

"I tried to stop them, but they took it," Bert pointed to a group of boys tossing something in the air just a few paces off. Jeffrey Claiborne, Matthew Erickson, Andrew Driscoll, and Charles O'Brien, local boys who made it their mission to let Bert know he wasn't welcome, that he wasn't one of them. As if the colour of his skin wasn't reminder enough. The four of them were laughing, but still managed to cast evil looks towards Bert and Weston. "How am I supposed to do my job now?"

"What did they take?" Weston said, his eyes trying to follow what was being tossed.

"Ms. Dumond gave it to me. She said it was my father's." A single tear streamed down Bert's face, threatening to make him sob. He didn't want to cry though. He wanted to scream and yell and gnash and roar. He wanted to take back what was his.

"Where is your father?" Weston asked, and Bert allowed his face to be drawn up so that their eyes met. He could feel the growing welt on his cheek, could feel the swelling start around his left eye.

"My father is dead," Bert managed through sniffles. "Ms. Dumond is at the saloon." He spat and wiped his face with his sleeve.

They both looked at the other boys again, their faces still grim despite the laughter they forced from their lungs.

"All right, boy. Stay here." Weston said and walked over to the boys, Bert watching his broad back as he went. For their part, the boys feigned that they didn't notice Weston standing beside them, another of their games.

"Hand it over," Weston spoke loud and clear without raising his voice, but Bert could hear the cold bite of his impatience in it, worried that it was aimed at him and not the others.

"What?" The biggest boy, Jeremy, said and slipped Bert's property into his pocket. He was a large boy, but he was no more than ten or eleven. His black hair, cut short on the sides, still hung in strands before his eyes. Dark freckles spotted his cheeks and nose, and he had a lazy sort of overbite. He was easy to dislike, and still he gathered others to him. Friends attracted to his maliciousness.

"Whatever you just put in your pocket. Give it here." Weston held out one meaty hand. The boys went quiet and circled behind Jeremy, waiting to see what he would do.

"What, this?" Jeremy said taking his hand out of his pocket and flicking open the blade of a knife. A funny smile grew about his lips.

"What did I say? Hand it over," Weston thrust his hand forward. Bert could see something working behind Jeremy's eyes, like the gears of a clock winding away.

Was Jeremy bold enough to do something, to use Bert's father's knife? *Please, Weston, please see the look in his eyes,* Bert wanted to yell, wanted to scream but his voice locked up, frozen between the conflicting emotions.

Jeremy's smile disappeared, replaced by a grimace. Bert sighed; his body relaxed.

"Fine. Have it," he tossed the small knife at Weston's feet, the blade digging into the soft grass between them. The boy's friends followed him, hooting and hollering as they went. Bert heard Weston curse under his breath as he bent to pick up the knife. It was a small blade that folded itself into a wooden sheath that doubled as a handle. It was well constructed, or that's what Ms. Dumond had said. Bert just liked the feel of the knife in his palm, the wood grain warm and smooth, shaped as if it were meant to fit there. Weston shook his head and Bert knew what he was thinking. Who would trust a boy his age with such a knife? Bert was aware that most boys got the hand-me-down blades that their fathers hadn't used in some time or had gone blunt. That was half the reason why Jeremy and his gang took the knife in the first place. What they didn't realize, or care to differentiate, was that it wasn't Bert's father who gave him the knife. It was Ms. Dumond.

"Here," Weston put the knife in Bert's hand.

"Thanks, mister," Bert said between sniffles, running his sleeve over his face.

"That's a good knife you have there. What kind of job were you doing with it?"

"Nothing… this time." Bert looked down to the ground, shuffled his feet some, and let out a loud sniffle.

"Sorry to hear about your father, that must be hard." Weston put his hand on Bert's shoulder again.

"It was before I was born," Bert said and pocketed his

knife with a shrug of his shoulders.

"And your mother?"

"Don't know." Bert had a vague recollection of a woman smiling down on him, but it was hazy, as if he were seeing it through a dirty window, or through water. Other than that, whenever he thought of his mother, he either pictured Sister Mejia or Etta Dumond.

"I'm new to town, Bert," Weston said. "How about you show me where you're working? I'm sure Ms. Dumond will want to know what you're up to."

Bert nodded and started back into town at a slow walk. He'd look back over his shoulder to see if Weston was following from time to time, the warm feeling of a crooked smile still on his face.

Weston returned the smile and followed the youngster into the heart of Millwood.

CHAPTER FOUR

I

While most buildings on the street were connected to their neighbors via boardwalks and shared sides, the Last Chance Saloon stood separate from those around it, ominous and solitary. Two stories tall, it was painted a garish blood red. The second floor was overwhelmed by a large hand-crafted sign that decried "Saloon," and was so gaudy Weston was sure it could be seen from Mejia's shack. The main floor had a large single pane window that stood open to the whole world. Weston could see several empty tables and chairs.

"Not busy this time of day?" Weston asked and let the boy take the lead.

"Nah, we see more business after dark. Ms. Dumond says that's because the funnest things to do are done in the dark." Bert chuckled.

"I bet she does," Weston said with a head shake.

A lamp post stood just to the side of the saloon. At about eye level the remnants of a poster were visible, the word "Vote" torn in half. The last words of a dead man hastily ripped asunder.

The Last Chance was open and airy. The smell of stale tobacco smoke and spilled beer was subdued under a fresh coating of sawdust but persisted all the same. A sturdy countertop of stained oak stretched along the far wall, an assortment of liquor bottles stacked on shelves behind it. A burly gentleman stood behind the bar, taking a break from buffing the counter. He slung his dirt spotted rag over his shoulder.

"Get you a drink?" The bartender said around a hefty moustache, his half-lidded green eyes on Weston. Then, as an afterthought, he nodded to the boy, "Bert."

"Whiskey," Weston said and bellied up to the bar.

"Get the dinner party order, boy?" the bartender said and poured up a glass of amber liquor.

Bert nodded and slapped a much-folded piece of paper on the bar top.

"Nice work." The bartender slid the glass to Weston and unfolded the paper. "Did ole Del give you much hassle?"

"I had to settle for the original price." Bert lowered his head as the bartender tutted.

"Ms. Dumond won't like that much," the bartender said and sucked his teeth. "Best get to work, the whores are going to want their breakfast." The bartender turned to Weston and raised his voluminous eyebrows. *"Liquid* breakfast."

"Ole Del wouldn't happen to be Del Cornish, would it?" Weston asked and took a seat.

"The same." The bartender poured something clear into five glasses and put them on a round tray.

"He runs a shop around here?" Weston watched Bert balance the tray on his shoulder and carry it to a set of stairs leading to a loft that overlooked the rest of the bar.

"Fella, you must be new. That black bastard runs *the* store around here. Has been running the general store here since before it was a proper town. He's the only dry goods dealer in the area, and he has connections that can get him just about whatever he wants." The bartender passed the tray to Bert who carefully carried it up the stairs to the second-floor loft.

"I heard that," Weston said and sucked back his whiskey. "Heard that he charged quite the premium too."

The bartender gave him an appraising look but after a moment he relaxed, and his smile returned.

"Between me and you," the bartender whispered, "he's the richest man in Millwood. The cheapest too." He filled another tumbler and slid it to Weston.

"I suppose it's even more likely now that the Puddicombe fella got himself killed."

The big man guffawed a laugh and slapped the bar top. "You got that right, mister."

"Begs the question," Weston said, the strong scent of turpentine wafting under his nose, "why send a boy to barter with a skinflint?"

"Because the old skinflint likes the boy," Etta Dumond purred from the railing of the loft. A lazy smile parted her scarlet lips and she sauntered down the stairs, grabbing a glass from Bert's tray as she came.

Weston took a slug from his drink and turned to greet her. She wore a low-cut purple dress complete with corset top, she paused for a moment to let him to get a good look.

"Sister Mejia's stray," she said and put a hand on one hip. "What brings a man with such holy companions to the Last Chance Saloon?"

Weston raised his glass to her and finished his drink. "Figured I could use a little pick-me-up."

"And your holy redeemer?" Dumond asked and made the exaggerated pantomime of looking around, a playful smirk on her face.

Weston gestured to the nearly empty room. Shrugged.

"Well, without your chaperone, perhaps we can get to know each other a little better. My name is Etta Dumond." She offered a gloved hand.

"Pleasure," Weston said, and took her hand. "Bill Weston at your service, ma'am."

"Oh my. Did you hear that Jed," Dumond said and swallowed her drink whole. "I'm sure I can find many uses for a man of your–bearing." The bartender, Jed, grunted and moved away to busy himself at the other end of the bar.

"So, Ms. Dumond, you spent your ace in the hole," Weston nodded toward Bert as he descended the stairs with an empty tray, "and it didn't pay off. Are you going to send someone of my *bearing* to balance the scales in your direction?"

"Del Cornish is a cheap piece of dung, but that isn't what our relationship amounts to," Dumond said with a frown. "Certainly not over a couple of bottles of wine I'd forgotten to order from my own supplier."

"Did he have that kind of relationship with others around town? I heard Horace Puddicombe wasn't too fond of Cornish's business practices."

"Oh, you heard that did you?" A sly smile curled Dumond's lips. "No doubt a cast-off lesson from our holy sister in waiting. Well, she wasn't wrong. Puddicombe didn't appreciate Del's ability to corner the market around here. Of course, Puddicombe was the last person who should've been complaining, what with him having hit it rich in gold. Del knew that, too."

"I gather Cornish wasn't about to vote Puddicombe in

for mayor?"

"Nobody was going to vote for that man," Dumond said with a look of disgust. "Mayor Winter is the best thing to ever happen to this town. We'd be foolish to give that up for an old prospector too rich for his own good."

"Puddicombe must have thought differently," Weston said with a shrug.

"That man was delusional. An outsider with the whiff of new money on him. Puddicombe wouldn't even spend time in the town after dark, so afraid that he might be robbed," she scoffed. "Instead, he'd spend his nights out there in his gawdy house on the outskirts, alone with those darkies he hired on." Dumond's face soured, her mouth in a snarl.

"Seems like he may not have been as well liked as he had thought."

"Oh, some people tolerated him. Ambrose and Dermot gave him the time of day, though I can't see why. The man was a chore."

"That why the town held a celebration the night he was discovered?"

Etta opened her mouth to say something else, a sneer cutting across her porcelain skin, but the thought must have bit itself off and she forced an almost pleasant smile.

"I think I'll go look in on a couple of friends." Weston stood and made a show of stretching out his back. "You have a good day now, Ms. Dumond. Bert," he raised his hand to the boy and made his exit.

Perhaps a few more days in Millwood wouldn't be so arduous after all.

II

Weston weaved his way through the dust covered streets, avoiding the swaying citizens who passed him, a goofy smile etched on their drawn and hungover faces. Unlike what Bert had said, it wasn't just the twilight hours that saw the townsfolk enjoying themselves, and Weston thought that more than a few of them had a run in with opium before heading to their local watering hole.

Opium addicts were nothing new, but in a town the size of Milltown, the Last Chance Saloon had no competition. That was unique, and so much the better for Ms. Etta Dumond, who seemed to have her fingers in just about everything except dry goods. She left that to the miserly Delbert Cornish. Both of whom seemed to have little good to say about the recently deceased Horace Puddicombe.

The urge to talk to Mr. Cornish brought a crooked smile to Weston's face. He thought something might be there, but it wasn't his business; he'd let the town figure it all out. All he had to do was drop off Javier and wait for his train to come in. Simple. And yet it didn't feel right.

Weston had no trouble finding Dermot and his nephew, Ambrose. He asked a slack-jawed local busy staring at his shoes where they kept shop. The livery stable was just down the road from the church. It was a large red building with barn doors. Clean and crisp white paint adorned the door frame. It surprised Weston seeing something so clean around a livery. It spoke of Dermot and Ambrose's hard work and dedication.

Weston knocked on one of the barn doors and pulled it open, his eyes following a slantwise shadow that struggled to keep the sun from entering the small barn. Gravel crunched under his boot as he entered the dimly lit room. Horses shook their heads or grunted on either side of him, nervous at his approach. At the back of the building was a single doorway that stood open. The white light of midday cut through the shadows and guided Weston through without tripping over a feed bucket, pitchfork, or water trough.

"Hello," Weston called out as he moved through the horses who were now sniffling and snorting.

On the other side of the door was a small, enclosed green space. In the centre there was a small circle where the grass had been beaten down by horses getting a modicum of exercise. The yard was surrounded by a high fence of red-painted boards and was occupied by well-used saddles and riding implements, as well as three bales of hay stacked atop one another and a barrel of rainwater. There was no sign of Ambrose or Dermot.

Walking back through the barn, Weston couldn't see anything out of the ordinary, or anything that might indicate where the men had gone, but he found it strange that they would leave their business unattended.

Exiting onto the street, Weston squinted his eyes against the risen sun, and moved his way back towards the hotel to put him up for a day or two. Turning a corner by the church he nearly ran into Ambrose, the young man jumped out of the way in surprise.

"Damn near gave me a heart attack, Weston." Ambrose clutched his breast and chuckled. "What are you doing about? Where's the sister?" His broad smile beamed as he did an exaggerated pantomime of looking for Mejia.

"Sister is at her house, I suppose." Weston said, pushing his hat back away from his eyes. "She let me use Javier to get here. Said I could leave him with you and your uncle. That you'd make sure he got back to her."

"Javier out and about without the sister? That's a

strange sight, I'd wager. Poor horse rarely can stand to leave her side." The young man straightened and rubbed his stubbled chin. "Though what she said was true, we'll get him back to her." He looked past over Weston's shoulder and pointed. "The livery is over this way."

"Just came from there, place was wide open. I guess this a friendlier town than I had thought."

"Uncle Derm wasn't there?" Ambrose asked. He moved around Weston and stared off at the big red building.

"Nope."

"That's strange." Ambrose shrugged. "I suppose he had to run out for something. Probably just getting us some grub. While we're waiting, why don't you take me to Javier. Won't old Derm be surprised to see him." A chuckle escaped the young man as he motioned for Weston to lead the way.

"Nearly clear on the other side of town," Ambrose laughed and slapped Weston on the shoulder. Ambrose was a tireless conversationalist, and Weston got the impression he would talk about anything and everything. As they navigated the streets of Millwood, Ambrose took on the role of tour guide, and tried to impress upon Weston the daily comings and goings of the town, which amounted to an unbridled rant about the townsfolk and their little eccentricities.

"One old buzzard who you may want to steer clear of is Delbert Cornish," Ambrose said, after a long and uninspired dressing down of another horse lender, Garfield Brown.

"He owns the dry goods store?" Weston asked. "I've

heard a good bit about that old fella. Haven't heard much good. Still, he seems to be quite a fixture here in town. Almost like he's indispensable." He watched Ambrose's wide smile falter, a nearly imperceptible quiver at the corner of his mouth. Weston tried on his own grin. "One person I've heard precious little about is the dearly departed." Weston pointed to another of Puddicombe's mayoral posters tacked to the side of a house. "Seems like no one has much to say about him."

"Horace?" Ambrose said and shook his head. "Well, I guess there isn't much to say about him. Not anymore."

"I heard he wasn't well liked around here. Nearly as polarizing as Mr. Cornish, it seems."

"From who?" Ambrose's ever-present smile soured again, and he turned on Weston. "Horace was a bit of a strange bird, but he was a fair man. He kept his word, and regardless of what others say about him, that makes him a good man in my books."

"Did you and he get along well?"

"We did all right. Horace and Dermot were chummier, but it was a loan from Horace that got us the livery. We owe him our livelihood."

"I suppose you boys would've voted for him if he had lived," Weston said and noticed some passersby take interest.

"I don't know about that," Ambrose said and waved to the people passing on the street. "I mean, Mayor Winter has done a lot for this little town. Without him we wouldn't see the business that we do, and I doubt we would be drawing in all the big wigs that we have been, or even have all the little perks of the city..."

"Like gas lamps," Weston added.

"Just like that," Ambrose nodded. "Mayor Winter has

his gasping throat.

"Mr. Weston?" Ambrose approached him.

Weston found the strength to put out one heavy arm. "I'm okay," he coughed, and he did feel better. It was a sudden change, the pain draining away from him, as if a blanket had been removed. He could feel his strength returning, could feel the darkness flee from his eyes and his breath came more readily. "I'm fine. Just felt a little woozy is all. Might need a bite to eat." Ambrose smiled at him, but there was no joviality in it. He returned to traipsing around the garden as if he might find his uncle hidden away somewhere.

Weston turned back to the barn, the horses quieter now, and if he squinted enough he could see Javier standing tall at the other end of the building. The shadows had lightened, had retreated. Weston wasn't sure how he knew that, but he did, could feel it in his bones. He rotated his sore shoulder and started to look around the yard with Ambrose.

"I don't know," Ambrose said at last, beating his hat against his leg. "It seems damned strange that Derm isn't here minding the horses." His face was strained, his worry-free expression vanished.

"Could he have gone home, been called away?" Weston said and took a seat on a nearby hay bale.

"Maybe. I don't see Olivia sending for him though. Maybe the sheriff. But I saw Port just before I bumped into you and he didn't say anything to me. You sure he wasn't here when you stopped by?"

"Not unless he can turn invisible," Weston said and made a broad gesture towards the empty yard.

"Dammit." Ambrose fixed his hat on his head and stormed around the yard one more time.

Weston watched him. The carefree boy had himself a temper. That rage wouldn't prove good for anyone, least of all Dermot if something serious had happened to him. It was time for Weston to take his leave.

"I'm sure he'll turn up," Weston said, "and thanks again for taking Javier for me. I'm sure the sister will appreciate it. I best be getting on my way, still have to find a place to put me up for the night."

"Wait a minute," Ambrose said. "Was this here earlier?" His face was close to the heavy timber that made up the door frame leading back into the livery.

Weston peered over Ambrose's shoulder and got a good look at a fresh, claw-like gouge in the wood. Weston's shoulder started to throb.

"No," he stammered and grabbed his arm, "I didn't notice."

"There's blood in it," Ambrose said, his voice shrill. "Is that Dermot's blood?"

"It wasn't there," Weston said. "It must've...must've..." He crumpled to the ground, the pain digging into his chest like fishhooks tearing at skin.

"Did you do this?" Ambrose's voice was vacant, his face slack. "What'd you do to Dermot?"

Weston felt the edge of Ambrose's boot before he saw it, the pain merely a dull thud in comparison to the sensation that crawled away from his shoulder. A cold sliver of pain wedged in his heart, he felt another kick, and then he slipped into darkness.

III

The cell was standard issue. Three concrete walls, one wall and door made of iron bars, and a matching window just within reach of Weston's fingertips. There was no cot, but a filthy mat lay in the dirt, and a bucket sat in the corner where he could piss and shit. Weston had seen worse places but not by much. He settled himself into one corner, avoiding the pale, slanting rays of moonlight that passed across the floor. He hadn't seen another human face since he woke hours earlier.

He'd been bleeding. He couldn't really tell from where, though his lips had certainly been mashed against his teeth, and he could feel swelling around his right eye. The pain in his shoulder and chest had faded away to a dull twinge during his sleep, and he had only to deal with the aches left by Ambrose.

Now that he could think clearly, Weston figured he was an easy choice for someone to pin the murder on. The sheriff made that clear the first time they met. He was new in town, he had few connections, and he'd been at the scene of the murder. If there was a murder. Being locked in a cell didn't give him much hope on that front; Dermot was likely dead.

If the sheriff wanted to look good, make it look like he caught a killer, Weston would be an easy target. Of course, that would mean the sheriff was one of two things: lazy or didn't want the real killer caught.

"There's something there," Weston said, and he *could* feel it. A little burst of excitement bolted across his chest.

He sighed, pushing that feeling away. Little use that realization did him now. He was in a strange town with no one to speak for him. Sister Mejia was a recluse. The priest, Father Mason, seemed to be at odds with Johnson already, and Ambrose—well, Weston wasn't exactly holding out for a sudden turn in Ambrose's beliefs. A fella like that would be out for blood. If that were the case, Weston would find out what Ambrose thought soon enough.

He managed to sleep. His back against the corner of the cell, his chin on his chest, Weston's body needed the rest and thanked him for it. The soreness and stiffness of the previous night had almost disappeared, though that would soon be replaced with a new soreness from the beating he took. Still, he had time to enjoy the little aches and pains before the big ones came back again.

It was the jailhouse's door that brought Weston around. It wasn't slammed, not even closed hard, but the click of the latch perked up his ears and brought him back to life. He tried to remain still, but it did him little good.

"Hello, Mr. Weston," the sheriff's deep voice carried through the small jailhouse "I'm sure these accommodations were adequate for your needs." Johnson smiled behind his big moustache.

Weston sat still in his corner, his eyes watching the sheriff who placed a chair in front of his cell and plonked his ass down on it.

"I'm sure a smart fella like yourself must've figured out what you're in here for. Although, some out there," he pointed over his shoulder toward the town, "don't think you're very smart at all. In fact, they think you're downright stupid. Not that you can blame them. You see, they understand that you came into town just two times, each time you were seen with Ambrose or Dermot. The second time you came back, of course, lead to Dermot's death. Chumming around with your victims before you kill them just isn't something a smart man does." The sheriff leaned back into a deep slouch and studied Weston over a smooth smile.

"Here's how it looks, Mr. Weston. A stranger like yourself, a stray brought around by Sister Mejia out in her shack," he paused there, seeing something in Weston's face. "Oh yes, Mr. Weston, you weren't the first stray the sister brought along. I suppose you may have been the first she brought to a murder, but that's neither here nor there. You see, Mejia's strays all had one thing in common: they were batshit insane. Yep, loopy from the sun, or from Sister Mejia's strange ways, or maybe they were just plain crazy their whole lives. It doesn't matter, not really. In each case they left after a time without any harm coming to anyone. Well, I'm sure Darrell Brahams' livestock will never be the same again, but we had no murders. Understand?

"Well, until a few days ago. You rode into town twice, once with the sister, once without, and you spent a little time with Ambrose or Dermot. Both I'm told. They had a soft spot for the sister, so I can't say it's a big surprise that you were introduced right away. Big mistake on her part, wasn't it?

"The town out there thinks you got pretty excited after hanging out with those boys, and you started to make plans. Plans that you couldn't hold on to for too long. Maybe you were trying to set up a simultaneous killing that didn't pan out, or maybe you just wanted to focus on the older man, hard to say. Either way you came back to town on a borrowed horse knowing those boys would take care of Sister Mejia's property at their livery. Smart, in a way.

"Now, we just found Dermot's body. Throttled like Horace and Percy. The only thing I can't figure is why you didn't kill both of them boys. You had the chance, why not take it?"

The sheriff's smile grated on Weston's nerves and a fierce streak of anger rose in his belly that he had to work to force back down.

"No," Weston said after several too long moments, and he moved into the middle of the cell facing the sheriff who peered at him through iron bars.

"No, you didn't have a plan to kill those boys, or no you didn't have the chance to kill them?"

"I mean, no. You don't believe any of what you are saying. You may not know who the killer is, but you know it's not me."

Johnson faltered some. It wasn't much, but Weston could see the corners of his mouth dip some. And it took him much more effort to maintain it.

"I know there is a killer, and I know it *is* you." Johnson said. "The only thing I need to figure out is how long you've been in spitting distance of Millwood. Maybe you killed a few more people, eh?"

Weston laughed; he couldn't stop himself. "Sheriff, you're an easy man to read. I can see through you quicker than glass. You don't really know much of anything do you? You just want someone to take the blame. Unfortunately for me, I fit the mold. New to town, no acquaintances…"

"And a pissy attitude," Johnson sneered through the bars.

"You may just be right there, but you're wrong on so many counts. You just need something to keep you afloat. I'm easy, I guess. I'm someone the whole town can get behind. It doesn't matter that Delbert Cornish and Etta Dumond had issue with Horace Puddicome. I'm sure it also doesn't matter that Dermot was friendly with Puddicombe. Tell me, Sheriff, have you investigated those people yet? Or have they given you enough money to look the other way? To look straight at me."

Johnson's hard-fought, smug facade crumbled and

fell. A frown, almost a pout, replaced it. The big man went sickly gray and sat himself up straight.

"You don't know what you're talking about," Johnson said, his voice a strained whisper.

"I know what treachery looks like, Sheriff. I know that you are doing your best to cover up something. Why that is, I can't rightly say, but I can only imagine it's because of money. Or fear. What scares you, Sheriff?" Weston tried on his own smug smile.

"Fuck you," Johnson shrugged. "Piece of advice, Weston. I'd watch myself if you want to start spreading those rumors. You may not like the response you'll get."

The door creaked opened. A warm breeze swirled the dust at Weston's feet. Johnson exploded to standing, up-turning the chair, and sending it across the wooden floor. He turned on the door violently, his cannonball sized hands rolling into fists.

"Who the hell..." he let himself trail off and dug in his heels. He took a deep breath, ready to call down whom-ever walked through the door.

The feminine form of Etta Dumond stood in the shad-ow, the sunlight at her back. "Am I interrupting some-thing?" she asked, one hand on a cocked hip.

Johnson deflated, his shoulders rounding and his head turning to the side. He kicked at the floor like a child caught in the act by his mother.

"Jesus, Ms. Dumond, I was just about to give you a hell of a tongue lashing." His voice cracked, but Weston couldn't tell if it was from humour or fear.

"You were, were you?" Dumond's smile faltered some, her eyes serious as she moved forward toward the sheriff and Weston.

"I mean, I wasn't expecting anyone, least of all you.

Did we have an appointment?" Johnson moved off to the side, one long arm reaching out to lean on the wall, a great sigh sending a shudder through him.

"No, Port, we didn't have a scheduled meeting," She rolled her green eyes and peeked around the large man. "I came here to see if you really did have Mr. Weston in custody. I can now see that you do." She frowned.

"Well, Ms. Dumond, as you can see, I'm busy here. Maybe I could call on you a little later…" Johnson moved to intercept her, his large hands open in front of him. Dumond wasn't having it.

"Why, Mr. Weston," Dumond sidestepped the laborious sheriff and moved closer to the cell. "What are you doing in there?" she asked Weston.

"Ma'am," Weston stood and tipped his head to the matron of the Last Chance. "You'll have to ask the sheriff about that, I haven't the foggiest idea."

Dumond let out a low chuckle, her eyes emerald slits.

"Porter Johnson, what is the meaning of this?" Dumond's voice went up an octave as she called to the sheriff. For his part, Johnson seemed to sag more, his face collapsing in front of Weston and the businesswoman.

"Well, Ms. Dumond, that is sheriff and town business."

"Oh please," Dumond waved her hand. "I pay my due diligence to the town."

"Yes, Ms. Dumond, but I can't go—"

"Can't or won't, Sheriff?"

"God damn it, Etta," the sheriff stood to his full height, towering over the woman. His eyes were a blue balefire that sought to bore holes into whatever or whomever stood in their path. Johnson grabbed her wrist and pulled it to his chest. "Let me do my job for once."

"Sheriff," Dumond said. Her voice was low, calm. There was no sign of fear in it, only pure, unfiltered authority. Johnson stared at his hand, held it there for another moment and let go, backing up with his hands open in front of him.

"He's suspected of killing Dermot." The sheriff spoke barely above a whisper, his eyes turned to the ground.

"Well, that's just ridiculous." Dumond turned to Weston, a broad smile stretched across her face. "When was he suspected of killing poor Dermot?"

"Sometime in the afternoon, according to Ambrose."

"Impossible," Dumond said. "Mr. Weston was with me."

Johnson's head shot up at once, his eyes roaming the woman's face for some sign of falsehood or deception. He didn't find it there.

"What do you mean?" The sheriff spoke slowly, drawing out his words to study them both.

"Oh, don't be so foolish, Port." Dumond waved her hand. "He was in the Last Chance. From what I hear he rescued our little Bert from some young ruffians and made sure he got back to work, safe and sound." She gave Weston a wink and faced the sheriff.

"You're sure he was there all afternoon?" Johnson tensed up and he approached Dumond again. It looked like he might make a grab for her again, but he thought better of it. "You can vouch for him?"

"Maybe not all afternoon, but I can vouch for him. Yes."

The sheriff straightened, his big eyes blinking in a moment's contemplation.

"Regardless," the sheriff said at length, "he's still a suspect. He can't be allowed to leave that cell until we have everything sorted." He crossed his arms and nod-ded to himself. That was the end of it.

"No, release him. Now." Dumond stood facing the sheriff, her hands on her hips. The sheriff's mouth dropped open.

"Etta, damn it, woman, I've done enough. The man will stay here until the killer is found, and that is the end of it."

Dumond put her hand to her ear and cocked her head to the side. "What's that I hear, Porter? Is that the sound of a train pulling into the station?"

Weston couldn't hear anything above the shallow breaths of everyone in that room. He didn't know what she was playing at, but it drew another reaction from the sheriff. His eyes hardened, but he also turned his ear to the door. Listening.

"I hear that Mayor Winter will be in town before sup-pertime. I suppose I could always bring this matter up with him when he arrives, perhaps we could even inter-rupt the planning of his dinner party with this. I'm sure he'll be overjoyed to learn about your work in the town, and in the Last Chance."

"Etta, you don't mean that." The sheriff had one hand open and in front of him as if he were trying to lull a feral animal to calm. Weston was a man who had been around guns his entire life, and for a moment, Weston thought he saw the sheriff's hand twitch on his holster.

"Oh, dear Port, I mean it. I think you'll find that I'm deadly serious." Weston wanted to reach out and shake her. Warn her.

The sheriff sighed and deflated once more. He allowed himself one single nod before he moved to the opposite wall to retrieve the keys from their resting place. His eyes, when they met Weston's, were pure indignation and hate. Weston would run into this man again.

Sheriff Johnson let him go without uttering another word. Dumond excused herself and left the room, leaving the two men alone. Weston thought that once Dumond had left, Johnson would turn his fury on him, perhaps finally draw that gun he was itching to loose just a moment before.

There was nothing.

The sheriff gathered up whatever belongings the deputies had given him and placed them on the small desk that sat over to the side of the building. With that done he walked out of the building, never uttering a sound or looking Weston's way. Weston was just fine with that. He'd rather not goad an already irate man into a fight when he had no guns at his side.

Weston took his time checking his things, taking stock of what was there: another outfit, what was left of a bacon sandwich, and the silver crucifix and chain that the sister had left him. When he was satisfied that he wasn't missing anything, he threw his satchel around his shoulder and made for the door. Etta Dumond was sitting on the other side waiting for him.

Weston tipped his hat to the woman once again. "Ms. Dumond. Thank you for speaking on my behalf. "

"You're innocent, aren't you?" Dumond was staring out into the town before her, a pipe sticking out from between her teeth, smoke rising from its bowl.

"Never saw a woman smoke a pipe before," Weston said and stood next to her in the courtyard.

"I'm sure there are plenty of things you haven't seen

a woman do," Dumond said and started to walk away from the building. She waved one hand behind her to call Weston to her side. As he approached, she stuck out one of her thin arms, crooked at the elbow.

Weston linked arms with the woman, let her lean on him some as she puffed away on her pipe. An elongated bowl, onyx in colour to match the stem, sat at the pipe's end and was cradled in Etta's gloved hand. The pipe's bowl had tiny specks of white, or silver, that shimmered as Dumond moved. The more Weston looked at the pipe, the more specks he saw. It was as if the pipe captured the night sky within its surface. She gave him a sidelong glance, a smile in her eyes.

"Mr. Weston," her raspy voice pulled his attention back to her, "walk me to my bar. I'll see that you get a nice glass of whiskey for your trouble."

Weston grunted his ascent. After what she'd done, it would be terribly rude for him to turn her down. Still, he had hoped he could get to a horse dealer and put some space between him and the town.

"You see them watching, don't you?" Dumond spoke in a hushed tone, he eyes ahead of her, pipe in hand, and smile beaming.

Weston looked around, could see that the crowded streets of Millwood didn't just have feet, but it had eyes, and each set was turned toward him.

"I see them. Is that because I'm on the arm of Millwood's sweetheart?"

Dumond barked out a small, forced laugh. "Not even close, I'm afraid. Why don't you look again?"

Weston turned back to the crowd. Most stared with some sort of curiosity, as if they were trying to figure him out. Perhaps trying to figure out what he was doing with

Etta Dumond. Others looked at him as if he were a novelty, easy come, easy go. Most of those eyes though, they stared at Weston with fear. Not just the healthy fear that keeps one man from killing another or keeps a sane man from fighting a grizzly barehanded. No, this was a primal fear. A fear that would turn into something else given half the chance. It would turn to anger and fury. Some of those eyes that were laid upon him already bared the marks of that burning rage. So intense that it nearly turned Weston back.

Weston's breath hitched in his throat. They believed he'd killed Dermot. Any moment he expected to see the crowd pull out pitchforks and catch him unawares. But they didn't.

As if reading his thoughts, Dumond said: "it's because of me darling."

"How's that?" Weston said, caught off guard.

"They won't attack because you're with *me*. The sheriff's failing manners notwithstanding, I garner my fair share of respect, karma, and well-being in this town. Unfortunately, I can't be held up babysitting jailbirds. After you drop me at the door of my bar, you're on your own."

Dumond gave Weston a side-eyed glare, and a broad bow-like smile stretched across her face. Weston had to give it to the woman, she was tough and smart. It wouldn't do her any favors to help him out, though it probably wouldn't hurt her much either. Which begged the question that had been nagging at Weston.

"Why help me?"

"I like to play against the odds," Dumond said, her face falling serious.

The rest of their walk was in silence, the heat of the stares from the townspeople weighing on them. Dumond put on a brave face, a smile and a nod to those she passed, but Weston thought there was something underneath that. Fear, maybe, buried deep down under her charm and strength. He absently ran his fingers over his scarred shoulder.

"This is it, Mr. Weston," Dumond said, pushing open the door of the Last Chance. "There's still a glass of whiskey in here for you if you'd like."

Weston shook his head and tried to gauge the amount of hostile looks surrounded him. "I think it's best I put some distance between this town and me."

Dumond smiled around her pipe. "You may be right. Stay out of trouble, Mr. Weston."

"Much obliged, Ms. Dumond." Weston tipped his hat and turned away from the Last Chance.

CHAPTER FIVE

I

Weston kept his head down. The urge to let his hands slip to his hips and his belt worked overtime. He'd always imagined that he'd die in a gunfight, a hail of bullets to send him to the great beyond, whatever that was, but not before he took some bodies with him. It was a violent death he had seen in his future after the war tore the country apart; since he fought in the mud and blood, looking his countrymen in the face as he shot or gutted them. It was a violent world that bred violent death.

To be lynched in some far-flung town in the West was not something he thought would claim his soul. Then again, maybe hanging would be the right way to go. His past had more than a few skeletons crawling about in it, more than a few things that he needed to bring to bear.

The streets emptied as he moved along. And though he could still feel the eyes of those that passed him, Weston felt much more at ease now that he was moving away from onlookers. He just needed to do what he had meant to just the day before and get out of town.

The distant sound of music and the hushed roar of gathered people talking surprised him. Something big was happening nearby. Weston couldn't help but think that a posse had gathered and made plans to ambush him in the plain daylight, hang him in the town square. They were so happy about it that they had hired a band to play music. A soundtrack to murder.

Weston expected to be mobbed, to have the entire town descend upon him in a righteous anger, but that didn't happen. All that he had to suffer through was some annoyed stares from the townsfolk whose path he stood in. His legs went weak, and he felt a little giddy, a bubble of laughter threatening to spill past his lips. Weston had thought he was marching to his death, but what he faced was more akin to a garden party than a lynching.

The area around the train station was crowded with people. They were scurrying around like ants from their hill. Bright streamers and ribbons covered the nearby buildings, and a stage was set up in the center of the courtyard with a four-piece band playing atop of it. Games were being played, people were laughing, and the death of their own forgotten. Again.

Weston made his way through the crowd. The station building was empty in comparison to its courtyard, and even the ticket person was missing from his post. The chalkboard sign had changed also. The times of arrival and departure was missing. In its place was a welcome in big, hand-written letters:

Welcome Home

Mayor Winter

And Governor Carlyle.

So, it's a triumphant return, Weston thought and scrubbed the palm of his hand with his beard.

"Mr. Weston?" Bert's voice carried across the pavilion drawing Weston's eyes back to the crowd. The boy was pushing his way through them, dark hair bouncing away from his face. His movements brought more attention to Weston. Heavy-lidded eyes turned his way, their unfriendly faces marking him in the crowd.

"Doing okay there, Bert?" he asked. The people around him kept moving, and Weston sighed with relief.

"Yes, sir. Ms. Dumond gave me some time to try out the games. Say, what happened to your face?"

"Never heard about that, huh?" Weston touched his swollen eye, ran his fingers across a scratch and some crusted blood in his moustache. He hadn't taken the time to think about how he looked. It'd have to go on the list. "It seems I ran across the wrong person at the wrong time."

"He sure worked you over," Bert shrugged. "Want to try a game? Might make you feel better." Bert gave him a half smile.

"You know something, Bert, you're probably right," Weston said. "I'm sure I can make some time for a game or two."

The boy led him from game to game, never tiring. Weston was quiet, and his smile was hard fought, but it found a way to burrow out of his doldrums. Thoughts of Sister Mejia in the forest, his questioning at the hands of the sheriff, and the death of Dermot were forgotten as he took part in the day. He let himself laugh at the boy's frustration with the BB rifle, a laugh that carried eventually to Bert, much to the boy's chagrin.

At noon, the music stopped. A cacophony of hushes flowed through the crowd, silencing them. The sound of a train coming down the line echoed in the silence, and excited chatting resumed. The mayor would soon be home. Early.

Weston drew Bert close, and followed the lead of what the crowd was doing: readying themselves for the arrival. There was whispering now, many people with smiles of anticipation beaming at one another. Weston allowed himself another sigh. It had been a long time since he was able to feel at ease, unburdened by anything. Despite the worries that had begun to draw around him in these past few days, he felt content.

Rough hands grabbed his shirt at the shoulders; fists curled around the clothing in bunches. He had no time to register what was happening before he was pulled backwards, falling to his back with a grunt, his air driven from his lungs.

"You son of a bitch," Ambrose said aiming a kick at Weston's head.

Not this time. Weston heaved his legs over his head and rolled to his feet, Ambrose's foot just catching his hat and sending it flying into the crowd. There was a sharp pain in his back from the fall, and he felt like he was sucking air through a straw, but he was up and aware.

If he hadn't recognized the voice, Weston would have never counted the man before him as the Ambrose he had known and talked with. The man's once infectious smile was drowned in a snarl that took over his entire face, his entire body. The young man's eyes were sunken and red from grief and the bottle. His strong thews were taut like springs, ready to launch themselves at Weston, and he wasn't alone. Circling Ambrose was a group of four other men, their faces alike in rage. Relatives or friends of Ambrose one and all, young like him and full of piss and vinegar.

"Ambrose, I'm sorry…" Weston said, his wind coming back some now. He held out his hand before him, open, empty.

"You shut your fuckin' mouth." Ambrose made another charge at Weston, his fists flying before him. Weston tried to dodge out of the way, move his head just enough to avoid being hit and grab the grieving man, try to talk some sense into him. Ambrose was younger and faster than him though, and he got a good clip on the shoulder before he could wrap the man in a bear hug.

"Listen to me, damn it." Weston screamed into Ambrose's face, hoping to clear the fog of rage that had overtaken the man's brain. "I didn't kill anyone. The sheriff let me go for Christ sakes."

"That bitch Etta Dumond got you free, you mean." A wild smirk overtook Ambrose's face and he headbutted Weston on the bridge of the nose.

Eyes filling with water, Weston let Ambrose go and cradled his nose in one hand, dried his eyes with the other. A surge of searing pain ran through his face and he cursed, trying to see what Ambrose might do next.

It wasn't Ambrose this time, but the others who came at Weston, grabbing him from all sides. They held him up for Ambrose but got their own licks in on him while they could. Ambrose wasted no time and landed a wild haymaker on Weston's chin that made him see stars and taste the iron of blood in his mouth.

"The sheriff might not hang you," Ambrose said through gritted teeth, "but I sure as hell aim to."

"No!" It was Bert, his voice shrill as he grabbed Ambrose by the arm before he could bring it back for another swing at Weston.

"Ambrose, please leave him be," Bert begged.

Ambrose wasn't in the listening mood, nor was he in the mood to be gentle. He flung off the boy, pushed him to the ground on his ass. "Back off, Bert, this ain't your fight."

Weston growled and tried to break loose from the hold

of the four men at his arms. They had to readjust some, but they held firm, laughing.

Bert rushed in again, dust kicking up around his boots. He clung to Ambrose's leg this time, muttering something about his mother. Ambrose cursed and pried the boy off, slapped him.

"Percy, hold this boy before he really gets hurt," Ambrose said over the cries of Bert clutching his cheek in the dirt. The whole courtyard had gone silent, the crowd circling around them to watch but doing nothing.

"George, make sure no one else interferes."

Weston could feel the hands release, saw two men jog over to Bert, one holding him tight about his arms and neck, the other standing guard before the gathered onlookers.

"Stand him up," Ambrose rubbed his left hand over his right fist.

Weston was dragged to his feet by the remaining two men, their grip tight on his arms.

Ambrose cocked his right hand for another punch, but Weston was ready. He flailed out with one foot, supported by two of his attackers, and kicked Ambrose in the chest. It was an action that knocked all four men to the ground, three in surprise and one with intent.

Grips loose from the confusion, Weston tore himself free, raining blows down on his two would be restrainers.

A set of strong arms wrapped around his neck, closing off his airway, choking him. Weston grabbed the arm in his two hands and, using a twist in his hips, flipped his assailant over him and fell to his own knees, throwing wild punches at the man even before he realized it was Ambrose.

"Bill!" Bert's voice called out drawing Weston to turn to him. The man who had held Bert had tossed the boy to the ground again and was rushing Weston with a drawn knife. Weston ran to meet him, grabbed the knife wielding wrist in his two hands, and wrestled him for control. With a kick to the man's knee, Weston was able to wrest the knife from the man's grip. Wrapping his own fist around the knife handle, Weston hit the man on the back of his head and dropped him.

"Percy!" the man on guard screamed and ran at Weston, his own knife drawn. Weston wasted no time. He faked meeting the man knife to knife, but instead ducked under his arms and plowed a shoulder into his stomach. He followed through by grabbing the back of the man's knees and putting him on the ground. The knife fell in the distance. A whistle seemed to sound in the distance.

Winded, George flailed on the ground, one arm on his stomach and the other trying to scratch at Weston's face. Weston took the time he needed and landed two good punches to George's nose and watched the man's eyes roll back in his head. Then Ambrose tackled him.

Weston rolled with the tackle and came out on top of the grieving young man. He had his knife to Ambrose's throat, trying to calm the fire in his veins.

"Go ahead, you coward, kill me like you killed my uncle." Ambrose's face was red. Blood ran from his nose and his face was twisted with hate.

Weston had a mind to grant Ambrose's wish. It would be easy enough, a quick slice across the throat and it would be done. He'd watch the life drain from the man's eyes and never have to worry about his retribution again. After all, he had been attacked by them, he was just finishing it.

A shot went off and Weston fell to the ground, trying to scramble back to his feet, the blade he had acquired tossed to the side. The scars on his shoulder and chest began to pulse with pain.

II

"Well, Mr. Weston, perhaps Ms. Dumond's trust in you wasn't so well placed."

The sheriff stood just a few feet away from them, his gun pointed in the air. The crowd around them had started to scatter, and, aside from some groans from Ambrose and his men, silence remained.

Weston saw Bert not far off, kneeling on the ground. His face betrayed a mix of confusion and sadness, but not fear or anger. Not hate. Weston was thankful. He didn't want the boy to look at him like that.

"Okay, Weston, step back, hands in the air." The sheriff walked forward and helped Ambrose to his feet. He was flanked by two men Weston didn't recognize. They didn't look like any of the deputies that Weston had encountered since he arrived in Millwood, and they didn't look much like the rough type. The first man approached on the sheriff's right. He was an older man, his balding head surrounded by white hair that was exposed for the world to see, and he wore a smart three-piece suit. There was a long gold chain that ran along the man's thin stomach that he was fingering in his black leather gloves. On the sheriff's left was a tall, sombre man. He stood more to the back, his large blue eyes seeming to take in the whole scene. He had a pale complexion that was accentuated even more by his dark black hair and moustache. His mouth was a tight line that spoke of grim tidings and quick decisions. He was dressed in a dark blue suit, his arms crossed behind his back making it taut around his chest and stomach as he followed the sheriff.

"What happened here, Ambrose?" The sheriff had his gun stowed in its holster and was giving the young man a once over. Ambrose continued to look over his shoulder at Weston, rage still contorting his face.

"I'm doing what the law ought to have done." Ambrose practically spit in Johnson's face. His anger was easily doled out it seemed.

"I know it's been a big shock for you Ambrose." The sheriff moved to put a hand on Ambrose's shoulder, but the young man shrugged it off and pushed the sheriff away from him.

"You don't know shit, Port. If you did, you would've hung this bastard when you had the chance." Ambrose turned back to Weston. "Or you'd let me and the boys at him for a while and let justice be done."

Johnson's face fell, his eyes darkened, and he gave the men flanking him a cursory look. "Didn't seem to help you and your boys out much today," he said waving a hand at the human wreckage around them.

"What the fuck did you say?" Ambrose launched himself at the sheriff, but Johnson was a quick draw, and his gun was to Ambrose's belly before young man could do anything else.

"I know you're having a rough go," the sheriff raised his free hand and waved it, his deputies came running in from the crowd. "I think all you and your boys need is some time in a cell while you clear your head of all that booze." He handed Ambrose over to a couple of stout men, who dragged him through the crowd along with his friends.

Weston watched the men go, being led to the jail he

had only recently left himself. He ran a hand under his nose, and it came back with blood. He started to feel those little aches and pains again now, the scratches and contusions that he had sustained were going to start smarting him before long.

"What am I to do with you, Mr. Weston?" Sheriff Johnson said as he sauntered up to him. "I can't seem to put you in jail, you'll just walk right back out. I can't seem to leave you alone in town because you'll be killed, or you'll get someone else killed. So, Weston, you tell me what I should do?"

Weston tried to look past the sheriff, but his sight was blocked by the two newcomers, their eyes intent on what Weston had to say.

"Who're your friends, Sheriff?"

Weston thought he saw Johnson freeze then. His eyes squinted as if Weston had figured out a secret or asked a question Johnson didn't want to answer.

"I'm David Carlyle," the older man said and extended his hand to help Weston out of the dirt.

"That's Governor Carlyle to you, Weston," Johnson said.

"Frank Winter," the other man said.

"Mayor Winter?" Weston dusted himself off. "I've heard a lot about you."

The mayor frowned.

"Weston, I'm getting annoyed," the sheriff took a step in front of the mayor, one hand on his gun.

"Don't get yourself frazzled, Johnson. I aim to leave town just as soon as I can." He pulled his train ticket out of his pocket. "Damn train doesn't leave for another two days, if it does leave."

"That's a mighty solid plan, Mr. Weston. But, if I were

you, I think I might make my way out of here sooner than that." The sheriff and his two shadows nodded and walked off, the older man keeping his large brown eyes on Weston as he passed.

Bert had gone. Weston was hoping that he might be able to explain to him what was happening, explain why he did what he did. It wasn't fair that he'd been drawn into this with him, and he was sorry for that. He wanted to apologize, but he didn't think he would be a much welcome sight for Bert.

The crowd was much more aware of him now than earlier. Fear tickled most of their faces—fear and unease. People squirmed away from him, scattered at the thought of having to touch him. Weston was fine with the distance, but the fear was something else entirely. Would he be able to buy himself into a place to sleep with his newborn infamy?

He moved to the empty train station, hoping the crowd would die down sooner rather than later. He could see the courtyard stage. The sheriff and his two charges were each taking turns giving speeches. Weston couldn't hear much, but the crowd seemed to be softening to them. Some laughs weaved their way through those gathered, and by the end of it they all seemed to be back to normal and going about their business as usual. Weston leaned on the window frame and watched the townsfolk peter away from the area, making their way home, to the bar, or wherever it was their life took them.

"Mr. Weston?" I soft voice of Father Mason surprised him, his adrenaline still hammering through his veins. "Sorry if I bothered you," the old priest said with a wry smile, "but would you happen to know if Sister Mejia made it into town for the celebration?"

"I'm sorry, Father," Weston said around a deep smile and a chuckle. "I don't. Is there anything I can help you with?"

"I don't think so, son. It's just the matter of, well, Dermot's body. He needs his…"

"Last Rites?"

"That's right," Mason said, his face brightening. "I was hoping the sister would help me sort things out."

"You know, preacher, I think we may be able to help each other. Walk me to church."

"Why the church?" Mason whispered, his face sank in confusion.

"Sanctuary," Weston said.

III

"You're not looking too good, son," Mason said, sitting him down in the front pew just beyond the pulpit.

"Not feeling too good either, preacher." The church smelled of burning incense. Weston cleared the flowery, acrid smoke from the back of his throat.

"I imagine those two things are connected." The father excused himself for a moment and returned with a small bowl of water and a white cloth.

"You ain't wrong," Weston chuckled through the aches.

"So," the father set himself up across from Weston and dabbed the wet cloth over his fresh abrasions. "You said we might be able to help each other?"

"I did," Weston took the cloth and bowl, pressed the latter to one corner of his mouth. "I'll go and fetch the sister for you, I just need—"

"Sanctuary," Father Mason said and leaned back, the shadow of a smile on his pinched face.

"Not exactly, Father. I'm looking for some...enlightenment."

"You don't strike me as a religious man, Mr. Weston." The priest folded his arms over his chest.

"Not that kind of enlightenment, Father."

"How can I help, son?" Mason said, eyebrows raised.

"Well, see, it's something that the sister said to me about all of this," Weston said with a broad gesture of his hand.

"The murders?"

Weston nodded. "The sister said that this had happened before. That she—that the both of you—had seen it before."

"Did she?" The priest took a battered Bible from his pocket and drummed his fingers along its cover. "And how can I help in that regard?"

"Tell me about it."

"It's not something I like to retell, Mr. Weston..."

"Bill."

"Bill. The last time we saw something like this was years ago, you understand. I was still just a young man. Colorado wasn't even Colorado then. Millwood certainly wasn't the same, run by breakneck crazy lumbermen. Outside of that it was only myself, Delbert Cornish and his wife, Darrell Claiborne, Sister Mejia before she took her vows, and a man named Bose Scarborough.

"Delbert and myself were setup from the beginning. I had the church, and he had the foresight to build a goods store. Darrell was akin to Del in that he had a business plan. He was the original purveyor of the Last Chance Saloon."

"Explains why it's the only game in town." Weston wiped at the dried blood around his eye.

"Indeed. Bose...well, Bose was a different story altogether. It seemed like he was blown into town on an illwind on the heels of Darrell's doors opening."

"A boozehound?"

"The worst kind. Of course, that's not the only thing that the Last Chance peddles. It still isn't. Bose was a man of flesh."

Weston nodded.

"Bose, though, he...he was unpredictable, and he was so large. So large and so strong that the lumberjacks wanted nothing to do with him. And that man was *mean*. So downright cruel that he'd put the devil to shame.

"After Bose roughed up a few of his girls, Darrell hired a few of the bigger boys around here to *take care* of him. Neither man walked right again after that. The town was at a loss. Bose Scarborough acted like he owned the place, and there was no one to tell him otherwise. That was, at least, until what happened to Amelia Hart.

"Amelia was only a young thing when she fell in with Darrell and his lot. Still, she was sweet and nice and even came to church. She and Mejia were close."

Strays, Weston thought, and nodded for the priest to continue.

"Bose took a liking to Amelia. It didn't take long to see the telltale signs of his affection. One night I heard a knock on my door. It's a miracle I did. It was such a small whisper of a knock. Even when I did hear it, I thought it might have been a branch banging against the walls, an animal trying to find its way in. But it was so persistent, so constant.

"When I found her, she was crumpled in a pile next to the door, blood everywhere. Her face was a mess, swollen and bruised into a mask of pain. And...and her nethers,

"God damn it." Weston wrapped his arms around his chest and slowed Javier to a walking pace. His body still wasn't done reminding him of the abuse it had been through over the last few days. Hell, it still wasn't over his first foolhardy trek into the desert. "Easy boy, I'll need these ribs when we get where we're going."

That was the problem—getting there. Though Mejia's place wasn't too far from town, at a walking pace it would take him well into the night, wasting time that he didn't have.

"Well, Javier, do I push you hard and half-kill myself in the process, or do we take it easy and enjoy a night under the stars?"

The horse offered a noncommittal whinny.

"Stars it is." Weston pushed the hat back over his forehead. "Take your time, boy. You know the way."

They stayed like that for some time, Weston watching the sky and Javier strolling forward, his head down, uninterested. Then he stopped. Javier's head perked up and his ears twitched. Weston pulled down his hat and tried to peer into the darkness. It was a bright night, the stars and moon providing as much light as could be expected in a clear sky. Still, Weston could only see a few feet in all directions. He cocked his head to the side, strained to hear what the horse did.

Javier shook his head and took a step backwards.

Weston patted the horse's neck. "Easy there. Easy now," he said and scanned the ground, praying they hadn't upset a rattlesnake.

The pain was sudden, and Weston grabbed at his shoulder with such ferocity he almost fell from Javier's back. Then he heard it. A crack in the distance, the scrape of rock on rock, the sounds of pebbles under foot. Weston winced and turned towards the source. Something black moved amongst the darkness. An ink blot merging and melding with the shadows but not quite managing it.

"Go," Weston said and kicked Javier into action. The horse hesitated for only a second, then took to the trail at full speed.

Pain exploded through Weston's entire body, but fear kept him upright. Fear that what trailed him was death. The mob of people from his former life. The lynch mob that killed Jack. He could feel the heat of their hate on his back.

Weston tried to regulate his pain, his anguish. He knew it wasn't the same people that killed Jack; they were back East. Still, the feeling was there. The certainty of their blind hate, their dedication to his utter destruction.

The cold sliver of pain in his shoulder brought him back, kept him alert. Again, Weston tried to force it out of his mind. He focused on Javier, on the horse's movements, the subtle feel of its muscles contorting under him. He held the reins tight, bent forward, and then he was airborne.

Javier squealed and thudded to the ground just as Weston made his own impact. The force drove him into a roll and his satchel flew away from him. It was hard to breathe, and his air came in thin wheezing gulps. Weston told himself to get up. Get up, check on Javier. Did the horse trip over something? Did he break anything?

Weston struggled to his feet; pain wracked his body. He patted himself—a quick check—nothing broken. He held one hand to his shoulder, where it hurt the most.

Eyes squinted against the gloom, Weston could just make out Javier wriggling himself up from the sand and dust and allowed himself a sigh of relief and started to jog to the horse. *What did we hit?* he wondered.

Weston was in the air before he could theorize. He landed hard—again. Fighting through the large gulps for air, he tried to piece together what had just happened when a large hand clamped on his arm and he was tossed through the air one more time.

"Bill Weston," said a guttural voice, breathless and ethereal, which made the little hairs at the base of his neck quiver. Javier snorted and whinnied, and Weston could hear him ride off.

He tried to stand, but the best he could do was get to his knees. His hand brushed against his satchel, the familiar feel of the old leather soft under his fingers. In the distance a giant shadow moved closer.

Weston reached into the bag, a small hope that he might find a weapon. He emptied the sack, the thunderous footsteps of the giant before him ringing in his ears.

Nothing. Just the clothes and the stale food that Mejia had packed for him. Weston cursed and swept it away.

"Bill Weston." The giant was bearing down him. That same large hand grabbed at his shoulder. Its thick fingers smothered Weston's bloated scars and a rush of agony coursed through him. He flailed, trying to get away from the pain and the giant inflicting it.

Something cold touched his hand and he grabbed it— thin, small, delicate. With all the strength he could muster, Weston thrusted it into the giant's face.

There was no loud cry, no grunt of pain. Silence.

The hand disappeared, as did the giant, and Weston sat alone in the open desert. Sucking in air as best he could, he let the pale night light fall on the thing in his hand, the object that drove the beast away.

Mejia's silver crucifix.

CHAPTER SIX

I

The jagged fingers of daylight clawed at the horizon as Weston shuffled into view of Sister Mejia's shack. He paused to stretch his back and beat the dust from his jeans. It was a long night of walking, the cold air only waylaid by his constant movement and his own arms tangled about his chest. The crucifix dangled from his neck and bounced with every step. The giant shadow never returned.

Mejia was out by her garden, as if she had been expecting him to arrive. She was leaning on her wagon, Javier already hooked up and ready to go.

Weston waved. Mejia offered him a slow nod that made him smile despite everything. She had forgone her religious wear, save for her veil, in favor of a pair of dirty old jeans and an old button up shirt.

"Glad to see he made it home," Weston said and nodded towards Javier. "I guess he wasn't too busted up."

"Mr. Weston, what did you do to my horse?" Mejia asked, her eyes taking him in.

Weston relayed the events from the previous night. Mejia sat in a stony silence as he spoke, scrutinizing each word as he went. She asked questions to clarify: no, he didn't see a face; no, he couldn't describe anything about his attacker; yes, he was sure that he wasn't followed; and yes, he was sure that whatever had attacked him left after it had touched the crucifix.

"La malora," Mejia said blowing out a long breath. "It speaks of an ill fate. Death." Mejia reached out her gnarled hand and ran it over Weston's scruffy face. "Not to worry, Mr. Weston, you seem to have your senses about you, what little you had anyway." She smiled and slapped his cheek gently.

"What brings you out here?" Mejia took a piece of grass out of her mouth and threw it to the ground. "I was expecting Dermot or Ambrose, instead I get a terrified Javier missing a rider. I was about to head out to see if someone needed help."

"The murders," he said.

Mejia nodded at the rising sun.

"I thought there'd be more. I suppose Father Mason wants me to help."

"He does, but, Mejia, there's something else." Weston reached out and took her hand into both of his. It felt small, fragile, and nowhere near as strong as it had when it had been healing him. "It's Dermot. Dermot was killed."

Mejia pulled her hand away from him, her face a veil of shock and anger. "Dermot, but... are you sure...why?"

"I haven't seen him yet, but the father has. He needs you." Weston put his arm around the older woman, her shoulders stiffened for a moment, but only a moment. She fell into him, her body racked with sobs.

They had moved into the kitchen, each occupying their old places. Weston related the last couple of days. Mejia had stopped crying, her face drawn and fixed, her eyes wide and staring.

"Mejia, I want to help, but I need to know more. What can you tell me about the murders?"

"I have two ways I can answer you." She chewed on her cheek. "No sé que tampoco te dará lo que buscas."

"I need to know more," Weston said and stared across the table, willing her eyes to meet his own.

"That's what you want." Sister Mejia poked a crooked finger at his chest. "But will it help you get what you need? No se."

Weston wanted to tell her to stop obscuring the truth. The sooner he could figure it all out, the sooner he could leave the town behind to sink or swim as its people saw fit. Instead, he sat on the edge of his seat. Waiting.

"I will say that what is happening in Millwood now, that's pure evil." When she finally turned her eyes on him a shiver went through him. "The problem with pure evil is you can't defeat it. You can't fight it. You can only over-come it. And that, Mr. Weston, that requires faith."

"I know about the other murders. The murders from before. I know about Bose Scarborough."

Mejia straightened, one of her withered hands pawed at her lips, as if she were slapped.

"Father Mason has been telling tales." Mejia stood and crossed her arms. "Bose was a very troubled, very angry man. He forced his will on more than one woman who then saw their way to me for aid and support." Mejia's mouth was a tight, white line.

"Mason said he killed the former owner of the Last Chance, a man named Darrell, in a way that resembled the recent murders. Is that true?"

"It's true. Bose Scarborough was an animal. When la furia took him, he didn't need weapons beyond his fists. His teeth." Mejia shivered; one hand glided over her neck.

"It seems like too much a coincidence that similar killings were done so long ago, only to return years later in the same town. What's the connection?"

Mejia didn't have an answer for him, and Weston hadn't expected one. They let the silence grow between them, only broken by Javier's soft grunts and whinnies from beyond the door.

Mejia reached out her gnarled hand and ran it over Weston's bearded face. "Perhaps it's time for a shave," she said, a hint of a smile on her old face. "Change may help you think."

She boiled water over her small stove and rummaged through her kitchen, eventually producing a straight razor and a bar of soap. After pouring the hot water into a bowl she arranged herself behind Weston, scraping the blade of her razor over an old leather belt. She lathered his face with the soap, the once flowery scent having grown stale after sitting in Mejia's kitchen for however many years.

"Do you trust me, gringo?"

Weston paused, his eyes meeting Mejia's one more time. He nodded and felt her warm hands on his neck and chin, pushing his head backwards. He heard the razor slip from its sheath and the rough, scraping sound of it brushing over his skin.

"I found something...out of place, in the back of the barn there," Mejia whispered, as she pulled the razor up his neck.

"And what did you do with it?" Weston was hoping that she would tell him that his guns were right there, waiting for him. He missed their weight on his hips, their feel in his hands, their smell.

"I left it back there," the nun shrugged. "I figure that if

they're needed, they'd best stay where they were."

Weston said nothing and let the nun continue. A pang of loss and disappointment turned over his stomach, though he knew it was for the best.

"Tell me, sister, what do you actually do when Father Mason calls you to look over these bodies?" Weston felt the razor catch before Mejia pulled it onward.

"Would you rather the short answer or the truth?"

"The truth."

"I suppose you're ready to hear it," Mejia said and rinsed the razor's edge in the still hot water. "The truth is, I administer Last Rites...in a way. I suppose Father Mason told you I wasn't a nun when Bose Scarborough ran roughshod over Millwood.. I had just come up from Mexico with my family. I was young, but I was still a woman grown.

"I lived in a small town near the Rio Grande before my father thought it wise to move North, probably with gold fever, though that I cannot say for certain. He was killed shortly after we arrived." Weston froze and she caught his eye. "Oh, nothing like that. It was an accident. He fell from a horse."

Mejia paused, took a deep breath, and continued.

"Just outside of my pueblo lived an old woman, though in truth she was likely the same age I am now." Mejia allowed herself a chuckle. "She was what is known as la bruja. A witch. La bruja always liked me. I helped her with some of her chores, brought her fresh fruit and vegetables when my village could spare them. In return, she taught me some of her ways."

"Magic?"

"In a manner, I suppose you could say that."

"I saw you that night, in the woods."

Mejia grunted. "I figured as much, Mr. Weston—"

"Bill."

"Bill. I figured there was a reason you were suddenly very interested in what I was doing." She let the razor drop into the bowl and passed Weston a hand mirror. "What do you think?"

"I haven't seen that face in a long time," Weston said and ran a course hand over his smooth features, his broad chin. The little scars from a lifetime ago peered out at him, and he could feel their pain as if he were experiencing them all over again. They were overshadowed by the bruises, the cuts, the scrapes from the last few days. "It's seen better days."

The old nun cackled and dried his face with a cloth.

"Sister, what did the bruja teach you? What do you do with the dead bodies?"

"I make sure they are no están maleficio; that they are not harassed by demons or spirits so they can move on. Then I make sure to clean up any mess left behind. Not physical, mind you. You see, whenever los brujas use their magic, as you call it, they leave something behind..."

"A stain," Weston said and turned to face Mejia.

"Si, a stain. I make sure that I clean that stain. That I remove it so that it can cause no more damage."

"Is that what the picture and candles are for?"

"You really were watching that night." Mejia smiled and fetched her bag, taking out half-burned candles, thick droplets of wax frozen along their sides, and a plain black picture frame. "The candles are a part of the process. The picture gives me focus." She handed him the picture.

It was a photograph of a young Mexican woman, dressed in a black, full-skirted dress. It was a little out of style, full-throated with large, puffy shoulders. Weston took all that in immediately, pushed it to the back of his mind, and focused on the face. She wasn't unlovely, her full lips unmoved, her eyes half-closed and staring off to the side. The young woman's long hair was worn in several elaborate buns and her hair was painted to look like a skull.

"What is this?" Weston handed it back to Mejia.

"That was mi hermana, many years ago. She's dressed as a Catrina to celebrate Dia de los Muertos. She also honors Santa Muerte."

"Santa Muerte? Saint of the Dead?"

"Si. I appease my ancestors and Santa Muerte to help rid us of the evil."

"And was there any evil around Puddicombe and Gulliver?"

"Oh yes. Very much so."

"Who or what is causing that? Caused the attack on me last night?"

"I don't know," the old nun said, staring Weston in the eyes, "but it frightens me."

II

The ride back into Millwood was slow, but with Mejia at the reins Weston allowed himself a few moments of rest. Eyes closed, the question that kept coming to mind was what did the victims have in common? It seemed that there was very little aside from some strained interactions and the town that they all happened to live.

He grunted. Ask the sheriff that question and he would likely say it was Weston himself. It wasn't hard to see his point, but only if you hung your hat on the idea that the killer was unknown to the victims. If Sheriff Johnson looked at it differently, if he ignored Weston's presence, he'd be asking about the connection between the dead men as well.

The first, Puddicombe, was a rich man. Had hit it big and moved to the outskirts of Millwood to live out his fortune. With him was one of his employees, Percy Gulliver. A hard working and kind man, by most accounts. The last was Dermot, the owner of the livery, and a local boy. He seemed to be on good terms with everyone in town, including the sheriff, Father Mason, and Puddicombe. Puddicombe and Dermot seemed to have had some issue with Delbert Cornish, but what of Percy? And what was the connection to the long dead Bose Scarborough? Too many questions without answers, too many loose ends. One thing was for sure, Weston would have to pay a visit to Mr. Cornish before too long.

Father Mason was waiting outside the church when Mejia pulled the wagon up. He was paler than Weston had remembered, his thin fingers drumming over his Bible.

"Sister, thank goodness you're here," he said and pried one of his hands from the good book to help Mejia from her seat. "I had expected you sometime last night."

"Sorry about that, Father," Weston said, moving around Javier to greet him. "I was waylaid."

"Mr. Weston? I almost didn't recognize you with your," he ran a hand along his own small chin.

"Yeah, I know the feeling," Weston said with a chuckle.

"I suppose it's best, what with the attention being cast your way in town," Mason said and beckoned for them to follow him into the church.

"What happened, Father?" Mejia grabbed her bag and

ran to catch up.

"I had a visit from our esteemed sheriff just a few minutes before you showed."

"I suppose he wasn't too happy that you wanted to keep poor ole Dermot's body for more Last Rites?" Weston said.

"Not at all. I convinced him to give us some more time, but it might have been after several threats to my own person."

"Cabrón," Mejia said under her breath.

"Where's Dermot now?" Weston said as they moved toward the back of the church.

"The cellar," the priest said and led them through a door behind the altar. The room they entered was small and cluttered with some of the priest's more formal accoutrements, an aged thurible, and a brass cup all on the lone table by the far wall. In the center of the floor was a large trap door, made of a thick dark wood. Father Mason pointed to it. "It's cooler down there."

The thick stench of earth almost concealed the fetid stink of death, but the telltale putrescence wafted through the enclosed space, invading wherever it was able. Weston put a hand across his mouth and nose and delved further down. Lit candles lined the walls on makeshift shelves dug in the dirt. They cast strange, misshapen shadows as Weston and Mejia passed them.

"Not coming, Father?" Weston asked.

"No, I...I think not." The old priest had a purple handkerchief clutched around his face. Weston nodded and moved on.

Dermot was laid out on a table cobbled together with little more than a sheet of plywood on a couple of sawhorses. He was naked, though Weston didn't think there'd be much left of the clothes even if they had left them. Gouges were ripped from his flesh, thick pieces of muscle and tissue were missing from his bicep, his stomach, and chest. His neck was a deep black, almost as if someone had spilled ink over him. Tendrils of the ebony crept out making jagged edges around his throat. It wasn't until Weston got closer that he realized it was a bruise.

"Strangled," he muttered.

"And much more," Mejia said with a wince, her hand hovered just above the missing skin.

"Bite marks?" Weston bent forward, his eyes staring at the torn remnants of flesh. "Has to be."

"This was done by hand," Mejia said, bringing her hand back to her chest.

A spasm wracked Weston's shoulder, he sucked on his teeth.

"That's...that's not possible. No man can—"

"And yet, we've seen these types of wounds before." Mejia frowned, placed a gnarled hand on Dermot's cheek, and muttered a prayer under her breath.

"I'll let you do your thing, Sister," Weston said and moved back upstairs, where the father met him.

"It's a horrible sight, isn't it?" The priest was sitting in a rickety old chair, his bible open on his lap.

"Where do you folks keep your boneyard around here?"

The forest stood before him, a hard border for the ever-reaching town. Weston could see the paths taken by the loggers each day, as wide as two men and clear.

The small path he'd shadowed to find Mejia and Mason performing Puddicombe's Last Rites wasn't too far down. The big clearing where the sheriff's men had ambled about blaming things on bears and the like was just to his right.

To Weston's left, a small wooden sign was driven into the ground, slip shod and crooked in front of a gnarled old tree. "Graveyard" was etched onto its surface with an arrow pointing down the tree line. Weston followed it, moving further and further away from the noise of the town.

The forest opened onto a small mound. Grave markers pointed to the sky—unadorned and lopsided crosses, the deceased's names carved into them. Others were proper stone markers, smooth looking, well made. Names and dates were engraved on them, clear to read. For a town the size of Millwood, the bodies buried in the graveyard seemed too few. There was perhaps a little more than a hundred. Though, there were two fresh graves of note near the entrance.

Weston sighed, pulled up his pants and went to work. He walked among the graves, his eyes seeking anything that may resemble Scarborough. It was a tedious process, made worse by the unsteady ground. Weston's hunt ended abruptly with a short fall over a freshly dug hole.

His foot and ankle caught, Weston wheeled his hands around to support himself, but fell in fresh dirt all the same, his cheek brushing the edge of a stone. Dull pain resounded through his leg, and he cried out in fright as much as in pain. Fingers grasping handfuls of dirt and grass, Weston dragged himself out of the hole. He had to keep his leg perfectly straight but managed to slide it out without further issue.

He tested his leg, moved the knee back and forth, and felt nothing out of the ordinary. Gripping onto a nearby headstone, he stood and tried his leg again. A dull twinge settled into his ankle.

Weston chuckled, a curse tasting his lips, and shook his head.

"What the hell am I doing here?" he said and felt around in his satchel. The ticket slip tickled his fingertips, and he sighed. One more night. He had one more night in this hellish town and then a train would carry him away. To where, he didn't care. Denver for starters, he figured. From a big town like that, he could likely head just about anywhere. Start anew.

Could he start new? Part of him wasn't so sure. Nothing Weston did now would erase his past, would cleanse him of what he had done. Of what he'd failed to do. He rubbed his thumb over his scarred shoulder, pushed down on those bulbous, purple lines as if he could flatten them.

"One more night," he said and dusted himself off, his eyes falling on a familiar name.

Scarborough's gravestone was a large and hulking thing, his name etched into it in big bold letters.. There was a puckering wound in the ground in front of the marker. Weston crouched to get a better look. First, the broken cover of a coffin lay atop the dirt, discarded and unneeded. Second, the dirt was scattered around in a large mound piled away from the headstone Third, it didn't look dug out as much as it looked pushed out, as if someone or something had clawed their way out from within.. The casket underneath empty. Bose Scarborough was dead, but no one had convinced him of that.

Weston ran his hands over the marker. He let his fingers fall into the grooves of the etched letters and into the space around them. He came upon something wet and he drew his hand back, angling it toward the light of the midday sun. The blood looked dark in the light, nearly black, and it was thick, almost creamy. Weston poked his head around the gravestone and found the source of the blood on its flat back surface.

There, hastily scratched in the coagulating blood was the name David Carlyle.

III

"What does it mean?" Father Mason ran a shaking hand along his narrow chin.

"Well, Father," Weston was squat down behind the gravestone once more, one finger grazing the bloody letters there, "judging by the dried blood here, and the nearly fresh blood outlining the governor's name, I'd say this was a list." It hadn't taken him long to gather up Sister Mejia and the father. The sister had just finished up with Dermot, and the father had arranged for some of the sheriff's boys to come around and gather the corpse.

"Esto es pavoroso," Mejia whispered; her hands clenched together.

"A list of what?" the priest's said around a cracked voice.

"Victims," Weston said and pointed to the dried blood. "See here, it's hard to make out, but I'll be damned if that doesn't say 'combe.'"

"Horace," the priest said and crossed himself. "I'm still not sure...I...I..." The priest wavered and Weston grabbed his arm to keep him steady.

"La brujería," Mejia said and bent over the ruined grave.

"I'm not so sure myself, Father," Weston said and patted the older man on the shoulder. "But at least we know who's next. We can warn him, keep him safe."

"Mejia..." Mason said almost leaning on the grave-stone but recoiling his hand before it touched the porous surface.

"You've both heard me speak of stains, of scars, of what's left behind. This," Mejia picked up a handful of grave soil and let it drain through her fingers, "I've never seen anything like this."

"It also brings us back to Bose Scarborough. It's his grave after all." Weston crouched down across from Mejia trying to read her. She was blank, her dazed eyes looking over his shoulder to somewhere far away.

"Bose Scarborough is dead."

"Are you sure?"

"Of course, I am."

"We both are," Father Mason said weakly.

"What about children?"

"He never had any," Mejia said. "None that we knew of."

"What about the girl he raped, was she pregnant?"

"Amelia," Mejia stood, one hand rubbing at her eyes. "Amelia was never the same after that night. She drifted, fell in with the other girls at the Last Chance. Then she disappeared into the woods. I never saw her again."

"So, she could have been pregnant. She could've birthed Scarborough's child. Maybe that child came back here to learn about their father. Maybe they weren't happy with what they found." Weston joined Mejia in standing.

"That seems very unlikely," Mason said. "And even so, how would he know who to put on the list?"

"And what do Puddicombe, Percy Janes, Dermot, and the Governor have to do with him?" Weston said and ran a hand through his hair.

"That brings us back to Governor Carlyle," Mejia

said.

"It'll be hard to get to see him now, even with your shave, Mr. Weston. People around here still suspect you of murder."

"I think I know a way, and I think I know someone who can help us."

Weston hadn't paid much attention to the mayor's residence in his trips around town. As he walked up to it now, he wasn't certain how he'd missed it. It was a mansion, decorated as such with its tall arches, many windows, and austere colours: black and grey. It was as tall as any other building in town, likely taller, and just as stout, its broadsides almost touching its neighbours. Just behind the main house was another building, smaller and a little more traditional looking. Both buildings were blocked from the street by an iron fence that seemed to run around the entirety of it; a thick gate stood closed to passersby. Bert stood just outside the gate, invitations stuffed into one pocket. A man who Weston recognized as one of the sheriff's deputies stood a little way behind the boy, beyond the gate, a scowl etched on his sun burnt face.

The boy looked uncomfortable in the tuxedo. His hands, clad in white cotton gloves, kept wandering to his pants to pull and tug at the legs, to his neck to loosen his bowtie. Obviously not custom made.

"Bert," Weston said, sauntering up to the mayor's house. The boy nodded and straightened out the arms of the tux.

"Looks mighty warm in that getup, boy," Weston said keeping to shadows as much as he could.

Bert nodded.

"Got you working the dinner party?"

"Yep."

"I thought as much," Weston said trying to keep Bert's gaze. "I know there's been some things said about me around town, I'm sure you've heard more besides, and I know I owe you some sort of explanation, but we need a favor."

"Who's 'we?'"

"Me, Sister Meija, Father Mason."

"Need something for the church?" Bert gave him a sidelong glance.

Weston smiled, leaned in close. "It's about the murders, boy. We're trying to save the Governor's life."

Bert took a step back, his nonchalant expression cracked and his eyes widened.

"I know it's a lot to put on you, but it'll be all right. I promise. Now, do you think you can get me inside?"

"Not looking like that," Bert said giving him a look up and down.

"Fair enough," Weston plucked at his dusty, sweat soaked clothes. "Think you might be able to get the Governor to come out here?"

The boy looked at his feet, shuffled them in the gravel and dirt road. "I can try, but I'm not really supposed to leave my spot here."

"Do what you can, Bert. If you can get him to leave, bring him around back. The sister and father are back there and will talk with him."

"What are you going to do?"

"Find another way in."

A cool breeze came from the east. It mixed with the

sweltering heat of the day and a thick fog twisted close to the ground. The mayor's mansion dominated the town, and Weston questioned himself once more on how he had missed it in the previous days. Its white exterior glowed in the moonlight, the dull orange of lantern light spilling out of its windows like spotlights on the fog. Weston watched from the alley across the street, his head peaked out from around an unlit house, its residents either asleep or in their drink.

Mejia and Father Mason were set up near the rear of the house, hidden in the shadows of another alley in case Bert was able to draw the Governor out. Weston wasn't so sure. The sheriff would be close to the mayor and Governor, and despite the celebratory nature of the party, there was a small detachment of deputies on guard. It was strange but prudent, as if the sheriff had set it all up for Weston's benefit.

Two men circled the house, crossing each other's path twice as they did. It left a space of a minute, perhaps less, where Weston could sneak in. There were more to the front guarding the gate, and Weston had to expect that there were more inside.

Weston cringed. The pain in his shoulder had returned. It was dulled some, but it persisted. Gripping his shoulder and keeping his arm close to his side, he crouched at the edge of the alley, still disguised by its shadow. Timing the deputies reminded him of his first night in Millwood, his first night in the woods, the beginning of all of this. Puddicombe was the first dead body,. though there were more before that, more at the hands of Bose Scarborough. Either way, it started for Weston with Puddicombe, Percy Janes, and Mejia's ritual.

The guards were on their way around the house,

backs to Weston in their patrol. He sprinted across the road as quietly as he could, which wasn't very. He made his way to the side of the house and came to a halt at a large window. He had precious little time, but he made himself slow down and take a deep breath. His muscles and nerves screamed for him to keep moving, to get inside before the guards could return. He took another deep breath and, fighting these impulses, looked inside. The house opened into a large foyer. Beige tiles gave the area a warm feeling that was contrasted by its white walls. An ornate chandelier hung from the ceiling, dollops of crystal shimmering in the light cast by the lanterns and gas lamps that spanned the room. The guests were dressed in their best. Women wore exquisite gowns that floated over the floor, jewels sparkling at their necks and wrists. Their male counterparts were equally well dressed in tailored suits. Toward the back of the foyer were two staircases, one on either side of the room. Each staircase led to the second floor, which looked out over the rest of the house. The guests moved about smiling and laughing, drinking champagne from flutes served by men in tuxedos. Not everyone was dressed to the nines though. Some men were dressed in their road gear, some with their hats still on, cigarettes jutting from their mouths. Weston recognized them as more of the sheriff's men. Each one was staring around the room, hands eager to drop to their guns if anything were to go wrong, or if someone started trouble. Weston looked for the sheriff but didn't see him. He still had time. He ran to the back, to the servants' entrance.

He jumped up and grabbed the lip of the low overhang. His fingers gripped the porous adobe, the warmth of the day's sun still radiating from it. He pulled himself up and rolled out of sight, keeping low to the roof to avoid being seen from below or even the second-floor window. The patrolling guards passed one another again. Neither man acknowledging the other, they just went about their business. The sheriff had them on a tight leash. Most deputies would be satisfied to half-ass their duties to gab with their fellows, play cards, get drunk, or generally just fuck off. Not these boys though. They were strictly by the book. That didn't bode well for Weston.

He waited for them to disappear behind their respective sides of the house then did a low crawl to the closest window, painfully aware of his boots scraping on the clay tiles; the hollow sound seemed riotous in the gloom. A lantern hung from the wall opposite the window, its flame dancing in its glass case.

Satisfied there were no deputies patrolling the hallway, Weston pried the window open and crawled inside. The carpet runner muffled his steps, and he followed the hallway to the stairs. Even before he peered around the corner, he knew there were men on guard. Their whispered conversations carried up the winding staircase. Hushed laughter followed talk of their nightly conquests, imagined or not. The lantern and candlelight cast their deformed shadows on the stairwell, dancing in a peculiar mockery of their patrol.

Too many, he thought and crept back the way he came. Lanterns lit his way, hanging from the wall every few paces. Some were kerosene, their fuel supply hanging below them, keeping their wick soaked behind a porous yellow glass. Others were gaslights, like those that were used to light the streets. The pipes that funneled the gas into the house were strewn along the wall, painted brown to disguise them against the background. If he had to guess, Weston would have thought they led to the first floor.

Weston came upon a loft area that overlooked a large dining area. It mirrored the aesthetics of the foyer: warm coloured tile, sterile white walls, high ceilings with an extravagant chandelier. There was more furniture there, and the guests were relaxing at their leisure. He cursed under his breath.

A bell rang from the back of the room, drawing people's attention and put an end to their conversation. Weston could see the governor in their number, his horseshoe of grey hair and bald pate stood out from Weston's position. He wavered some, had a drink in his hand.

Frank Winter stepped up to face those gathered, a smile pasted on his square face under a thick, black moustache. His blue eyes were startling in their intensity. The sheriff walked up behind him, his own eyes shifting around the crowd.

"Friends!" The mayor's voice boomed through the foyer. It was a smooth voice, and it dripped like wine into Weston's ears, pleasant and warm. The Governor didn't seem to feel the same, and he shifted some at the sound of the mayor's voice.

"Friends, thank you for coming. I have been away from the fair city of Millwood for far too long. I've missed it." He paused and looked over the crowd, his smile still strong but out of place.

"I've seen the other towns and cities that we share in this great county, in this great state, in this great country, and you know what I discovered? There's no place like home." There was a soft round of applause, smiles all around.

"There is no place like Millwood, friends. None. At first, well, at first that made me sad. It made me think, perhaps we're doing something wrong here in Millwood."

A gasp or two rose from the mayor's audience. Weston looked around but couldn't pinpoint the source.

"Right," the mayor responded, a bigger smile on his face. "I couldn't fathom that for very long either. So, I started to think: if we're doing it right here, in Millwood, how can we help our neighbours attain such greatness?" The mayor lifted one hand to the air, shaking, and mimed grabbing something that was just out of reach.

"Well, friends, I don't think it will be easy. You see, we have a government that's forgotten about us. That's right, they've forgotten about us now that the war is all said and done. They focus on New York and Boston and even San Francisco. Well, that's going to change. You see, I've served you well as a mayor for these past few years, but I think it's time that Millwood got what it deserves. I think it's time that Millwood stood shoulder to shoulder with the rest of these cities and got what it's due.

"I've decided that in order to give Millwood its best shot on the national scale, we need someone from our fair city representing us on the federal level. As such, and with the blessings of our fair city, I have decided to put my hat in the race for governor of our fair county." A cheer went up amongst the guests, and the mayor's eyes scanned them. "Thank you all, I look forward to representing you and your interests in the near future." He stopped on Carlyle and gave the governor a nod, his smile much more believable.

The governor made a beeline for the door. The mayor was one cold bastard, but Weston had to admire him—at least he was doing his business out in the open and giving his opponent a fair shake. Of course, that wouldn't matter much if the governor ended up dead.

Weston cursed and ran to the window, not caring about the sound his boots made as he thundered across the floor and launched himself into the night air. His feet skittered across the adobe roof of the servant's entrance and he fell to the ground in a roll.

What connection did the Governor have with any of this? Weston thought and broke into a run.

"What the hell—," a deputy walked into his path, his face a mask of surprise. Weston recoiled and flailed backwards, his hands wheeling to avoid the burly man.

They collided, a harsh clash that drove both men to the ground on their backs. The clatter of the deputy's rifle rang in Weston's ears as he forced himself to sit and ignored the aches and pains.

"Reg, everything all right?" The other deputy turned the corner, his eyes widened, and he brought his own rifle to his shoulder. "Hold it!"

"Shit," Weston clambered for the iron wrought fence, his feet unsteady below him.

Reg's hand shot out like a snake and latched onto Weston's ankle. "Got you, you son of a bitch," he said panting.

"Christ," Weston said and tried to kick Reg's hand away, but the deputy adjusted his grip and grabbed a fistful of Weston's jeans.

"Get over here, Orville," Reg said. The heftier deputy nodded and made his way over.

"Not him," Bert's voice floated to them from the front of the house. "He's over here, trying to get away." Bert pointed into the street. The deputies gave each other a look and ran off towards the boy.

"Thanks, kid," Weston said and jumped the fence in search of the governor.

IV

David Carlyle wasn't a fearful man. No, David Carlyle, governor of the great state of Colorado wasn't fearful, but he was cautious. He had been that way since the day he was born, or so his mother had said over many a yarn. His mother would often recount the time that, as a child, he faced down a rattlesnake poised to strike. No fear in his face, no cry on his lips, just a stern eye that watched the snake's every move. After that, well, after that was another story. The boy that would become governor stalked around the home of his parents, putting toys and furniture in the way of any gaps or holes that might allow some wayfaring critter to enter. Not fearful, but cautious. Practical is the way the governor himself would have put it.

Of course, like any man when he was drinking, his nature would often play against him. David Carlyle, governor of Colorado, threw caution to the wind, and, with more alcohol in his system than sense, he stormed out of the mayor's mansion and into the streets of Millwood.

Carlyle had been in Millwood several times, maybe half a dozen, and had convinced himself that he knew it well enough to get back to his hotel. His driver, a fat, greasy man by the name of Otis had asked him if he needed the carriage brought around, a cigarette hanging precariously out of the corner of his mouth. Carlyle waved the man off, and stumbled away, cursing the uneven street. Otis shrugged and went back to a conversation he was having with another driver.

When Carlyle had first been to Millwood, it wasn't much to look at. He was just an up-and-coming politician then but was setting his sights on the governor title and thought he should get to know the smaller parts of the state. Millwood was a logging town made up of a general store, a mill, the saloon, the church, and some loggers' houses. Some of those places still stood from what Carlyle was led to believe, but he couldn't see why. The town was a completely different animal than it had been all those years ago. It was the trade routes that really did it, opened the place right up. Carlyle had recognized that side of it himself all those years before. The prime location, the central location, and the natural resources to make the train companies and the government feel it was worthwhile. So, a train station was gifted to little Millwood, Colorado.

Carlyle paused to lean on a building and pissed on the street. Some people were walking around him, but that's the type of place Millwood had become. Carlyle sneered and zipped up. After the train station came to be, more opportunities opened up for the small logging town. More people came to town, and more businesses followed. The livery was set up then, the blacksmith, a bank, and a post office. Then, to slow down all that fun, the undertaker and that failed nunnery set themselves up as if the town were trying to keep itself honest. The town grew and grew some more. Out of necessity more than desire. Then Frank Winter stepped onto the scene.

Frank Winter was the mayor by the time Carlyle had paid his second-to-last visit to Millwood. A charming fellow—deceivingly so—underneath that strong brow and cool eyes. Winter was a hometown boy, grew up in Millwood before it was much of anything. Maybe that's why he was so dead set on seeing the town grow into something more. Carlyle shrugged as he made his way up a familiar looking street.

When Frank Winter came on board things started to change for the town. He did a lot of posturing for the crowd, but he followed up on it. In Carlyle's time as governor, he hadn't been so inundated by any other mayor than by Frank Winter and his Millwood. Of course, tenacity is to be admired, but it can push someone too far. You get too far, and you might go over the edge.

Carlyle had been to Millwood four or five times. Maybe less, maybe more. In either case, as he stood wavering in the middle of the street that had looked so familiar just a mere moment before, Carlyle came to a realization: he was lost. He spun around some, trying to check for familiar buildings or locations, to get his bearings, but all he got was dizzy.

"Shit," the governor said, a gut full of alcohol threatening to expel itself. He leaned forward, his hands on his knees, and coughed, a dry gag that was almost enough to send him and the alcohol over the edge, but it didn't. It passed. He did a quick look around to see if there was anyone who had seen him. No one. He must have wandered away from the pack.

"Thank Jesus," Carlyle grumbled, running a sleeve over his mouth and belching loudly. The night was warm, but the fresh air and the walking seemed to clear his head some, especially after the near vomit experience. He didn't know where he was, but he could see the large, dark trees that chewed on the outskirts of town before him. During his visits into the town, he would often be brought to the forest. Not to go in to explore, that was what the loggers did. No, he was brought there to bask in the magnificence of nature that still held sway over the town. Carlyle always put on a show of being impressed, of enjoying the simple majesty of nature. It was all bullshit, of course. They were dealing with the governor of Colorado. The state was teeming with trees and lakes and ponds and mountains. Millwood was nothing new. The only good thing about all those visits was knowing that he was on the opposite side of town to where he was supposed to be. He cursed again.

Pulling up his pants, the governor turned around and started to walk the other way. His legs were still unsteady, but he had started to come around some. In the distance he could see a small group of people turning a corner around a building. He started towards them.

Frank Winter, the overzealous mayor of Millwood, was now running for governor. Carlyle really couldn't say why that bothered him. After all, he'd faced opposition before. He'd had opponents who were twice as politically savvy as Frank Winter. Real politicians with a sense of propriety and ability in them. Carlyle always beat them though. He always came out ahead. Winter would probably get the votes coming out of Millwood, but that was only one town. A growing town, but a town all the same. Carlyle would focus on the cities, on the state as a whole. He'd get his aides to run the numbers and the odds for him. They could do that, bless them.

Still, Frank Winter made him nervous. Perhaps it was his unwavering stare, or his quiet contemplation during every conversation. More likely, it was how he played the favourite with Carlyle during their recent Colorado tour before turning coat and isolating Carlyle against everyone.

"I hate 'em," came out of Carlyle's mouth in a croak. That was the real answer right there. He just didn't like Frank Winter.

A scuffing sound made Carlyle jump. His heart racing, he turned on shaky legs to see what it was. Nothing. His heart pounded against his chest, and the sick feeling returned like a blanket draped from his head.

The hairs on the back of his neck were sticking up, and there was a sensation that something or someone was looking at him. He started to move again, faster than he had intended. His drunken legs and numb feet tripped over one another and he fell to the ground. Dirt and gravel dug into his palms and scratched at his knees.

"Christ," he said, blowing some dust away from his face. He stood up, favouring his hands, and looked behind him again. A large man stood there, his shoulders slumped, and his head cocked to one side as if he were studying him. The man seemed to have very long arms, long enough that his hands seemed to reach below his knees. He took one step towards Carlyle, the same scuffing sound he had heard following him.

"I had a bit of a fall, but I'm all right," the governor slurred, backing away from the strange man. "You go on about your business now. No need to look in on me." Carlyle managed a nervous laugh.

His hands were out in front of him, scraped and bleeding, hoping to ward off whoever it was. The man took another step forward, tilting his head the other way this time, a large hand reaching towards the governor.

"That's enough, now. I'm fine. You go on home." The governor was backing up, trying not to let himself go too fast again in fear he may trip but afraid of not going fast enough.

Silence filled the air. The sounds of the town seemed to be so far away that they didn't matter, and the sounds of the nature that the town had been so fond of, seemed to have abandoned him as well. He was alone with this strange man who just kept moving closer.

David Carlyle was a cautious man, but when the hulking form stood before him on the empty road of Millwood, he threw his caution to the wind and ran. The idea that he would be safe just around the bend, where the group of people had gone, echoed in his brain. He just had to reach that. Nothing would happen to him if he was around other people. Nothing.

His stomach squelched, his throat burned, and his legs pumped. Vomit began to flow from his stomach and throat, but he kept moving. Until he couldn't. The vomit interfered with his breathing, made Carlyle panic. His panic caused him to run faster, but that was the opposite of what he needed to do. To compensate for this, his body gave him a warning: more vomit. It was enough to curl him over, to feel his muscles work against him and heave out the content of his stomach. He tried to keep moving but anytime he did, he'd heave again, stopping the work of his other muscles, just so his abdomen could focus on getting out whatever was within its reach.

Panic still gripped at his brain, and he turned his watering eyes in the direction of the man he'd been trying to escape. Nothing there. But the feeling of being watched remained. He stumbled forward, his breath coming in wet gasps. He could feel the vomit on his chin, but it didn't matter. The only thing that mattered was getting to that building. Getting to other people. He moved slowly, bent forward. Pain pulsated through his stomach and back, and his hands and knees stung from his fall. His brain shouted at him and told him to get to the people. Be with the people.

He could hear the far-off chatter of people. Could hear their movement on the streets. A dry smile crossed his face. His heart beat hard but began to ease. He forced himself to stand up straight, to walk normally. He felt much better now that his stomach had emptied, and his legs were warmed from the walk and run. He was thinking clearer. More confident. He took a moment to look over his shoulder, just to be sure there was no danger. Obviously, there wouldn't be, he was so close to the people. So close.

It was a large, grey hand that grabbed him. Rough and cracked, its strong fingers and jagged fingernails dug deep into the flesh and muscle of his chest, clawing all the way through his suit coat, vest, and shirt. The pain was immediate and blinding. He wanted to scream, to call for help (he was so close), but he couldn't. Nothing came out.

Another large hand blocked out his vision, its cold, clammy skin closing on his face leaving him in dark. It smelled of earth and filth. The hand squeezed and the governor screamed.

CHAPTER SEVEN

I

Weston squat next to the grave, his hands swollen and sore and stained with fresh dirt.

He, Sister Meija, and Father Mason had spent the night looking for the Governor, but they didn't find any sign. They split up and Weston wound his way through the town, drifting aimlessly like a ghost. When even the tireless population of Millwood staggered behind closed doors, Weston wandered. He stumbled through the town until it brought him to the graveyard. The dim moonlight led him through the twisted path compounded by grave markers, leading him to Scarborough's resting place. Scarborough was dead and so was the governor.

It wasn't until the sun had cast its light on the edges of the cemetery that Father Mason and Sister Meija had found him. Their faces pale, their hands fidgeting, their teeth chewing on their lips.

"He's dead," Weston said and halted their advance.

"He is," Meija said around a deep sigh.

"Figured." Weston pointed to Scarborough's grave. "His name was crossed out." He found himself sighing and clenching his painful hands. Another name to add to his ledger, another name taken from under his nose. The dirt on his hand might as well have been blood, a stain that would not wash out. "Same as the others?"

"Yes," Father Mason said in his withered voice. The father had seen better days. His eyes pouched in purple rings. were swollen and bloodshot.

"Did you see to it?"

"Si," Mejia said and placed a hand on Weston's shoulder. "There was nothing you could do."

"I could've waited here. The bastard had to come back out here to attend to his list." Weston stood and looked down on the open grave. "You may want to let the sheriff know about this. Maybe he could set up some deputies out here. In the meantime, might want to set up here yourself, or get someone else to do it. I'd wager he'll be back unless he's done."

"You... you won't help us?" Father Mason stepped forward some. The effort made Weston smile.

"No, Father, I won't." Weston fixed the hat on his head and made to leave, his boots sinking into the black earth.

"Why?" It was Meija, her voice was quiet but clear. Maybe even sad.

"I got a train to catch," Weston said and held up the ticket.

The town was quiet, waking late after the mayor's party. Few were up and about. Among them was a lone boy making a slow march through the streets ensuring the gas lamps were out. Weston couldn't remember if it was one of the boys he'd seen lighting them on his first night in town, which felt like months ago.

He headed for the train station, such as it was, to see about the train. In truth, he didn't know if the track had been cleared or not, or if the train would be on time. It didn't matter. He'd failed. The town would deal with it in its own way, Father Mason and Sister Meija leading the charge if the Sheriff wouldn't.

A bell tinkled to his left; a door closed. The building surrounding the door was singular and appeared more akin to a small home or cabin than a business. All the same, "Del's Dry Goods" stood like a marquee above the door. A sign crafted with time, patience, and skill.

Delbert Cornish's name had come up more than once over the last few days, Weston thought, and stared into the sky. He had time.

The bell tolled again, a tinny sound that was more practical than musical, a warning and not a welcome. The little building opened into rows of shelves and counters, each stocked full of supplies. Burlap sacks of seed, fertilizer, oats, and wheat layered the wall to Weston's left, pots, pans, and sundries to his right. Through the center of the store the shelves were a mixed bag of fresh produce, cheese, and clothing. The mishmash of scents was confusing but welcoming.

Even from the doorway, Weston could see the counter and register at the far end of the store. No one stood behind it.

"May I help you?" A small man crept around the side of one of the shelves. He was old. His dark skin creased and wrinkled under a cap of tightly curled white hair. Glasses sat precariously on the end of his nose, and his brown eyes gleaned with intelligence and appraisal. He was sizing up Weston just as Weston was him.

"Looking for Delbert Cornish," Weston said pushing back his hat and making a show of taking in the entire store. "That you?"

"Depends on who's asking," the old man said, screwed

up his face, and walked back to stand on the other side of the register.

"Bill Weston. Mighty strange, a business owner being so curt with a potential customer."

"Mighty strange times we're living in, Mr. Weston. Especially when the wealthy and influential are being murdered just outside that door." Cornish pointed vaguely towards his entrance.

"Wealthy and influential people who didn't seem to like you much," Weston said and picked up a loose apple, shined it on his chest.

"Oh, I see what this is," Cornish said, a sour smile stretching his lips. "Trying to find a scapegoat, eh, Weston? Well, I know they got you over a barrel, son. No one's going to believe a crusty old man like me decided to kill anyone. I can barely stand straight anymore, let alone rip a man to shreds."

"Maybe you hired someone?" Weston shrugged. Cornish was awfully hot under the collar for a man his age. Weston could see why he rubbed people the wrong way. He also could see the need for a hot temper and a sharp mind. A black man running the most successful business in town? That had to really needle some. The old man fought for what he had, and Weston respected that.

"Mr. Weston, you've got some funny ideas in your head."

"Not just in my head. I'm not from around these parts, Cornish, I'm only telling you what I heard." He took a bite of the apple. "Afterall, Horace Puddicombe was bad-mouthing you around town and his pal Dermot felt cheated by you. Two of them together might have made your life a little rough. Maybe even hurt your business. Especially if Puddicombe had become mayor."

The old man chuckled. A low, rumble of a laugh that rose and filled the room. The kind of laugh that took the breath away, made tears run down your cheeks, and hold your ribs.

"Puddicombe as mayor," Cornish said between gulping breaths. "Boy, you really aren't from around these parts."

A surge of anger rose in Weston's throat. A dark bile that turned his stomach. He slammed the apple down next to the register, watched it explode. "You think this is funny, old man? Four men are dead. Torn apart. Now, you better start talking sense, or..."

"Or what, Mr. Weston? You'll do to me what you did to those other men, hmm?" Cornish hadn't flinched, hadn't move. His deep brown eyes stared at Weston over his spectacles.

"No, I...I just..."

"Listen, son, I don't know what you did or didn't do, but I ain't got time for you and your temper tantrums."

He was right. Weston had exploded, obviously in the wrong direction. The face of Mary danced in front of his face. Carlyle might soon join them.

Weston lay his train ticket on the counter. "I'll be out of your hair soon. Tell me about Puddicombe. Why wouldn't he make it as mayor?"

Cornish let out a long sigh and pushed the ticket back to Weston with his fingertips. "Frank Winter won't let anyone take this town from him."

"Winter is going for the governor's seat, not much need of him around these parts if he gets that."

"Doesn't matter. Frank Winter is not about to give this town up, least of all to a man like Horace Puddicombe. Winter owns this town. He's a part of it and it's a part of him. He gets Governor, well, either he'll put a flunky in charge or he'll dismantle the role all together. Sheriff Johnson will likely take over."

"And the town's okay with this?"

"Most of us. Look at what he's doing here. We're on the map. Next we'll rival those fancy east coast cities. He brings in money, people, business. He's been looking to expand the town again recently. Bring in another attraction, maybe a theatre or games house. Something to keep the masses distracted. As a man who keeps his ear to the ground, I can tell you that it might be best that Dermot passed when he did."

"Why's that?"

"That livery is in a fine spot for expansion."

"Why would Ambrose give up his business?" Weston eyed the smaller man, his gaze falling on the growing smirk of someone who knows something and eager to tell it.

"Without poor Dermot around, I fear the lust for business has gone out of our young Ambrose. That and I'm sure the mayor had a word with the good sheriff about the boy's recent incarceration. Maybe Ambrose felt he owed something to him."

"So, Frank Winter is looking to expand the town and he's buying up the abandoned businesses and land?"

"Just so," Cornish said, and his smile stretched around his round face, exposing bone white teeth.

"It's the mayor," Weston said, his breath hitching, his body aching. He ran from the store as quickly as he could, his feet carrying him back to the graveyard where he'd last seen Mejia and the father.

"Bill," Mejia said, "what are you talking about?"

"Frank Winter, he's behind it. He's the killer." Weston sat with the help of Mejia, wiped his brow free of sweat.

"Mr. Weston, I'm not sure what you mean," Father Mason said and gripped his Bible tight.

"Winter is the killer and I know why." Weston knocked the hat of his head and pulled the coat from his shoulders. "He's doing it for two reasons. One, control and power. He doesn't want anyone to control the town besides him, and he wants the power that comes with being governor..."

"Horace was running for mayor," Mejia said. "He didn't seem to have much chance of winning if I'm going to be honest though."

"Sure, but if Winter was to go off and become governor..."

"Then Puddicombe would be a shoo-in, especially after his announcement last night. If Horace had lived the election would be in just a few days."

Weston nodded along. "Exactly, and with Carlyle dead and gone, his chances of becoming the governor increased drastically."

"You mentioned another reason," the old nun said, her brown eyes glinting in the dim light.

"His second reason is expansion," Weston said around a big gulp of air. "With Dermot out of the way, and Ambrose too drunk and revenge-minded to care, he can destroy the livery and expand to the north. With Puddicombe gone he can get rid of his house and push further west."

"I admit it's probable," Mejia said at his shoulder. "It fits, but he wasn't in town for the first three murders."

"And why not kill the governor while on the road with him," Father Mason spoke up. "Seems a lot easier than waiting to come back here."

"I don't think he was doing the killing, not directly," Weston said through the edge of a smile. "Bringing Carlyle back here brought him back to whomever is doing it."

II

"I'm not sure about this, Bill," Father Mason said and tapped away on his Bible. "I don't see how or why Frank Winter would do any of this." They'd made their way back to the church, each of them tired and desperate. Mejia set to work gathering some belongings and disappeared into the backrooms of the house of God. Weston and Mason set themselves up in pews in opposite aisles and stared at the pulpit.

"It's the best we got," Weston said and spun his hat by its brim. It was the only thing they had. It'd been three days of snooping around and asking questions and this was the only thing that made sense. Sure, Bose Scarborough was a nice story; some wronged ghost come back to haunt the town, but it was just that—a story. Mejia helped with that, her cleansing and Last Rites. It had almost convinced him. Almost. But there was no such thing as ghosts or Weston himself would be carrying them around like a sack over his shoulder.

"Don't misunderstand, I'm as compelled at what you say as Mejia, but I've known Frank Winter since he was a babe."

"I'm sure it isn't easy seeing him this way, Father. I'm sure it doesn't paint the picture many people here in Millwood see when they watch the mayor walk about town. Still, it makes more sense than anything else."

"I suppose, it's just..."

"Either way, Father, we're going to have to watch his

comings and goings. If he isn't the killer, or working with him, then we'll know shortly."

"I thought you had a train to catch," Mejia said and sat next to Weston, the edge of a smile cushioned by her cheeks.

"I guess I missed it," Weston said.

Bert ran the wet cloth over the table's hard surface. There was hardly a need; the Last Chance had been slow. Times like these usually made him antsy, annoyed, and, eventually, bored. Not tonight. Mr. Weston had asked him to be a spy, to keep an eye to the comings-and-goings of the mayor. A strange feeling gripped his stomach. Excitement, Bert guessed. He'd never been a spy before. And a real spy, like a Pinkerton, would be professional in circumstances such as these.

Why can't you do it? he had asked and pushed that feeling down as much as he could.

It wasn't until he got to work that Bert found out about the town service for the dead governor. Jed pronounced it as soon as Bert swung in the door, heady with his new-found responsibility. A township service for the deceased meant business would be just as dead, for a couple of hours at least. It'd pick up again once the appropriate amount of mourning had been observed and the urge to forget took over. Bert wasn't even sure the mayor would show up after something like that. His first job as a spy, and he had little to show for it. He could feel himself deflate as he feigned work. Deneen, the other server, gave him a knowing smile and grunted her ascent. He shrugged and wrang out his cloth.

The door creaked open and Bert's head shot up. An

older man with long blond hair strolled in brushing dust from his coat. He gave the man a wave and a nod, and Jed started to pour him a drink. Mr. Weston was sure that there was something going on with the mayor. His steady brown eyes were serious and stern when he asked Bert to keep a look out around the saloon. The look in those eyes, it was the first time Bert could believe that Weston was a stone-cold killer. He'd only ever seen that look once before, in the eyes of the preacher and missionaries that came to his village. The same look he'd seen just days before his family was slaughtered.

Bert sighed, "Jed, when do you think it'll pick up again?" He rested his cheek on one hand and stared at the burly man as he wiped out glasses for the third time since he had been there.

"I can't say, boy," Jed said and blew out his cheeks and shook his head, his hairy forearms twisting with the cloth. "Death is a funny thing, but it's never done us poorly."

Jed was right and soon after the first customer more and more townsfolk poured in. They crowded around the bar and squeezed shoulder-to-shoulder at the tables. Bert and Deneen ran around the floor, delivering drinks and food as fast as they could. There was no sign of the mayor, but Bert was kept busy and was able to distract himself from his disappointment. It had been some time since Bert had even noticed anyone at the door. He'd been so preoccupied that he only saw the people bustling around him, their voices loud in his ear. When he could, or when he remembered, Bert would keep an eye on the door.

As the night crawled on, the telltale squeak of the door rose above the uproarious crowd. Bert turned at the door opening again and was in time to see the tall figure of the mayor enter flanked by the sheriff and deputies. His pale face solemn under his black hair, he nodded to the staff as he made his way into the bar. The watery feeling returned to Bert's gut; maybe it wasn't excitement after all.

"Frank, how are you?" Etta Dumond's husky voice sounded from behind Bert and it set him on edge.

"Ms. Dumond," the mayor said accepting the woman's embrace. "How have you been?"

"Oh, I'm getting through, Frank. Getting through." Etta looked about the bar, her dark eyes prowling about like a cat on a hunt. "Bert, I think I saw some detritus in the back. Perhaps you could get to it when you're able." A frown framed her scarlet lips.

Bert felt his cheeks flush and he hustled to the back, rag in hand, feeling Etta Dumond's hard stare on his back.

"Come with me, Frank," Etta purred, taking the mayor by the hand. "You can leave your guard dogs down here." Etta gave the sheriff a crooked smile and dragged the mayor towards the stairs.

Bert tried not to make it obvious that he was staring as Etta and the mayor made their way toward him arm-in-arm. He had to look though, had to stare.

The sheriff joined him in watching the two slink up the stairs, the wisp of a snarl on his marred lips. For their own part, his deputies desperately tried to avoid eye contact with anyone until the sheriff led them to their usual table for cards and drinks, driving other patrons away without issue.

Jed waved Bert back to the bar, drinks lining its surface. "Here you go, deliver these to the sheriff and his boys. They look thirsty." Jed leaned both hands on the bar, his round stomach balancing at its edge. His kind green eyes gave him a sympathetic look that told Bert to take it easy but get to work.

Bert looked to the second floor, the line of doors where she'd seen men lineup each night to rent a room with one of the painted ladies that Etta kept on hand. "What do you think they meet about?"

Jed raised one voluminous eyebrow, a smile growing on his face. "That's between the mayor and Ms. Dumond. If I were you, boy, I wouldn't even attempt to find out. Trouble brews for anyone that crosses the path of either one." He nodded in the direction of the sheriff who had a sour look on his face, his gun drawn and laid on the table.

With a deep sigh Bert hefted the tray to his shoulder and brought them to the sheriff and his deputies. Bert's eyes and thoughts flitted back to Ms. Dumond and the mayor and what they were doing that room.

The crowd continued to trickle in. Bert weaved through them, a large smile pasted on his face, cleaning up where he could. Deneen took the orders, and Bert helped to deliver them. The heat in the room was a living thing, thick and stifling. It made his hair stick to his forehead, put a shine on his skin, and a flush in his cheeks. He could feel the sweat running down his back, over his face, but he had to move. Had to keep going.

"Boy!" Jed yelled from the bar his arm waving him in.

Bert slapped his empty tray down on the bar top, panting despite himself, and waited for the next order.

"Our poor, soiled doves need refreshment," Jed said and nodded to the second floor.

The whores were busy airing themselves, leaning over the railing of the balcony, smoking cigarettes from black and shining cigarette holders. Smoke flowed from their salaciously open mouths while oversized fans made of feathers in their hands dried the sweat they'd accumulated.

Bert sighed and hefted the tray up the stairs. The girls floated around him, laughing and playing as they always did.

"When are you going to let us deflower you, Bert?" one said and slid a drink from the tray.

"You'll enjoy it. Less time on your feet," another cackled and made to grab at his leg. He jerked away, careful not to slosh the drinks around too much.

"I think Anita is hoping to retire, you like the older ladies?"

Bert ignored them, his eyes turned to the floor until his tray was empty save for one drink. He looked over the railing down to Jed, but he was busy sliding drinks down the bar.

"That's for the boss," Anita said, sitting on a chair besides her open room door. Her painted cheeks caving in around a cigarette, her eyes half open under their heavy lids of makeup.

"Ms. Dumond?" Bert looked at the glass, short and half full of dark gold rye.

"Yep, but if I were you, I'd be very careful. The boss doesn't like to be disturbed when she's in a meeting with the mayor." The prostitute stood, wrapping a shawl around her bared shoulders, tossed her cigarette to the floor. "If I were you, I'd just lay it inside the door. Get in and out."

"Hey, that's what I just told Harold," one of the girls said, pretending to writhe around and causing the others to renew their shrieking laughter.

A smirk on her face, Anita bent close to Bert, whispered in his ear. "Just do it, hun, get it over with." The woman's breath smelled of smoke and gin, a sweet smell that turned unpleasant.

Bert moved towards the door with a light push from Anita, the women behind him still cackling. He took one more quick glance at Jed, hoping he might provide him with a guiding look or some direction, but Jed was still too involved in slinging the drinks. Bert had been in Etta Dumond's employ for some time, but he'd never served her himself. Deneen usually did that, or Jed. He cursed under his breath and moved to the door at the end of the balcony.

It was a particularly ornate door, a dark lacquered oak hand carved with filigree images surrounding another carved image of a large tree towering above a small house. It was beautifully crafted and elicited both awe and fear. Bert reached to knock and stopped himself, his hand frozen in front of the door.

Withdrawing he chewed his lower lip and dropped his hand to the doorknob. Weston had asked him to be a spy, to keep an eye on the mayor, and this was his best chance. With a quick look around, he pushed open the door, slowly. As slowly as he could. In all his time at the Last Chance, Bert had never seen the inside of Ms. Dumond's office. She had forbidden anyone from entering unless she had specifically requested their presence, and it was always kept closed and locked. Bert was surprised when the door pushed open, the warm glow of lit candles spilling out from within, the fragrant smell of perfume and spices tickling his nose. The floors were the first thing that he noticed; the deep caramel colour of wood polished to a shine in the candle's glow. The room seemed bigger as Bert looked up, like it spread out farther than the building could handle, farther than it possibly could on the outside. Books were strewn about in piles, and a ponderous amount were clumped together on the bookshelves that surrounded the room. All of this Bert could see from just the sliver of an opening. He pushed further.

There was a desk at the back of the room, equally as ornate as the door and larger than Bert thought any business man would need, let alone a tavern owner. Oddly shaped bottles stood upon the desk, implements for cooking and cleaning lay there was well. He caught the scent of something unpleasant on the air that almost made him withdraw from the door. He was this far now, though, and he wouldn't turn back.

Of all of that though, as Bert placed the glass of rye on the ground just inside the door, the thing that drew his eye was the forms of Etta Dumond and the mayor, Frank Winter. They were on the floor, Etta sitting up with her legs curled underneath her, and her arms wrapped around the prone mayor, hugging him tight into her. Their heads were touching, forehead to forehead, and Etta seemed to be whispering something as she rocked the mayor back and forth. Bert nearly yelled for help, screamed that the mayor was dead, but saw the steady rise and fall of the mayor's chest and stifled his call into a muted whimper. The mayor's eyes opened and twitched towards him, but he didn't or wouldn't move away from Etta's embrace. Bert fell back and scrambled to close the door. It closed with an audible click that seemed to echo above the roar of the busy tavern.

He returned to the bar in a daze, confused about what he had seen, and worried what would happen if the mayor had truly laid eyes on him. Not much of a spy after all.

"Head's up, lad," Jed said in a growl. "The people need their spirits replenished."

III

Weston sat close to Mejia and Father Mason in the shade of the boneyard. The moon was no more than a sliver of light, its unwavering barrier pushing against the shadow in a hopeless battle for supremacy. Weston had to squint to make out the individual markers that stood in their own shadows.

"You sure he'll be back?" The priest sat cross-legged on the ground, his old legs unable to handle the constant tension of the half-squat Weston remained in. He'd only returned a little while before, having played his part in the town-wide spectacle that was disguised as grieving the dead. Arrangements had been made to send the governor back to Denver on the next train; his family wanted him close by. Millwood took the unburied body, stuffed it in a pine box and hefted it on a makeshift platform in the middle of town. "What if the governor was his last target?"

"That's possible," Weston said, his eyes focused on the big shadow he knew to be Scarborough's headstone. "But we don't have much choice. The boy is watching the mayor, we'll watch the grave. Best case scenario: one of us will see something suspicious. Worst case: we'll miss out on a night's sleep. Pretty good trade off, wouldn't you say, Father?"

He couldn't see the priest nodding, but Weston knew he was.

"Este lugar no se siente bien," Mejia said and ran one rough hand over her face. "It feels...different."

"How so?" Weston was surprised she could keep up the crouching as long as she did, and there was no sign of her stopping. A smile slid over his face.

"It's as if *algo malo* happened here," she shivered. "Something very bad."

"Well, you two have been here the longest. Can you remember anything happening out this way?"

"No," Mejia said. "Father Mason has kept this place well, has tended to it."

"Not as much as I used to," the priest said resuming his stance next to Weston. "The murders, well, they've been terribly draining."

Weston nodded. He supposed that he hadn't noticed it in the same way as Mejia and Mason. There was a lot riding on the line for them; it was their town after all, their people. Weston wondered what that would be like, wondered if he was ready for something like that again. The image of Mary fell, unwarranted, in front of his eyes and he stuffed the thoughts down with a clearing of his throat.

"How do you think the *niñito* is doing?" Mejia asked.

"He's a good kid," Weston said with another cough. "He'll do what he can."

"Do you think you put too much trust into one so young?"

Weston turned his eyes to Mejia to find her staring back at him. Her old face calm, warm, disarming. "I don't. It's not so much to ask the boy, no danger in doing his job *and* keeping an eye on a customer."

Mejia nodded.

"Is... is that fog?" Father Mason asked and pointed toward the graveyard.

Weston turned back, skeptical. Sure enough, a thick, grey cloud weaved its way along the ground and through the graveyard. It rolled down from the mountains that lay just beyond the forest, a nebulous snake that wound itself about anything and everything. As it went, it obscured their sight and made everything fuzzy, dreamlike. Weston cursed.

"No bueno," Mejia said with a sigh.

"There's no cover any closer," Weston said. He took a look around and stood when he was satisfied that no one would notice him. Mejia and Mason followed his lead, the latter groaning behind cracking joints.

"La niebla esconde el bien y el mal por igual," Mejia said. "We can hide in the fog, even as we move closer. Come on." The nun patted Weston on the shoulder and moved forward. Her steps were slow and careful, picking the safest path.

Weston signaled the priest to follow Mejia and let him pass. He wanted to take another look around first to make sure there was nothing that he missed. It was a strange fog, he thought, his eyes trying to pierce it. Weston was accustomed to the fog coming off the ocean in a cool mass. Though there were no body of water nearby, this fog brought an icy chill with it and it was heavy, thick. It weighed Weston down, slowed him as if it were pushing against him.

The fog twisted around his ankles. A chill crept up his body and he felt it rush up his spine. It was freezing. As he made to follow Mejia and the priest, it felt like he was dragging his feet through snow.

"Can you see it?" Weston had stumbled upon his companions just a few feet away. They were both crouched down, their faces strained in concentration.

"Barely," the priest said and pointed to a group of shadows in the distance. "Just there. The big shadow."

"It's no good," Weston said, "we'll have to get closer."

"We might scare him off, Bill," Mejia whispered, her eyes glued to the fog shrouded tombstone.

"You two stay here." Weston settled himself into a low crouch and worked his way closer to Scarborough's grave. He made his way in a broad stroke, trying to keep an eye on the marker and the ground before him. The fog was fully formed at his feet, thickest at the ground and wispy as it carried upward. It wouldn't be long before it concealed everything and their whole mission would be pointless.

The chill of the fog sank into his bones. Weston fought the urge to move faster and kept himself at a slow pace. No need to make any more noise. Still, the cold dug into him, gripped him hard like a vice, and he wanted to move, to try to shake it off. He didn't, but he discovered that he'd crossed his arms over his chest and was rubbing his biceps with his hands.

The night darkened. Weston stared at the horned moon. Its pale light had dampened, as though a scarf had been thrown over a lamp. The thick fog surrounded him, suffocating him. And in a moment of confusion, Weston thought that stretching out his arm might push the curtain of fog aside. Arms out, he flailed in the darkness.

He wasn't sure how long he'd taken to get closer, but it felt like hours. He looked towards where he thought he left Mejia and the priest, but he couldn't see much of anything. He shrugged. They'd hear him call out if needed. Unless the fog did more than obscure the eyes. It was a foolish thought, but a persistent one.

He hunkered down behind a small headstone, Bose Scarborough's grave marker just ahead of him. It wasn't much cover, but the fog provided for the rest. The graveyard had been empty, but the coiling walls of grey cloud could hide just about anyone or anything. The damn Confederate Army could be standing just beyond him and Weston wouldn't have been able to tell.

The scratching sound wasn't obvious, not at first. It was a subtle noise, a noise that was easily overwhelmed by the thoughts bouncing around in Weston's head, by the thundering of his heart in his chest, by his quick inhalations. Such an innocuous sound. When he did hear it, Weston didn't think much of it. Focused on Scarborough's final resting place, he figured the scratching was just some animal scrounging for something to eat. He wouldn't have been surprised to see a fox or deer roaming through, the graveyard a part of their migration or hunting patterns.

The more he heard it, though, the more Weston thought it sounded familiar. A noise he'd heard, but an origin he couldn't quite place. His mind played with the thought, happy to have a distraction from the swirling fog. The more Weston focused his mind on it, the harder the sound was to grasp. He coiled his hand into a fist. *What is that sound?*

It was another moment before he started to track it. His head swiveled to let his ears take in everything around him. It was close. Closer than he thought. Louder, too. It was a jagged sound, a grinding sound, that began to set his teeth on edge. Whatever it was, it took its time. One long scraping sound after another with a short pause in between before it began anew.

The sound was coming from somewhere in front of him. He chanced a quick move forward. Nothing. Just the grave of Bose Scarborough. The scratching continued, something sharp running against something hard. Like a blade and its whetstone, but that wasn't it. It was more like...

Weston ran forward. His hands danced at his hips for a moment before they settled into fists. He heard some shuffling off to his right: Mejia and Father Mason. It didn't matter, he'd be there long before them.

He came to the grave, the gaping hole still laying before its marker. Bose Scarborough still missing from his resting place. There, on the back of the tombstone, the source of the scratching revealed itself. A new name had been scraped into the stone, blood dripping from it, but there was no one else there. It was just Weston and the stone. To his horror, he saw the mystery writer finish its business, crossing a t with a pinched off scratch and then it was gone. If anything had been there to begin with.

"What, what is it?" Mejia asked coming up on his right, Father Mason on his left, both short on breath.

"We're too late." Weston pointed at the fresh blood. No fingers had applied that blood, no animal was sacrificed to write this message. It was the stone itself that bled a thick and stringy ichor. It was a phantom, a spirit that etched the message. Weston cursed.

"What does it say?" Father Mason asked and crossed himself. His face drawn and pale, he wavered where he stood.

Weston squat down one more time, in a familiar place just behind the grave marker. He heard his knees crack as he descended, and he almost jumped up again but stopped himself short. He probed the blood with a finger—sticky, coagulating. "Delbert Cornish," Weston said. "It says Delbert Cornish."

CHAPTER EIGHT

I

The end of the business day was always bittersweet for Delbert Cornish. On the one hand, going home to Martha after all day was wonderful. The poor woman would have his supper laid out and ready for him, would be sitting in her seat at the table just waiting for him to come home. Martha wouldn't eat without him. No, that wasn't their way. They ate together or not at all.

On the other hand, he loved his business. The activity of it, the competition, the money. It was a toss-up every day when he locked his store's door.

This evening had been more bitter than sweet. Delbert dragged his feet running through his usual rituals of tidying the store and counting the stock (the money was already counted. The amount recorded in his head). David Carlyle was dead. Had been killed, in fact. Carlyle and Del had been acquaintances for some time, had known each other before Carlyle had started making regular tours of the state to scout out political connections.

They'd never been close, but they were kindred spirits. They shared a kind of familiarity with one another that, even tested through distance and time, would flourish when the two were in conversation. Carlyle and Del shared a deep respect for business, capital. They were very much alike indeed.

Del thought about his trek back to Martha, thought of passing the alley where Carlyle's body had been found that morning. It had been in the back of his mind throughout the workday, when he was speaking with customers or just counting the money: what would he do when he went to pass that alleyway? Not look of course, was his initial thought. Sound and logical thinking. If he ignored it, he wouldn't have to acknowledge it as true, and could live a life of blissful ignorance. If he did look, he would surely let his imagination run wild. Del couldn't imagine going through those thoughts anymore, but they'd be there, waiting for him in the shadows. Of the two options he favored the latter most. And yet he didn't want to be seen as a coward either.

"Perhaps just a quick look," Delbert said to himself, checking his door to ensure that it was securely locked. A quick look might do it. Might meet the needs of both options. A quick look and it would be over. A brief moment to assure himself that everything had been done. That David was gone and not coming back. That the monster that killed him was no longer skulking about.

With that resolved in his own mind he made his way back to his house and to his wife Martha, now likely staring at two cold plates of supper. Despite that sad image, he still walked as though he were in quicksand. As if he were a man going to his own death as opposed to a man revisiting the scene of his friend's. The thought made him shiver. Delbert Cornish's world was a compilation of two streets, an alley, and several buildings. Chief among them were his home and his store. Anything that occurred in the rest of Millwood was usually brought to him through his business, and, in that way, he needed not expend his energy to cross the town. It was a short walk that he took every day. A walk of which Delbert Cornish knew where everything should be, where everything was. Whether it was according to God or himself, he knew. The rocks, the animals, the flowers were all in a particular order that he could recite as if it were his alphabet. If something was off, the old shop owner felt it necessary to set it to rights. Things in their places, it had its own sort of beauty.

Walking along his pathway (because if it wasn't Del's whose was it?), Del felt something cold creep into his mind. Something or someone was watching. He froze mid-stride, his head moving about so quickly that it threatened to dislodge the bowler from his sparsely haired pate. Nothing had changed, nothing was different or new. It was all in its place. Del, stooped a little more now, cast a glance at the alleyway up ahead. He couldn't see it clearly, his eyes not what they used to be, but it was dark and full of shadow.

"Damned superstitions," he said to himself, and pushed onward. He kept his eyes down, watched his feet shuffle over the ground, his cane leading the procession. Del didn't want to look the blasted alley square in the eye until he had to. Instead, he monitored it from the corner of his vision. In that peripheral view he kept vigil on the alley, on the shadows that dwelled there swirling like smoke. And that cold feeling of being watched continued to set in.

This is it, he thought, just one quick look and be done with it. He hobbled forward, his legs shaking, fighting to keep him from that alleyway. Despite their mutiny, Delbert Cornish forced himself to turn his full gaze on the place where his friend met his death. The dark. Shadows, oil-like and murky. That's all that met his glance, nothing more and nothing less. A heavy sigh shook his body.

Relief, or something like it. Disappointment too. Had he wanted something to be there? The soul of his dead friend, perhaps? Del shrugged out another sigh and made his way home to Martha.

The shade of the alley now behind him, a burst of warmth flowed through his chest and crawled to his limbs, fingers and toes, and eventually to his head. A smile had made a surprise appearance on his weathered old face. He felt lighter, better. A simple act of catharsis and now he was as right as rain.

Guilt has a way of eating at a man, Delbert thought. *You just have to find a release.* His thoughts were now focused on Martha, on supper, on returning to the store the next day. For some bizarre reason, the thought of having children came into his mind. The joy of having the little tykes around, of their playfulness, their ever-positive outlook. He shook his head; he and Martha were far too old to have children. Still, the thought was a nice one.

So distracted by his daydreams was Delbert that he failed to notice the looming shadow that had grown out of the alley he'd just passed. The shadow grew and stretched until it had fallen upon the old man's heels, legs, and back. Delbert was so distracted that he didn't see the pan-sized hand reaching from those shadows to grab ahold of him.

"Cornish!" a voice boomed from behind him. "Watch out!" Delbert had been moving to see who had called his name when he heard the last part of the warning. A warning that came too late. The large hand clamped down on the old man's shoulder. Thick fingers jabbed into flesh to pierce it, digging into bone to crush it. A squeal of pain fell from Del's mouth.

Another large hand grasped him around the neck, wrapping its thick fingers around his throat and larynx;

he'd been silenced. As his breath was cut off, as his eyes bugged, and as his vision blurred, the image of Bose Scarborough, disheveled, clothes torn and old, appeared before him. Bose Scarborough was supposed to be dead.

Del wasn't sure about what had happened next, but he did know that in one minute he was fighting for his life, and the next he saw someone else fighting for theirs.

Weston was almost too late. He ran all the way to the store but found that it was closed and locked. With his lantern as aide, he looked in the large window, but saw nothing. He thought about breaking into the store, kicking in the door or breaking out the window, just to see if Delbert was dead inside. Nothing was strange or out of place though, not from what he could see. With an angry curse, he ran on. And that's when he saw it.

He saw the shadows act strangely as he unknowingly followed in the same footsteps as Del, saw them melt and change into a man, tall and broad-shouldered. Weston shouted a warning, but Cornish's small frame was overwhelmed by the attacker as it emerged. Cursing, Weston ran and lunged toward Del Cornish's attacker.

The connection of Weston's shoulder and the lower back of the large man was more solid than he'd anticipated. So much so that it took both men by surprise when they fell to the ground. Delbert fell with them too, grasping at his throat and coughing for air. Scarborough twisted underneath Weston and scrambled to his feet, his huge hand reaching out for Delbert once more.

With few options, Weston shrugged himself out of his coat, hopped to his feet, and dropped the jacket over Scarborough's straining face and neck. Scarborough grunted and grappled with the jacket, giving Weston the time he needed to lunge again. This time he managed to enclose his hands around the dead man's body, just as Scarborough had freed himself from the jacket over his face. He stared down upon Weston, a groan escaping his slackened jaw, his green eyes covered in a viscous white film.

"Delbert Cornish," rolled out of the dead man's mouth, a groan filled with sadness. His fists began to drop on Weston like a man swinging hammers in alternating hands. The thuds from Weston's back echoed through the buildings. Weston grunted, taking the pain long enough to twist his leg around the dead man's and tripped him to the ground again, this time on top of him and throwing punches of his own.

"Delbert Cornish," Scarborough yelled, a gurgle rising from his chest as he bucked and jostled to get away from Weston. Weston held fast, his legs now wrapped around the dead man's hips, his hands clamped around Scarborough's forearms fighting to keep them still.

"Cornish!" Weston caught the eye of the recovering old man, still holding his throat and rubbing his forehead. "Cornish, run!" he panted, still fighting.

The old man's face had started to swell, bright red finger marks wrapping around one side. At Weston's voice, Delbert's eyes focused on the two men fighting in front of him, his mouth gaping in shock or fright.

"Come on, Del!" It was Father Mason, bug-eyed and taking in the sight of Bose Scarborough even while he pulled and dragged on the old store owner.

"Delbert Cornish." Bose Scarborough's voice was strained and high pitched, his dead eyes bulging from their sockets. He broke free of Weston's grip and flailed hard and fast. Weston was close to being knocked clear all together.

Delbert was up on his feet, Mason's hand clutched around his bicep pulling on him. They were stuck, unable to choose where to go. Neither man could stop looking at Bose Scarborough.

"Run!" Weston yelled at the old men. Scarborough had broken free and scrambled away from him. Weston made another lunge at the dead man's legs but couldn't get a grip. As the hulking dead man made his way towards Delbert, the old man finally gave in to Father Mason's urging and started to move.

It wasn't enough. Scarborough caught up with him within seconds and pushed Mason out of his way. The dead man's huge hands grabbed Delbert's jacket around the shoulders and threw him into the wall of the nearest building. A sickening crunch resounded around them.

Weston jumped on Scarborough's back, wrapping one arm around his neck, while the other tried to pry the silver crucifix free from beneath his shirt. If it worked on the open road, it might work here. The dead man paid no heed to Weston hanging from him and continued to stalk Delbert. The old man moved weakly against the wall, moaning. Cursing, Weston tried to pull his chain free, but it was lodged under his shirt between him and Scarborough. With a curse he attempted to drag Scarborough down once again, but Scarborough wouldn't fall. He was focused on his prize and meant to finish it.

As Scarborough approached Delbert, he made a quick and sudden movement that took Weston off guard. Losing his grip, Weston slid from the dead man's back and into the same wall Delbert had been crushed against earlier.

Weston's vision waned and blurred at the edges. Darkness seeped in to his sight, and he could feel himself drifting into unconsciousness. He fought it, tried to force himself out of his stupor, but it was out of his hands. Where did the priest go? The last thing he saw was Bose Scarborough's large bloodless hand reaching for Delbert Cornish's throat.

II

Sunlight pierced the shadowy veil that hung over the familiar, small jail cell, blinding Weston as it did. His head hurt, and he could feel the dried blood when he ran his hand through his hair.

A cough drew his attention to the small desk that sat outside his cell. A broad-shouldered deputy sat there, feet up, and sunken eyes closed, his sausage-like fingers intertwined on his stomach that rose and fell in a gentle rhythm.

"Where were you last night?" Weston said before being overtaken by a series of harsh barking coughs. His head shook with each cough, and a sharp pain strobed within his head each time.

The deputy groaned some, set his big boots on the floor and turned to face Weston, a yawn wide in his mouth.

"Hey," Weston said, his hands gripping the cold iron bars, "what's Johnson got me in here for this time?"

It wasn't a far stretch of his imagination to figure out what happened, but he wanted to hear it from someone else.

"Humph," the big man said stroking his chin and pursing his ample lips. "Boss don't want me talkin' to ya."

"No, I guess he wouldn't." Weston said resting his head on the bars. "How's Mr. Cornish?"

The deputy bent forward, his red-rimmed eyes bulging. "'How's Mr. Cornish?'" He repeated. The deputy's face turned red. "You damn well know how ole Del is, you bastard. You tore him to shreds didn't ya?" Spit flew from the deputy's bulbous lips.

Weston raised his gaze to the deputy. "I suppose it would be hard for you to believe I didn't do it."

The deputy scoffed. "Hope you like them bars." He walked out of the room and left Weston to stew in his thoughts and the slow throb in his shoulder.

Weston woke in a sweat, grasping his scarred shoulder. His breath was ragged, his mouth dry. The bulky deputy hadn't returned. To his knowledge, no one had entered the small jail. No one to light a lamp. When the sun had finally set, a painfully gradual process, Weston was left to think on things.

It would take an awfully stubborn man to ignore the fact that there were things that crawled across the plains and forests of Colorado that weren't meant to be. They manifested and stayed by some evil force of will. A will that was unparalleled in its maliciousness, its ability to corrupt. Weston thumbed the scars on his shoulder.

He knew what Mejia had meant before, knew that evil hands left stains and caused sour deaths. Sour, because that's what they were. Soiled, rotten. Bose Scarborough was different though. He had the same scent of evil on him, a hint of the monsters that truly held on to that power, but it wasn't the same, it wasn't as strong. Bose Scarborough was human to start, maybe that was the difference. Or maybe he was the consequence of that evil. Weston ran his hand over his shoulder, feeling the dullness there and wondered how Bose Scarborough had died.

Light fell in through the opened door followed by the

shadow of a small figure. Weston rose from his cot, his eyes squinted.

Sister Mejia crept around the corner and shimmied into the slash of moonlight that peered in through the bars of Weston's window. In the light, the nun's face was pale, her wrinkles compounded around her eyes and mouth. She looked like a woman who hadn't spent much time sleeping or who spent too much time drinking. She'd donned her full nun's getup, but they were disheveled, as though she'd slept in them, and she clutched her satchel as if it might fly away.

"Sister, I didn't expect to see you here." Weston put his arms through the bars, leaning on them.

The nun shuffled closer, her brown eyes focused on Weston, her mouth a straight line of concentration. She reached for the bars like a drowning woman reaching for land.

"Bill," she said, barely a whisper and looked as though she were going to faint.

"Sister, what's wrong?"

"It's Father Mason," the old nun said through chatter-ing teeth. She gasped for air, her back shuddering as she spoke. "He's been killed."

The words tumbled from the nun's mouth and un-corked the well of sorrow that had been building up in-side of her. She sobbed now with her face pressed against the cold iron bars.

Weston took a step back, untangling himself from the bars that Mejia now embraced. He tried to make sense of the news and stared at the brick wall that separated his cell from another. He wanted to see the pattern there, wanted something that made sense, but his eyes wouldn't focus. Vaguely, as if by some distance, Weston aware that he was saying "what" over and over again. Stammering over it, whispering it.

"He's dead," the nun shrieked in her own sorrow.

Weston shook his head and shook himself free of his stupor. Anger, his old ally, rose up in his chest and latched on to his heart. He grabbed the bars so fiercely that Mejia pulled away.

"Bose? Bose Scarborough killed him?"

Sister Mejia fell to the floor, tears still running down her face, her satchel sliding across the floor.

"Bose Scarborough? No, he was shot."

"He was... shot. But Mason was with me. He tried to help Cornish. Scarborough tossed him. I didn't see him after that, but..."

"I wasn't in time," the nun had stymied her tears, her thin hands wiping them from her wrinkled face. "Neither of us could keep up with you, but the father, he pushed himself. He moved faster than I'd seen him in years. I couldn't keep up, damn it. I couldn't keep up."

Weston gripped one of Mejia's hands and she got to her knees, hands on the bars once more. The anger that had just overcame her vanished just as quick.

"Llegue demasiado tarde. When I got there, I saw you all on the ground. Each in your own separate piles, unconscious. Del was dead, the same as the others. I was about to check on you and the father when I heard footsteps. Several footsteps. I hid in the...the oscuridad between houses, but I could see them. I could see *him*—pendejo," Mejia spat a curse.

"Who shot him, Mejia?"

"They helped the father up," the old nun continued as if she hadn't heard Weston at all. Her voice shook in the aftermath of his sobs. "The father was coming around, you see. He had a...a el chichón on his head, a nasty bruise, but he was waking. I knew once I saw him pick up the father, I knew..."

"Who, Mejia, who?" Weston grabbed her thin wrist and pulled her towards him.

"The sheriff," she whispered. "Porter Johnson."

Weston deflated and fell to the floor. Mejia fell with him. They sat in silence for some time, their ragged breaths calming as their minds raced.

"That night in the woods, the sheriff, he didn't want you to do anything," Weston said, his head resting against the bars. He looked out the small window at the sharp, sickle of a moon.

"Si," she said. Her hand finding his shoulder, her warmth comforting.

"The sheriff knew then. He knew when he hauled me in here after Dermot was killed. He was working for the mayor all along. It makes sense. Even Cornish's death makes some sort of strained sense. The old man was aware of the mayor's schemes, though he didn't seem too perturbed by them. I guess the mayor is shoring up his opposition. Shutting mouths before they can open."

"That would explain why Johnson killed the father," Mejia said.

"With Cornish out of the picture and me on the scene, he had a perfect scapegoat. But Father Mason had witnessed it all. That could have ruined things for the mayor, the priest being well-liked and all."

"Si, but did the sheriff have his orders or was he being ambitious?"

"I'd bet on the latter," Weston said and turned to face the nun. "Though I'd call it more cautious than ambitious. Better to do something and ask for forgiveness than not do it and get the whip." Weston's face screwed up. The words coming out of his mouth felt old, rotten. "The only question left is the biggest. Why Bose Scarborough and how are they doing it?"

Sister Mejia looked around frantically. Catching sight of her satchel she scurried to it on her hands and knees.

"Here," the nun said and removed Father Mason's Bible and handed it through the bars. "Maybe this will help us understand."

Weston took the book, frustration rising in his gullet once again.

"Sister, I appreciate that, because of your calling, you have to tell yourself that all answers come from God. But, with all due respect, I've read this book, and there ain't nothing in there that will explain what the fuck is going on here."

Mejia straightened, and jabbed one gnarled finger in the soft leather cover of the book.

"Read," her voice stern, her eyes set. In that moment Weston could picture the nun as a young woman, her heart full of fire, eager to help, and brave enough to stare down evil men like Bose Scarborough. A fiery Valkyrie fighting in the Lord's name, sword in one hand, a Bible in the other.

So, Weston read, and he soon discovered this wasn't the Bible of his childhood, nor the Bible of his father.

III

Bert made his way to the church after Jed let him go for the night. He took his time, made sure that he wasn't in a rush; a spy wouldn't rush. Even though he was careful, cautious, he had the strange feeling of eyes burrowing into his back at every turn. Bert's heart raced, his lungs burned to catch up with it, but he managed to keep them in check; a spy wouldn't give away their feelings like that. When he turned back onto the main drag, the church grey in the early morning light, relief swept over him. Weston would be there, so would Father Mason and Sister Mejia. He'd be safe. He pulled open the church door and stepped in.

Weston wasn't there. No one was. The church was dark and empty. Every step Bert made echoed under the oak beams. The pews sat in silent audience to the un-manned pulpit. His heart thumped against his chest, and his breathing was ragged. With no one around, he lay on the altar and fell asleep.

He woke later that afternoon and went back to work. Resolved to himself, Bert knew he was still a spy until he was relieved. He had to keep watch over Mayor Winter.

Bert knew that he shouldn't have been snooping, least of all on the mayor and Etta Dumond, especially after he found out about Delbert Cornish and Father Mason's death, about how Weston was being held responsible. Still, there was something strange, even fascinating about them. He figured that was partly because he had no idea what they were actually doing.

He tried to bring it up casually with those around him, just to see if anyone knew anything. They all had their own opinions. The painted ladies would say something crude, or mime something cruder. While he thought that might be a possibility, it didn't seem to line up with what he had seen with his own eyes. The bartenders would just shrug and say that it was none of their business. That was true enough, wasn't any of his either, but he had to know. All in all, he didn't know much more than what he had seen the previous night when he had delivered drinks to them.

Of course, he'd tried to get another look. He was eager to bring the drinks to the girls, hoping he'd have one extra to slip into the door for the mayor or Ms. Dumond. It had been no use. Despite his efforts he was never given the opportunity. There were never extra drinks when the ladies had their fill, and anytime Ms. Dumond ordered something another server delivered it. Mostly Deneen.

She was an old one, Deneen. Rumour was that she'd been one of the painted ladies years ago, probably would've kept it up too hadn't she aged so; customers didn't want to pay for her anymore. Ms. Dumond offered her another job in the bar, just to keep her from going poor.

Deneen had never married, had never had time nor the desire for it. Too busy with the work, Bert supposed. Though, as tough and as rough as most of those girls were, Bert always suspected that they wanted to find a man, get married, and move away from the Last Chance. Not Deneen though.

"She's been around for so long, Ms.Dumond trusts her with damn near everything. It doesn't hurt that she can't talk," Jed said under arched eyebrows, eager to divulge his secrets to the young Bert.

"She is awfully quiet, isn't she?" Now that Bert thought about it, he couldn't recall a single time Deneen had spoken to him. The old woman's vocabulary consisted only of nods, grunts, and the seldom jabbing of a forefinger in midair when she was really adamant about something.

Jed shook his head, a smirk crossing his scruffy face. "Oh, that ain't it either. The poor ole thing ain't got no tongue." Jed punctuated this by sticking out his own tongue, as wide and cracked as it was.

"What happened?" Bert said, letting his own tongue

feel around inside his mouth.

"T'was before my time," Jed winked, "but they say it was an unsatisfied customer back in her glory days. That sounds about right to me, you know how saucy them girls get." Jed nodded his head to the girls hanging over the railing on the second floor. "Others say it might've been Indians that done it, but no one knows for sure. And Deneen, well, she ain't saying." He gave him another wink, and let out a rough chuckle.

Bert tidied around the room, served when he had to. The usual crowd had rolled in including the sheriff and his deputies. Most people were still in shock over Delbert Cornish and Father Mason's death and happy that Weston was behind bars. Jed thought that part of it was just a story, something the sheriff made up to make himself look better.

"If they caught 'em, what're all the deputies doing here?" Jed whispered to Bert after pouring up their drinks. If they were all at the Last Chance, who was watching Weston?

Bert shrugged. It was a better story than saying it was a bear that had done it. He was amazed anyone actually bought into that story. Then again, Millwood was an odd town.

Bert's thoughts came back around to Weston. Did he really kill all those people? Did he kill Father Mason and Dermot? He couldn't quite believe it. Then again, people were seldom what they appeared. The sheriff was a prime example of that. A big tin star pinned to his broad chest, but here he was drinking and whoring with the rest of the town. And then there was the mayor. A calm and collected man, an obvious product of education and good upbringing, and so beloved by the townspeople. Progressive, assertive, motivated, and confident. Though he never married, he spent his nights in the arms of the old maid who ran the local tavern and brothel. An obvious secret to boot. No, people were never what they seemed. Mr. Bill Weston was no different than the others.

"Boy," Jed called from the bar, his big hairy arm waving high above his head. "Time to water the ladies," he said and nodded to the second floor. Bert counted the glasses: seven.

"That's too many Jed, who ordered more this time. Anita?" Anita was always a heavy drinker, had been more so as of late. Bert thought it might have been that she found someone to love. Or at least a halfway decent man in the young Ezra Hames. Drinking took her mind off the work—for now. Bert speculated that it was only a matter of months, maybe weeks, until they saw the last of Anita.

"Nope," Jed said sliding a drink down the bar to some old-timer. "That's for Ms. Dumond and the mayor." He tipped a wink.

"What about Deneen?"

Jed shrugged.

Bert looked around the room, trying to find the elder barmaid. The greying tower of black hair that Deneen piled high on her head was nowhere to be seen.

He grabbed the tray full of drinks and moved toward the stairs, excitement and fear gnawing at his stomach and a plan forming in his mind.

Bert was nervous. The drinks he carried clinked and jiggled on his tray as he made his way up the stairs. He watched the drinks carefully. The alcohol inside bobbed and sloshed toward the edge of each glass, threatening to overflow.

The ladies wouldn't like it if their drinks had spilled. They'd cause a fuss. They'd ruin his chance to silently approach Ms. Dumond's ornate door. They'd make it impossible for him to see what was happening in that room.

"'Bout fuckin' time," chirped Molly, pulling her robe around her thin hips and small chest. "I'm dying of thirst." Molly was the youngest of the Last Chances' whores, the newest. She grabbed a glass of rum, hurrying to sling the amber liquid down her gullet. Her make-up was ruined by sweat and tears. Mascara erupted from around her eyes creating a mask of her face. Bert could see red welts in the shape of fingers around the young woman's throat, scratch marks on her neck and chest. Molly noticed Bert looking and gave him a sneer. But she had sad eyes, Bert thought.

"Fuckin' right, Mol," Clarissa clambered over, a loosely rolled cigarette sticking out of her mouth. An Irish import, Clarissa let her long red hair hang over her back. It was unique; something she could charge extra for. "You're going to have to lay Jacqueline and Denise's drinks beside their doors. Their suitors called early." Clarissa pointed towards the closed doors, snickered at the moaning, at the creaking of springs. "Them boys must've saved themselves up. They have a lot to get out." She elbowed Bert knocking the tray askew some.

Anita stood waiting for him, hands on her hips, bags under her eyes. She had a sad pout on her scarlet red lips. Bert gave her a questioning look: a fat lip?

"Appreciate it, honey," Anita said grabbing a glass and taking a loud, slurping sip followed by an audible sigh of delight. Anita helped Bert deliver the remaining drinks, laying them delicately next to the closed doors.

"For the boss?" Anita pointed towards the remaining drinks on the tray, huddled together.

"Yeah," Bert said, his eyes darting to the floor.

"Think you'll get a good show tonight, darling?" Anita's face split into a smile and took another sip of her drink.

"I don't know what you're talking about." Bert could feel his face burn red, his lips pull tight into a line of white.

"Sure." Anita took a seat next to her door. Her legs crossed automatically and she lay her drink on her knee. "But take it from someone who knows what desire looks like. And not that silly, romantic bullshit you hear coming out of young girls' mouths. Real desire is a need, a need that has to be quenched." She raised her drink to Bert and took another sip. "No darling, you desire that, in there. You need it, and I don't think you even know why. Maybe you ain't got nothin' goin' on in yer life right now. Maybe you just need a little thrill. Either way, you need it. You've got the desire. It's as plain to see as that nose on your face."

Bert stammered. His mouth and body shook with indecision. He couldn't decide whether to walk away or stay. He stuttered; the glasses sloshed. "I…I don't know what you're talking about," he repeated lamely.

"All right, darling, have it your way. I won't tell no one. Though, if it's a cheap thrill you're looking for, you only have to ask." The prostitute winked, took out a cigarette, loaded it in her cigarette holder, and took a long draw, her big green eyes turning toward Molly and Clarissa, watching the younger girls have their chat.

Unsettled, Bert walked away and turned his attention towards the ornate door with the small shack in the centre. His stomach was tied in knots. He hadn't believed that he had been so obvious. *Some spy I turned out to be*, he thought. Did he ask too many questions? Maybe he just asked the wrong people. All of them too close to the bar, too close to those involved. He sighed, trying to dispel some of the butterflies that had taken up residence in his stomach.

He ran his free hand over the door, feeling the smooth curves and indentations, feeling the outlines of the images preserved there. There was an impulse to knock, to announce himself before he opened the door. Bert stood before it, hand closed in a fist, poised to bang on the door, deliver the two remaining drinks, and excuse himself. That would certainly prove Anita wrong. Then again, it wouldn't answer any of his questions—any of Weston's questions. He let his hand fall to his side.

Bert looked over at Anita. The aging whore chugged her whiskey, fixed her breasts in her tight-fitting dress, and moved off to try and sway the men of the bar to come to her room. She gave Bert a quick look over her shoulder and tipped him another wink. She linked arms with Molly and Clarissa and guided them to the bar floor with her, three whores on the prowl. Bert was left alone.

His hand fell to the brass door knob, hissing through his teeth at the slight jangle that emitted from it. He turned it slowly, waiting for the soft click of the latch and then pushed in the door with just as much care. He only dared to open it a crack, edging his head and eyes so that he would gradually see the room unveil itself.

The familiar soft glow of candlelight creeped out of the opening, the smattering of books and overturned jars and bottles still strewn about the floor. As Bert pushed the door open, he was prepared to see anything. Part of him hoped to see the mayor in Etta Dumond's strange embrace once again, foreheads touching, a soft cooing on the air. Another part of him wanted to see them engaged in something more vigorous, their muscles pumping, their limbs quaking. He could still hear the moaning from the rooms behind him, would he hear more of the same once the door was completely open? Could he risk opening it that far?

The sound of quick breathing perked up his ears. He imagined the constant in and out of a woman's chest, her hot breath panting into a man's neck, her teeth grazing his ear. A low grunt emerged. It sounded as if it was hiding just behind the door. A man, his hands entangled in the loose blonde hair, his mouth exploring the woman's breasts, his hips moving in a rhythm with hers. Bert caught himself breathing heavy, his hand clamped to his trousers' leg, the tray swaying in his arm, almost forgotten during his daydreams.

Quickly, he placed the glasses to the side of the door, the tray stowed under his arm. The breathing and grunting continued just out of his sight. As he pushed the door open, he could see Etta Dumond, her face painted with something red and dripping. Etta's naked body writhed and gyrated on the floor, while her lily-white arms, stained red to the elbow, were raised to the sky. Her eyes were pools of white amidst a mask of shadow and blood. With her pink lips open in a grimace of pain and pleasure, her breathing become more and more rapid.

Next to the Etta was the mayor, Frank Winter, also naked, his chest painted in red circles, his face in lines of blood as if Etta had run a blood-soaked hand over his face. He grunted as his muscles strained under his skin. His mouth was closed so tightly Bert could hear his teeth grinding. The mayor retained his human-looking eyes, but they were unfocused and staring straight in front of him, at Etta.

Bert stumbled back, his hand clamping around his mouth to keep him from shouting out. *Close the door!* his brain screamed at him. Close the damn door. But he was already a step or two away from the handle, a step that equalled a mile. He swallowed hard, one hand still against his treacherous mouth while groping for the door knob with his other. As he reached, he noticed the body. Deneen's long hair, the grey streaking through the black, was splayed above her head. If it weren't for the blood, she may have been asleep. Gripping the doorknob Bert slammed the door shut. He dropped his tray and ran down the stairs and out of the bar. He was aware of Jed's eyes on him, of Anita's, Molly's, and Clarissa's . He was even aware of the sheriff's squinting eyes as he rose from his seat and looked towards the second floor. He was aware and he didn't care. He had to get out of that room, out of the Last Chance, and out of the town. He had to get to Weston.

CHAPTER NINE

I

The book lay opened on the ground in front of Weston, the highlighted words staring up at him. Spreading out from the book, like wings from an eagle, were the papers that didn't belong to the ible. Handwritten notes mostly. Observations, ideas, conclusions. Anything that Father Mason thought was important had been stored in that book.

Weston stared down upon it all, the strange font of knowledge that was splayed before him. It had been about two hours, the book laid flat in front of him as he read it, cross-legged on his cell floor, fingers steepled in front of his mouth. Mejia watched him, sitting as still as she could from the ground on the other side of the bars. She didn't utter a sound.

"This...this doesn't make sense," Weston said at length, rubbing his eyes with the heels of his hands.

"How so?" The nun's voice cracked some, dry as it was and ill-used from her sobbing.

"Well, how did a Christian priest hunt down all of..." he waved his hand at the knowledge that surrounded him, "...all of *this*."

"Me," Sister Mejia said and entertained Weston's securitizing look. "Well, partially. Lo digo sin orgullo. When

Father Mason saw what I was doing, when he learned la intención, he wanted to know more. I have a lot of the same knowledge, what I was able to glean from la bruja of my homeland. The father…well he sought out whatever else he could. Letters to fellow priests, conversations with travellers, freed slaves, he even gained audience with a Cherokee medicine man." She smiled. "He once said he didn't have the stomach to do what I did, but he could help in other ways."

Weston nodded and sifted through the papers one more time, giving the nun a moment with her recollections. He gathered them all together in a pile and put them back in the desecrated Bible, closing it atop of them. Mary would never had stood for it. He still remembered her face alight as she strolled to the church to pray. He loved that about her, and he hated it. Mary was kind and gentle and thoughtful. She would always help around town, taking care of older women and younger children. Then again, she took the Bible's word for law, listened to their local priest as if he had all the answers. When she was faced with something that couldn't be reconciled by either, she ignored it. "Ignored" was a gentle word. Weston never said this to her, never said this to anyone, but if something didn't match up with her religion, Mary hated it. It wasn't a hate that was full of rage, but a quiet hate. A judging hate. A hate that was silent behind a wall of ignorance. She just pretended it wasn't there. So, when Mary was actually faced with it, she reacted. Badly.

She was a religious woman, virtuous even. It was a surprise to even him when she killed herself. Weston saw what religion did to some people. He saw it and he wouldn't forget.

"So," he said running his hands down the length of his

face, "what am I supposed to be taking away from all of this?" He sighed, his forefinger tapping the leather cover of the book, hard.

"The father had made notes on what I was doing, yes," Mejia said. "But, as I said, he also collected some interesting information from others. There's more there than I have myself."

"And you think there is something that can help us?"

"Bose Scarborough is dead, Mr. Weston. We know silver protects against him, somewhat. I believe there is something very similar mentioned in that book. Something the father labeled as a revenant."

Weston sat in his small cell, legs crossed under him on the hard, concrete floor, and read through Mason's bible once more. The father was a meticulous reader and researcher, his ink marking nearly every page on the old book. In it he offered aid for learning and practising, chicken scrawls that could be just an anecdote, or a great ritual for banishing evil. Weston couldn't say.

He re-read the section marked "Revenant" and sent Mejia to fetch some things that might be included in the ritual. The nun had jumped up and ran out the door with a list of things to do, eager to help in the only way she could. Meanwhile, the jail was quiet. The noises of the building kept him on guard, and he was hungry, thirsty. Ever since that broad-shouldered guard had left, no one, aside from Mejia, had entered the jail. True, it had allowed him to converse with the sister in loud and open exclamations, but it left him with no food or drink for hours, and it strained his patience.

Still, it was strange. The sheriff seemed to butt heads

with him on principle at this point, but Weston had yet to see his gloating face. The sheriff that Weston had become familiar with wouldn't have missed a chance to condemn him, even if it weren't true. Weston felt a little disappointed he wasn't going to get a chance to explain how this whole thing happened, even though he knew it would fall on deaf ears. He would be lucky enough if he got the time to do anything before they strung him up. Just another swinging body six feet in the air.

Weston crawled onto the cot, the thin mattress only slightly more welcoming than the floor he had just vacated. The purple glow of sunset receded slowly from the cell. No lamps had been lit and Weston would soon be in complete darkness. He sighed, laid his head on the mattress, and tried to think of anything other than Bose Scarborough and the deaths he had wrought. He thought about Bert, how he was supposed to meet him the night before. He hoped the boy didn't think too harshly of him. Did he think he had left town? Worse yet, did he hear about Delbert Cornish? The father? Did the sheriff's poison against him seep so easily into his ears? Weston hoped not, but, in truth, they hadn't known each other very long. In that time, he'd been in more trouble than reasonable. Weston wouldn't have blamed Bert for stepping away from him. Renouncing him and wiping his brow in relief that he hadn't fallen into some torturous trap laid by a notorious killer. And yet, behind his closed eyelids, he continued to picture himself with Bert that day at the train yard, playing games, having fun.

His eyes popped open as the click of a door opening sounded in the small space. It was almost complete darkness in the little jail, the white glow of the unhindered moon casting a dull light in Weston's cell that didn't extend beyond his bars. Shadows danced out there, swirled and stalked, offering him nothing to latch on to. The door closed. Someone was out there.

"Finally come to gloat, sheriff?" Weston groaned, sitting up on the small cot. His eyes darted around the room, hoping to find purchase on something solid and tangible and finding nothing.

Something solid moved in the darkness, a tangible shadow that lurched through the small room in front of him. A heavy stomp of a large foot shook the floor, followed by another.

"Bill Weston," the deep, watery voice of Bose Scarborough grumbled through the dark silence.

"Shit," Weston said backing himself into the corner of his cell, eyes forward as the dead man wrapped his thick fingers around the iron bars of the cell door.

"Bill Weston," Scarborough said again, shaking the door with such force that the Weston could feel the wall at his back shake.

Weston scanned the contents of his cell in the dull light, hoping to find anything that he could use as a weapon, but he was running out of options and time. Scarborough shook the cage again, a grunt escaping his throat, and an unnatural creaking emitted from the door.

Tearing the mattress off the cot, Weston looked for anything he could remove from the metal frame to defend himself. Nothing there but springs and thin scraps of metal. He cursed again. The dead man was gripping the top corner of the door now, pulling on it with his foot placed on the bars for extra leverage. The door whined and started to bend under that strain.

Ripping some long strips of cloth from the mattress, he wrapped the ends around either hand, leaving enough to dangle between them. It wasn't his first choice, but it was all he had. The door moaned once more, bending further and further.

Bose Scarborough's expression was flat, his eyes cold and vacant, as he bent the iron door so that it rolled in on itself. Grunts and groans of effort escaped his slack lips, but no strain showed on his face. He just stared off, not focusing on Weston, the door, or anything Weston could discern. Scarborough just went through the motions, doing what he had to do to get to his goal.

"Bill Weston," came another grumble, one large arm now pulling on the cell from within.

When the door finally broke open, the crack of the thick metal echoed through the room. Weston prepared himself, waiting for the dead man to charge in and start his attack. Scarborough, though, just stood within the doorway and blocked Weston's exit, the broken door swinging loosely behind him.

The dead man came at him with a speed Weston wasn't counting on. The big hands wrapped themselves around Weston's neck, their grip crushing. Gurgle and spit escaped from Weston's mouth as he ground his teeth and tried to shake off the powerful hands.

Blackness threatened at the edge of his vision when he finally knocked the dead man's hands from his neck, scuttling himself sideways to avoid a return attack. He kicked himself off the back wall and made it past the large man's grasping arms. He was coughing and trying to suck in air in the process.

He landed just short of the door, his lungs still burning from the effort to regain his breath. A grunt uttered from behind him and one of Scarborough's hands grabbed his ankle and dragged him back. Turning to his back,

Weston aimed several kicks with his free leg at the dead man's head, landing each in succession. Scarborough just shrugged them off and clenched his free hand into a sledgehammer sized fist.

Weston braced himself, hugging his elbows into his ribs, his fists to his face. Scarborough struck like a snake, explosive and powerful. Weston tried to time the punches as they came at him, and managed to deflect some off of his forearms, but he took more on the chin than he hoped. It left him dazed, bruised, and bloody, but he was getting his timing. The dead man didn't get tired. Each punch was mechanical, with the same intense power in each strike. It was like the engine on a train, constant and powerful. Predictable.

As Scarborough was about to land another haymaker, Weston moved to the side and grabbed his arm as it hit the ground next to his head. Wrapping his mattress strip around the arm and holding on to it with all the desperation her could muster, Weston then buckled the dead man's leg by locking his own legs around it, driving Scarborough to his knees.

Grunting, the dead man tried to pull his arm away, but Weston was too quick, and managed to use his hips to turn the fumbling Scarborough to his back.

"Bill Weston," Scarborough cried as he tried to grab a hold of his target to rip and shear. Weston wasn't fool enough to try and out fight the dead man though. As soon as he was stable, he jumped up and ran to the door, away from the jail cells and his would-be assassin.

Scarborough wasn't a man to be denied, and he was soon back to his feet and chasing Weston through the door, and out into the open air of the warm summer night.

II

Sister Mejia's hands trembled, dropping papers and books alike. All things Father Mason had collected over the years. Things she supposed she had inherited now that he was dead.

She left the papers where they lay and clutched for the old wooden chest that Mason had stored in the corner of his office. It was a gift from his parents, he had told her once. A going-away present from when he'd left home to join his order. For years it was filled with objects of his youth: toys, books, clothes, and the like. Things that he kept for sentimental reasons. She craved those things now, the silly old fool that she was. Craved the familiar scent of her old friend, the feel of something he once handled and cared for. Something that might comfort her. But no, those things were long gone now. Given away, donated. Destroyed.

"Mujer tonta," she said, her chin digging into her sternum and tears running down her lined face. She opened the chest with her fumbling hands, stared into the shadows within. Her tools were there. Supplies so that she wouldn't have to take the time to return to her cabin and retrieve more.

No matter how long she'd done this, how long she'd attempted to push off the evil spirits, Mejia couldn't quite shake her distaste of the tools she used. She had strong convictions, but they were pulled in two different directions. Learning from a Bruja was an honor, but so was serving God. There were times when those beliefs didn't come into conflict, when they coincided quite well. It was the other times that weighed on her so. She was getting too old to have her soul torn in two different directions.

Mejia would have to choose soon how she would end her life: as a bruja or a nun. She wouldn't be able to do both for much longer.

The doorknob jostled so violently that she flung herself back and away from the chest, the lid slamming on her supplies.

"Who's there?" she demanded, her hands clenched into tight fists.

"Sister Mejia." The young voice of Bert seeped around the edges of the door. "Is that you?"

Using the heels of her hands to wipe the tears from her eyes, Mejia opened the door.

"Entra niño, entra." The boy's face was pale, his eyes wide, and remnants of tears stained his cheeks. "¿Que pasa? What's wrong, boy?" Mejia guided him into the room and closed the door behind her.

"I need to speak to Mr. Weston," he said through shallow breaths. "It's about the mayor."

Mejia knelt before the boy, their eyes on the same level. "What happened?"

The boy's eyes overflowed, and he collapsed in her arms, his back heaving with sobs.

"All right," Mejia said with gentle shushes. "Esta bien, chico. I am just getting some things here, then we will go see Mr. Weston. ¿Si?"

The boy nodded his head through sniffles and moved to lean against the wall. One hand made the effort to wipe at his eyes.

Mejia forced a smile and went about packing up what was needed. Bert stood behind her. His sniffles remained, though they became fewer and further between. She had known the boy for quite some time. No parents, no family. She had wanted to take him on with her, have him help her around her home, but Etta Dumond managed to get her clutches into him first. Money was such an easy distractor to the young and needy. Especially for those who never had any to begin with. She had been much the same as Bert when she first came to Millwood. She had her parents though, her sister, and the Bruja's teachings. Still, none of that saved her from Bose Scarborough. Etta Dumond may not have been as obvious as Bose in her methods, but she played against the soul just the same. Mejia hoped that Bert hadn't been hurt in some way. Hadn't been defiled.

Taking the boy by the hand she led him to the door. The boy was slow, hesitant. His breathing quickened as Mejia opened the door.

Sister Mejia turned to check on the boy but, in his place, saw a length of dead men, each one lashed together by some horrible green rope, a vine. What had once been the boy, Bert, stared up at her from the floor, his blackened hand, a wreckage of the human form, gripped Mejia's own tight.

Horror gripped the old nun, and a scream tickled the length of her throat. She tried to pull away from the putrid form lying before her but couldn't break the dead thing's grip. A smile crept over the dead face, its milky eyes alight with intent. Its smile stretched over the dry and cracking skin, enlarging more and more until it started to open on the creaking hinges of its jaw. The unnatural maw, now reaching toward the dead thing's chest, slammed shut with a shuddering bang, the horrible vibration of teeth grinding and chomping under his skin.

A hand at her shoulder brought her around. Weston faced her, sweating and out of breath. There were bruises and scratches along his neck and throat, and a desperate look in his eye.

"Sister," Weston said, still sucking air. "He's coming."

A small squeeze on her hand brought Mejia back around to Bert, who had returned to his old self. The trail of dead men was gone. But their fading memory still held sway over Mejia. She shivered and jolted, never releasing Bert's hand.

"Jesus Christ," Weston said, his eyes lighting on Bert for the first time. "Mejia, quick. Take the boy and hide in that room." He pointed back towards the office. "Grab your things and meet me at the graveyard. I'll lead him away."

A crash on the door punctuated this point, buckling the door inward. It drove Weston away for a moment, and he had to struggle to regain his footing. The crash caused Mejia and Bert to jump. The boy let out a yelp. Weston turned his eyes on them, sweat pouring down his forehead and face.

"Get in the room. Now."

Mejia dragged the boy back towards the room. Bert's soft cries echoed in the empty church that had gone strangely silent. She put the boy in the corner of the room and slid the desk across the door when the crash sounded again accompanied by a cracking sound and a round of curses from Weston.

"Bill Weston," said a deep and vacant voice that brought fresh shudders up Mejia's spine. She hadn't heard that voice in years, and now with those two words, all the pain and suffering its owner had caused flashed through her mind. Sister Mejia's mind was stained with equal parts anger and regret. Bose Scarborough was back, killing again.

III

Weston's shirt hung from his shoulder, torn by grasping hands. He could feel the fresh gouges in his chest and neck, could feel the trickle of blood as it ran down to his stomach. Fresh pain exploded from his wounds at each bouncing step. Still, the pain in his old wounds on his ugly shoulder was much worse. The throbbing there felt like ice water trying to freeze him from the inside, trying to stab at his heart and crawl to his brain. The pain forced his eyes wide and stilted his breath, but the trees were in sight and the graveyard wasn't much further than that.

"Bill Weston," Scarborough's voice carried behind him, the light summer breeze doing nothing to keep it at bay. Weston cursed.

Scarborough reached his meaty hand out for Weston, his jagged fingernails scraping the exposed flesh of Weston's shoulder. The tree break opened before them and Weston dodged towards it, the arm of his scarred shoulder hanging limply at his side.

The graveyard rose up before him on its small hill. Weston skirted the path, his tired legs pushing him up over the rise. He jumped the cold iron fence and headed for Scarborough's ruined grave.

"Bill Weston," the dead man cried. Weston chanced a look over his shoulder. The massive Scarborough was standing on the other side of the fence, his black silhouette blocking out the crisp, white moonlight.

The grave was in its state of disarray. The broken lid was strewn across a mound of fresh dirt. Weston bent at the waist, hands on his knees and his breath ragged. The dead man was nowhere in sight. His constant braying of

Weston's name had gone silent, as did his stomping foot-steps.

The moon coloured the sky an uneasy white behind turbulent clouds. Still, the graveyard was clear to see in the pale light, its crosses and headstones illuminated more so than Weston's last visit in the fog.

The earth that hadn't been disturbed by Bose's exhumation seemed to sprout dead and dying grass that was yellow and dry. It was as if the grass had been burned by the sun or sapped of its life. The grass around Scarborough's grave was in stark contrast to other nearby graves. Those touted green grass, lush and full of life.

Weston crept around the grave, intent on the tombstone's back. He had a notion that was playing with his mind since he had seen it the other day. There in place of Delbert Cornish's name was Bill Weston. Like the name that had been there before it, Weston's name was written in blood, scrawled there as if by some jagged pen.

"Come on, Mejia," Weston said, scanning the graveyard for anything he could use as a weapon. He hooked his thumbs in his belt and felt a pang for his guns. He felt foolish now for thinking he could do without them, thinking that he'd be able to avoid the life that had brought him to this point. He shook his head and rubbed at the back of his neck.

There was a shovel not far from the grave, its blade driven into the earth. With the rate of death in Millwood of late, it was no wonder it was left out for easy use. He grabbed it, tested its weight in his hands. "Better than nothing," he said.

A chill came first, an icy spider crawling up his back. Weston's hands tightened on the shovel. The throbbing pain in his shoulder came next, and it put him on edge; his teeth clenched tight.

The menacing silhouette of Bose Scarborough appeared on the opposite side of his own grave. No features of the dead man's countenance were visible; his staring, unfocused eyes and slack jaw were hidden in the shadow of the moonlight overhead.

It was him though. Of that Weston was sure. He had the same broad shoulders and torn clothes. And his massive hands, when he reached out to Weston, were an unnatural grey.

"Bill Weston," escaped from the dead man's throat in a croak of a whisper. It was said with finality. As if the game was done and Weston should turn over his cards, fold. Weston wasn't done though. Not by a long shot. He tightened his grip on the shovel, feeling the grooves in the wooden haft. He just had to hold off the dead man until Mejia arrived to do what needed to be done.

The nun had waited for at least fifteen minutes. She and the boy had sat on the floor next to the desk she'd pulled across to block the door. Sister Mejia waited and listened. The soft cry of the scared boy was all she could hear. The ragged breath of Bill Weston, the thunderous knocking of the dead Bose Scarborough had faded away. They were alone.

Mejia squeezed the shoulder of the crying boy. "It's okay Bert, they are gone now."

The nun stood, one old hand using the desk as support. The boy remained in his place, sniffling and wiping his face with his sleeve. It didn't take long for Mejia to set the office to rights. Coercing the boy to move was the hardest part. Once that was done, however, it was straight forward. She hurried to pack up some things she thought she might need for another ritual. Candles, matches, cigars, brandy. She'd gathered some of the papers she'd dropped earlier and packed them in her satchel as well, not knowing if she'd need them at all, but wanting to take every precaution.

"Sister?" the boy said, his voice cracked.

"Si," Mejia said without looking, and continued to pack her supplies.

"Sister," Bert was very close to her now. "I need to leave."

"No, es más seguro así," Mejia turned to the boy, another forced smile. "I just need to help Mr. Weston, then we'll be right back. You'll see." She nodded, not sure if she was doing it for his benefit or her own.

"They saw me," Bert said, trembling. "They know."

Mejia took Bert's hands into her own and crouched before him. "Who saw you, chico?"

"The mayor, Ms. Dumond. They..."

Mejia placed her satchel on the floor. She wouldn't press the boy. He needed to get this out on his own time. She crouched there, encouraging the silence, and waited for Bert to speak again.

"They... they were both naked."

Mejia allowed herself a modicum of relief. A sigh was loaded and ready for release, a genuine smile prepared to crack her wrinkled face.

"They were covered in blood and Deneen's body... it was... it was..." Bert trailed off into more sobs. The smile and sigh died with Mejia's sense of relief. She reached out and grabbed the boy, pulled him into a tight hug.

"It's okay, niño. I am here."

Mejia let the boy cry into her shoulder, his back heaving. Covered in blood, she thought. Deneen. That was a name she hadn't heard in years, not since Amelia found out she was pregnant and confided in a young woman who would become an old nun. Not since Bose Scarborough first terrorized Millwood.

"Bert, chico, I need you to think. Think back to what you saw." Mejia could feel the boy's head shaking against her. "I know it is hard, I know what you saw was horrible, but I need to know—did they paint any symbols in the blood."

The boy pulled back from her, his eyes wide, his mouth agape. I've pushed him too far, Mejia thought. It was more than he could bear. But she had to know, had to know what part Etta played in this, if any.

Mejia tried to pull the boy back into their embrace. "I'm sorry, child. I ask too much."

He pushed against her, his mouth working. Rolling a thought around, not sure if he could contain it. "How did you know?" he asked finally.

The old nun released his arms and they sat, facing each other, on the floor of the old church. Bert's eyes were red and tear-rimmed, his mouth a grimace of fear and grief.

He doesn't want to tell me, Mejia thought and forced yet another smile. Perhaps she did ask him too much. Perhaps the best thing to do would be to let him cry out his pain, put it behind him, and let him flee. Perhaps. But Mejia needed to know.

"What symbols did they paint, child, and where did they paint them?"

Weston landed on his back. The grass of the graveyard did little to cushion his landing, and the air left his lungs with a loud groan. He still held the shovel, and that was the best that he had right now.

"Bill Weston," Scarborough loomed above him, his long, thick arms reaching down to grab him once more, to rend him limb from limb if he could. Weston slashed out with the blade of the shovel, catching the dead man in the ribs, slicing across his chest. It did nothing but stagger Scarborough back some. No blood flowed from him, no grunt of pain or even discomfort. Instead, the dead man just stumbled backward. More like a feign of being alive, a reflex leftover from his life before.

"Bill Weston," the guttural voice whispered as Weston rolled out of his reach and brought the shovel back up, ready to defend himself once more.

"Stop saying my name," Weston growled through gritted teeth. He was sure that the dead man hadn't heard him, or perhaps it just fell on deaf ears. Scarborough was dead, a puppet being dangled by some unseen hand. But whose hand, and could they hear him?

Weston lashed out with the shovel again, a stabbing motion as if with a spear. Scarborough slapped the shovel out of his way and rushed in. He grabbed for Weston's neck, but Weston moved out of range, the shovel awkward in his one hand. Readjusting his grip, he swung the shovel like a bat. It landed true, slicing into the knee of the extended front leg of the charging dead man. Scarborough may have felt no pain, but he was as subject to gravity as anyone else. The dead man fell to the ground, his arms still outstretched, reaching for Weston.

Scarborough was working himself back to his feet, but the laceration at his knee slowed his progress. Weston turned to look in the direction of the town. Where was Mejia? He'd expected her by now, cresting the hill with supplies, papers sticking out haphazardly from the father's small leather satchel.

Weston swung the blade of the shovel into Scarborough's head knocking the dead man back to the ground.

The old nun was nowhere to be seen. The ritual they'd planned, the ingredients needed, were all with her. Weston gritted his teeth and swung the shovel into the back of the dead man's head. A satisfying crunch followed, and Scarborough fell to the ground.

"That feels better," Weston said and scanned the horizon once more.

"I'm here!" Mejia's voice carried to him, a salve to his nerves. Weston smiled and allowed himself a sigh of relief, bent over with his hands on his knees.

"Better get el hechizo ready," Weston nodded towards the open grave. "Not sure Mr. Scarborough is going to be this obliging for long." The dead man grumbled into the earth, his thick fingers digging into the grass and dirt.

Mejia rummaged through her satchel, taking out candles and placing them around the perimeter of the empty grave. Lighting them, she drew out some of the papers and shuffled through them. She sighed. Weston hit Scarborough with the shovel once more.

The nun pulled out something covered in a white cloth. She held it before her face for a moment, her old eyes studying the shape of it in the dim light. A shudder went through her body followed by a heavy sigh and she moved towards the tombstone. With care she placed the small object on the ground and removed the cloth covering it. Mejia took a step back, her eyes averted from the small figure she had just placed.

It was a white figurine, small but visible from where Weston was keeping the dead man at bay. It appeared to be a robed figure, a skull grinning out from the under its hood.

Weston nodded to the effigy. "What's that?"

Sister Mejia lit a cigar and placed it in her mouth. The red ash at the end of the cigar glowed in the night. She blew the smoke on the small statue. "Help," she said and placed the still-lit cigar next to the statue. Nodding to herself, she took out a glass flask with amber liquid in it and poured it into a small tumbler. Taking a quick swig from the flask, Mejia placed the tumbler on the other side of the figure and backed away.

"Bill Weston," Bose Scarborough grumbled at Weston's feet. He had managed to get to his knees while the nun was meandering through her rituals. Weston swung the shovel in a sharp arc towards Scarborough's head, but it brought up solid in the dead man's hand as he caught it, a powerful opposing force causing Weston's arms to vibrate.

"Bill Weston," leaked out of the dead man's blackened lips, his milky eyes focused on Weston's own.

"Shit." Weston tried to pull the shovel free, but the dead man's hand held fast.

Scarborough stood and tossed the shovel somewhere behind him. The night was still and quiet. Sister Mejia's whispering as she said prayers or chants stood above the eerie silence. Weston just needed to stay alive until the ritual was done.

He ducked under one of Scarborough's meaty hands, backed away from the other as it swept towards his face. A low grumble emitted from the dead man as he moved forward, his objective certain, his target before him.

Weston moved away, his eyes flicking toward Mejia hoping to judge her progress. The old woman's narrow shoulders were hunched over, her head lowered in a quiet chant. It wasn't working.

Scarborough's big hand gripped Weston's neck and lifted him off the ground. His feet dangling, Weston kicked at the large dead man to no effect.

"Bill Weston," Scarborough purred and squeezed Weston's neck harder. Black spots began to explode in Weston's vision, his throat stung with lack of air, and his tongue flailed. He was grudgingly aware that he was making guttural, choking noises. A ring of blackness shrunk his vision. The dead man's face with its grey complexion and brackish blood slicking his hair and cheek would be the last thing Weston ever saw.

Raising his arms above his head, Weston brought them down onto the joint of Scarborough's outstretched arm. Despite the dead man's unnatural strength, the arm faltered, and Weston was on his feet once more. His lungs burning for air, Weston ignored that Scarborough had grabbed a handful of his hair with his free hand and continued to hammer away at the dead man's choking hand. Finally breaking the hold, Weston took a deep breath and kicked away from Scarborough, only to be dragged back by his hair. A tearing sensation sent fire through his scalp.

Weston moved into the dead man, ducking as best he could, and wrapped his arms around the backside of Scarborough's knees. They toppled over together. Weston rolled over the large man, his hair now loose from the man's grip. He could feel blood weeping from his scalp; his heart pounded in his head.

Scarborough was up just as quick, a snarl curved around his yellowed teeth. He lumbered towards Weston, arms out and grabbing at him again. Timing the dead man as he came, Weston dropped to his back, planted one foot into Scarborough's stomach and tossed him over his head. The toss was followed by a crash that interrupted the chanting nun.

"Finish it," Weston said pointing his finger at Mejia. He looked to see Scarborough, readying himself for a quick reprisal, but couldn't find him. The nun scrambled away from the open grave.

"It… it's done." Mejia shrugged. She was still trembling, the pages in her hand shaking with her. "I fear that it is by someone else's hand that Mr. Scarborough roams the land of the living once more. A blasphemous union that even la Bruja couldn't sever." She gesticulated towards the bleached figurine. "It's up to her now."

Weston looked into the grave. Scarborough lay there atop the broken casket his body had just crashed through. He wasn't moving.

"Maybe she's already done it." Weston nodded to the grave.

Sister Mejia crept forward, bending just slightly so she could look in. Scarborough was still, his eyes were closed, and there was a sad, sagging expression on his face. The sister' s body loosened, her hands fell to her knees, and she breathed in the earth-scented air. "Alabado sea el Señor," she said with a nervous smile on her wrinkled face.

Nodding, Weston lay an unsteady hand on the old nun's back and started off to look for the shovel. He could feel his own trembling now, the aches and pains from the last few days sinking into his muscles and joints. His throat was swollen and fiery, and his ribs ached, a leftover from his time in the desert, and, of course, his ruined shoulder. By the time he returned to the graveside, he was limping with one hand wrapped around his chest.

"I may need your help with this, sister," Weston nodded towards the mound of dirt that was piled on the other side of the grave. The sister wasn't looking in his direction though, she was moving backwards, away from the grave. Her mouth open in a silent scream.

One large hand gripped the edge of the grave, fingers digging into the soft dirt. A grumble erupted from the open hole: "Bill Weston."

Cursing, Weston twirled the shovel around and swung it one-armed at Scarborough. It connected with the dead man's head, laying him flat in the grave once more. His alabaster eyes were still open, flaring with something approaching anger or hate. Pointing the shovel blade side down, Weston drove the shovel through the dead man's stomach, driving it in until it pierced the dirt beneath. Scarborough twitched, a growl rising from the back of his throat. Weston pulled the silver cross from his neck and let it slide down the shovel handle.

The dead man collapsed, his limbs lying loosely around him. His face fell into a peaceful expression, a sad smile upon his dirt layered face. Weston fell back, planting his backside on the sparse grass that surrounded him. Bose Scarborough, the walking dead, was at peace. He wasn't sure how he knew for certain, but he did. It was over. His shoulder stopped throbbing for the briefest moment, and he let out a sigh.

"Is he…" The nun stood behind him.

"I think so." Weston crawled towards the grave, the dead man still lay there, almost peaceful. "It's a shame really," Weston said getting to his feet and brushing himself off.

"W-what?"

Weston hitched a thumb towards the grave. "No

shovel. We're going to have to fill in the grave with our hands."

The sister nodded, a smile crossing her face then disappearing just as quickly. "We have more to talk about," she said and Weston's stomach sank.

"The mayor," he said with a nod of his own and then went to work covering up Scarborough.

The brown dirt fell easily on the dead man. His grey skin disappeared until all that could be seen was the edge of a shovel handle sticking from the ground.

CHAPTER TEN

I

Bert rocked back and forth and hummed quietly. Thoughts of Deneen's dead body, her maroon blood pooling on the floor of Etta Dumond's office, fluttered through his mind. Every so often he'd feel a slight tremble come over him, a flutter of his eyes, of his heart, and the horror of what he'd seen would come flooding back building a scream that ached to be released from his throat. Each time that happened Bert would squeeze himself tight, his arms wrapped around his chest. He became vaguely aware of his own moaning, and that was enough to keep him from losing his mind, if only just.

The small room was dark. Bert was hesitant to light a lamp in fear of the scary man coming back and seeing it. The outlines of the furniture stood in stark, black shadows, and he couldn't make out what most of it was. A chair here, a chest there, maybe a safe. Nothing that he could be sure of except for the large, heavy desk that he leaned on, which he had dragged across the floor once the sister locked him in. A brace to keep the monsters out. Feeling the wood against his back, Bert doubted anything could keep him safe from what he had seen just hours before.

Sister Mejia had asked him to stay in the father's office,

to keep out of sight, to be quiet until she returned. It felt like it had been hours. The desk wouldn't do. He needed to get out of town, to get far away from Etta Dumond and the mayor, Frank Winter. Then he'd be sure.

Only when he started the process of moving the desk was Bert reminded of its actual girth. It was a solid oak table, likely made by a local logger from a choice piece of a fell tree he was keeping for something special. It was a habit of the lumberjacks to do this, Bert had discovered. They made gifts in place of payment, donated items instead of money. Bert was never sure why they did this, but no one in the town argued with them, and the pieces were usually worth it.

His trembling hands gripped the desk with a white-knuckle tenacity. The books and papers that had been strewn upon the desktop when he'd first arrived at the church that evening were now scattered around the floor. His feet slipped on papers and the desk jammed on the books, making for slow progress. He remained as quiet as he could. His grunts and groans swallowed back the threatening screams. He would leave town just as soon as he could gather some of his things.

Allowing himself a moment of rest, bent forward and sucking wind, Bert gripped the shaking, ill-fitted door-knob and pulled. It came up solid, a loud bang echoed through the small church. Still locked. Bert cursed. He wanted to throw himself at the door, pour his fear and anger out against it. Instead, he wiped the sweat from his forehead and dug into his pocket.

His father's knife slid open with ease, the blade only a shadow in the dark room. He took his time and let the knife work into the gap between the door and its frame. He felt for the latch and, when he found it, pushed with the knife and turned the handle again. The door came free. He squinted his eyes against the gush of brilliant orange light. Through the slits made of his eyes, he watched himself close his knife and put it back into his pocket.

Bert moved through the church slowly, his feet moving cautiously past the pulpit and through the aisles of pews. There was a tingling on his neck as he walked before the cross, a sensation as if Jesus actually had his eyes upon him. As if He urged him to turn back. No, he had to get out of town in case Etta or the Mayor came after him. Before they killed him to keep their secret.

Knock, knock

The sharp rap of thick knuckles echoed in the empty church and stopped Bert in his tracks. His desire to leave evaporated, and a hesitant sniffle escaped his nose as he stared at the closed door.

Knock, knock

Bert weighed his options. Should he return to the small office? Return there to hide away and never to come out again. Or should he continue, and make his way past whoever it was? Bert's widened eyes flittered around the empty church in a desperate hope that something or someone would solve his problem, would tell him what to do. But the church remained silent.

Knock, knock

"Sister Mejia, you there?" The sheriff's surly voice rushed through the thick front door.

Bert's mind raced, he squeezed his eyes shut and tried to remember the layout of the church. There was no back door.

He hurried back to the office and breached the threshold just as the church door was flung inward. Bert slammed the office door shut. With a burst of speed and determination, he managed to partially push the desk in front of the door again just as it buckled from a harsh impact.

Grunting and cursing came from the other side punctuated by constant, incessant slamming. It was only when the attack ceased that Bert realized that he had been screaming the entire time. His voice hoarse and throat raw. He cowered in the corner, his arms wrapped around knees.

Silence invaded. The loud, hammering blows still echoed in Bert's ears. He took a deep breath and held it. He had been holding the desk in place, barely across the doorway, and made to push it into a better position.

Bert bent forward over the desk. His breath was tight now in his lungs, burning. His ear caressed the rough wooden door, and he listened. It all fell to silence. The gentle thumping of his erratic heartbeat grew in his ears. His lungs screamed to release the breath he hadn't realized he was holding.

When the door was thrown inward it struck him in the head. A sharp pain exploded in his temple. A short yelp caught in his throat. The door was open, and light spilled in from the church. As the hands wrapped themselves around his shoulders, neck, and throat he could feel a thick and sticky liquid flow from his temple. A more complete blackness came over his eyes. Bert fell into it, Deneen's staring, dead eyes haunting him as he did.

II

Weston squat next to the grave and looked at his hands. Swollen, sore, and coated in brown earth. Sweat coated his forehead. He rubbed it away with his forearm, one rolled-up sleeve feeling coarse against his skin. The silver cross he'd retrieved from the grave felt cool, refreshing.

He imagined the haft of the shovel was close to the surface of that pile of fresh dirt. That if he brushed away even a little of that sweet-smelling earth, he'd see the last inch or two reminding him of what he'd had to do.

The nun sat some ways off, leaning against a sturdy tombstone. After the business with Scarborough was through, and the dead man was buried, Sister Mejia walked through the graveyard, visiting friends and neighbours.

"So, what did the boy find out?" Weston asked, plucking his eyes away from the grave and turning them towards the old nun.

"¿Que?" Sister Mejia replied, roused from her thoughts. With a grunt, she used the headstone to push herself up. "Has it moved?"

Weston cast a sidelong glance at Mejia, the image of the shovel handle wiggling back and forth, dislodging some of the dirt broke into his mind. He glanced back at grave and shook his head. "What did Bert have to say?"

The nun tucked her chin into her chest, cleared her throat, and told him what the boy had said about the mayor, Etta Dumond, and the blood ritual he had witnessed. "It was an easy story to believe," she said. "Scarborough was an evil man in life. So evil the devil cast him out of hell." She gestured toward the grave. "What we hadn't considered was that Scarborough was a puppet, his strings being pulled." Her wrinkled face collapsed; her eyes closed.

Weston shook his head. "So the mayor has Etta in his employ as well?"

"I think it may be the other way around." Mejia opened one eye to give him a look.

"And, what, you think Etta Dumond is some sort of...

witch?"

The old nun shrugged. "Maybe. Bert mentioned a six-pointed star painted on Etta's left cheek, a sign of dark magic. On her right, was a spiral commonly associated with rebirth or spirituality. In the centre of her forehead, an X with a circle above it—the sign of a bane, of the deadly." She pointed towards Scarborough's grave. "Every symbol is associated with dark magic, witchcraft. If she is not a witch, she is playing with some powerful and dangerous forces."

"And what about the mayor, did he have anything painted upon him?"

"Oh yes," Mejia nodded. "He had the sign for winter painted on his cheek, or at least that's what I think Bert described. A little hut, snowballs gathered at the top, not falling."

"That would make sense," Weston said with a nod.

"Si, but he also had what Bert described as a 'house with one window' painted on his chest. I can't say for sure, not without seeing it, but I believe that to be a sign of protection. Specifically, the protection of a child."

"Whose child?"

Mejia shrugged. "As I said, I'd need to see it myself. In any case, the use of blood, fresh *human* blood, is not good. It is a sure sign of evil magic, an infection that will ooze its pus all over this town—its people." She spat on Scarborough's grave.

Weston's shoulder throbbed at the mention of infection and he stood to roll it. "We know that the victims were rivals of the mayor in some way. Someone who might threaten his position within the town or the state. So, what connects Etta to Scarborough and them both to Frank Winter?"

"No se," Mejia said. "But there must be something we are both missing."

"I'm not sure about Etta, but after meeting Mayor Winter, I can assume that he wasn't around during Scarborough's reign of terror. He must've been, what, just a couple of years old?"

"Maybe less. There were no family of Winters here when I left for my convent."

That is strange, Weston thought. A man so connected to Millwood and his family isn't even from here. Weston could feel the beginnings of something stirring in his mind. "Where are the mayor's parents? I'm sure they must be proud of their politically successful son."

He could see something click in Mejia's eyes as well. A subtle twitch of recognition. "I have never known his family. I believe I heard that they died when he was a boy, but I have no recollection of that. Nor do I recall news of what he did once they died. How did he make his way, earn his life and money, for instance?"

"I suppose we could look for them here," Weston said, and a humourless smile creep across his lips. "Though, if I'm right, I doubt we'll find anything."

"De acuerdo."

"Sister, I'm afraid that this has been building in your town for quite some time," Weston said and turned his eyes towards the entrance of the graveyard.

An orange glow grew in the haze of the summer night. A luminescent orange eye opened in the distance. It started with one, unblinking as it got closer and multiplying as it came. All told there was fifteen. Fifteen orange eyes staring into Weston, their glow cutting through the darkness.

"Looks like they finally noticed the jail was ransacked." Weston straightened, cracked his back, and stretched.

"Speak of the devil and he shall appear," Sister Mejia said.

The sheriff walked ahead of his posse, a lantern held in one meaty fist, a rifle slung over his opposite shoulder. As they approached, Weston could hear the jangle of irons that were meant to wrap around his wrists and ankles.

"I don't think he's here to congratulate us." Weston took a look around him. The only way to escape would be through the trees behind him. The thought of that sent shivers of pain through his abused shoulder. There wasn't much that could be done for it. He'd rather run than be captured by the likes of Sheriff Porter Johnson again.

Sister Mejia laid a hand on his shoulder. The old nun's brown eyes met Weston's. "Stay," she said. "I'll reason with the sheriff. Stay here." The nun nodded and gave Weston a weary smile. The old woman's eyes were harder though, determined. The nun only walked a few feet ahead of Weston and then stood her ground.

The sheriff and his men came at a slow pace, their guns drawn. Most held revolvers in their hands, some carried rifles like the sheriff, but only one held restraints—a pale-faced man who stood to the right of the sheriff, his dark eyes focused on Weston.

"Sheriff." Sister Mejia nodded towards the group of men who were brandishing their lanterns and guns. "I have good news. We have disposed of the killer."

The sheriff gave the nun a strange look before gazing over Mason's shoulder. "Weston, you're gonna pay for wrecking my jail." There were some appreciative nods from his men, some who echoed the sentiment.

"Easy, sheriff, Bill here just stopped the murderer. He's a hero, not a criminal."

"And just who was the killer, sister? I ain't see no one

about here save you two."

"It was Bose Scarborough, returned from the grave." The sister pointed a gnarled finger towards the grave, guiding the sheriff's glance. "He has been returned to his final resting place."

There was a rumble of chuckles from the posse. Weston noticed that of everyone there with their crooked grins, the sheriff's face had fallen, had gone cold. His crooked smile had disappeared altogether, and his pouched eyes went dead, his marred lips slack under his moustache.

"Scarborough has been dead these thirty years. Even I know that, and I was only a boy when that bastard died." It was the man holding the irons speaking, his voice raspy and his dark eyes still on Weston.

"And yet his grave is fresh. The shovel driven through his sternum is new. Without any of that, he hasn't decayed. It's as if his evil couldn't be contained by death. Come, see for yourselves." The sister leaned towards the sheriff and whispered just loud enough for Weston to hear: "but you already knew that, right, Sheriff Johnson?" The sheriff nodded and tossed his rifle to another of his men. Sister Mejia turned towards Weston and tipped him a wink, her head inclined towards the trees.

It was the movement that Weston saw first. Just a hint, a blur before the boom. Sister Mejia had enough time to clutch her chest, blood leaking beneath her fingers, and give Weston a pained look before she collapsed. The malformed smile had been reborn on the sheriff's face, a pistol outstretched before him.

Weston hesitated for just a moment, a sudden need to go to the nun that passed as quickly as it came. The sheriff began to take aim on him. Weston took off towards the forest.

His body ached and his throat burned as he lurched forward. A single shot fired behind him and a piece of earth flew off to his side. Weston cursed. Other shots began a moment later, panicked and clumsy. More pieces of earth and stone flew up around him. He was already through the trees before he could feel the pain in his thigh. Warm, sticky liquid made his pants cling to his leg.

The forest closed in around him. Branches slashed at him as he stumbled through, his hand awkwardly clinging to his newest wound. The sheriff would be on his tail, but he could lose them in the woods. If he could keep up his pace.

He heard the deputies breach the trees behind him, the rough shouts of Sheriff Johnson and his men as they tried to organize themselves carried through the forest. In all the noise it was the jangle of the irons that Weston missed; they weren't looking to take prisoners.

Weston ran as far as he could, but a sharp, creeping pain spread from his shoulder to his chest. The pain took the breath from his lungs, and he fell to the hard forest floor unsure whether he should clutch his leg or his shoulder.

The shouts faded in the distance, heading away from town and from him.

Weston pulled himself through the loose branches, twigs, and rocks of the forest floor. He flinched every time his thigh scraped the ground, biting his lips to keep himself from crying out in pain.

He didn't know how long he was crawling before he found a small clearing. He rolled onto his back, sucking in as much air as he could. Trees still haunted the clearing, but they were spread thin; their giant roots needed the space to grow. These trees were old, some greying and

gnarled, as if dead. And yet they lived on, their branches reaching far up into the sky still covered in the spring
growth of leaves, lush and green.

The pain in his shoulder got worse, a stabbing ache
that now ran from his shoulder to his neck to his forehead.
It throbbed at his temples and over his eyes. He forced
himself onward, he couldn't rest. He had to get away.

III

The pain kept him going. The harsh throbbing flamed
in his shoulder, angry and unrestrained. Weston twisted
himself to sitting, his hand rubbing over the tendril-like
scars that pocked his shoulder's surface. Through watery
eyes he could see the sun as it bent through the branches, and the pollen floating within its beams. As the pain
dulled, or as he became accustomed to it, he examined his
leg. It was as he expected, a flesh wound, deep though it
was. He tore off some of his sleeve and wrapped it around
the wound in hopes that he could staunch the blood and
waylay any infection. It still felt tender to touch and pained
him as he stood.

The clearing was silent. The animals of the forest
seemed to avoid it, and the stomping efforts of Sheriff
Johnson and his men had already passed it by. The gnarled
trees that lived within it stood sentinel over the land and
the strange bent cabin that stood in the middle of it all.
Weston's shoulder flared in pain once again.

The cabin itself was a squat building, as if it had been
constructed with only bowed wood and board. The moss
that grew around the eaves and the roof bespoke of its
age, and one of the large malformed trees seemed to have
taken a liking to the small shack and leaned one large,
coiled branch upon its roof, protecting it.

Weston approached the cabin, the eerie silence of the woods heavy on his shoulders, an echo in his ears. It was deserted. Not as though that was a surprise for Weston, but he had thought something might be waiting for him there. A cursory glance in the window revealed only destroyed furniture and nests of long dead animals. He sighed and leaned against the cabin. "I'm done here," he said aloud. "Scarborough is dead. I'm done."

He sighed. The image of Sister Mejia clutching her breast and falling to the ground raced through his mind. The smirk on the sheriff's face as the old nun fell. Weston struck the greyed boards of the ancient shack. The sheriff deserved to die for what he did. Weston was only one man, and the sheriff had the town and deputies on his side. The mayor and Etta Dumond too.

Weston rubbed his knuckles. He had to find the boy. He wasn't sure how much they knew, but he had to make sure no harm came to Bert. The boy, of them all, deserved to live. He could strike out from Millwood, make his way somewhere else. Make his way somewhere less evil, less poisonous.

What if they know what he saw, Weston asked himself. *What if they already have him?* Then, if that were the case, Weston would just have to take matters into his own hands. To do that, he'd need his guns. His hands reached to his hips, the odd sensation of the guns' absence still haunting him. First, he would need to get to Mejia's house, and that meant a trek through the woods and into town to retrieve Javier from the church. He assessed his leg and bandage, tightened it. He was in for a long walk.

Weston had stayed in the trees as long as he could, keeping to the shade of the early morning when he couldn't. He was still thinking about Winter's motivations, about his connection to Scarborough, and the significance of releasing that old terror on the town. He thought he might have it figured out, snippets of conversations over the last few days playing through his mind like a picture show. Flickering, unsteady, but there and very real. That didn't matter to him, not right now. His focus was on the boy.

The church was ransacked. The front door beaten down, splintered and half-torn from its hinges. Weston's heart lurched in his chest. The urge to run inside, find out what happened to the boy, tugged at his nerves, which were already spring-loaded with adrenaline. He held himself back, hiding in the shadows of an alleyway, his ears perked for any movement. He heard none. Millwood remained consistent in its lethargy.

The inside of the church was in as bad shape as its door. Pews were overturned, left askew, Bibles and hymn books scattered about. The priest's office was a warzone. Bert had done what he could to avoid capture, but he was a child. Droplets of blood trailed from the office door, leading outside. Weston clenched his hands into tight fists and dragged himself to the back.

Javier snorted his return. A sigh of relief deflated some of Weston's temper.

"Come on, old fella," he said and rubbed the old horse down. Javier snorted its approval and nuzzled its nose into Weston as they walked.

"Been lonely?" Weston scratched Javier behind the ears, patted him on the neck.

Javier gave Weston no trouble when he was hooked up to the cart, he even seemed eager. When Weston clicked his tongue and flicked the reins, Javier moved with a vigor Weston wouldn't have given him credit for.

Mejia's cabin was as he had remembered it. Cozy, tidy. He stared in at the bed where Mejia had nursed him back to health. The sheets were white and crisp. He wondered if they may be as cool and comforting as he remembered.

Still, he thought, there was something off. The old cabin was missing some of its warmth, missing some of its colour and comfort. With Mejia gone the energy was sapped. Without her busying herself in her garden, tidying, or cooking in her small kitchen everything seemed less. As devoted as Mejia was to the church, this house was where she prayed, the land where she worshiped.

Weston sighed and cursed himself. What had the sheriff done with her body? Did he toss her atop of Scarborough to be done with it, leave her out to the elements? Or did he have his deputies dig her a shallow grave, unmarked? Mejia deserved more than that. She deserved to be buried where she was happiest, in her own home where she kept her strays from harm and, sometimes, brought them back from the dead.

The barn was more of the same. He admired his handiwork on the barns new door, kicked around through the hay, but everywhere he went Mejia's absence was felt.

His guns weren't in the barn.

Did Mejia remove them? Did she donate them to some other stray she had come across?

The thought had crossed his mind to dig deeper into the house, to go into Mejia's small room and sort through it. Pretend to look for his guns, but really investigate Mejia. Did she have more papers like those collected by Father Mason? Something more obscure, perhaps. Was there anything about her life before the church? Weston gripped the doorknob, his shoulder pressed against it, ready to push it forward. All those questions ran through his mind, but none of them mattered. Mejia was who she made herself to be; there was no point dwelling on the past to see how that happened.

Javier snorted outside, probably hungry and thirsty, and drew Weston out of his doldrums. He moved toward the door and stopped again. The small, stained window where St. Jude—Mejia's favourite saint, the patron of lost causes—overlooked the household from the doorway was cracked. The old nun's pride and joy was split, a bullet lodged in it. St. Jude stood there, brandishing his club, on broken wings. The bullet had sent fissures trailing in a webwork, their edges stabbing at Jude, cleaving his side and wings without mercy. Weston ran his hand over the broken glass only to pull his hand away with a hiss of breath. Blood spotted the saint and ran down the window like tears.

Stray bullet, he thought, maybe from a hunter. Or did someone pay a visit to Mejia's house as well? Weston surveyed the small home; it didn't look like it had been touched. Then again, there wasn't a boy in here fighting to get away from captors.

Weston used Mejia's sink to clean his wounds. He came upon a set of clothes that looked to be his size and he claimed them as his own. He sucked on his injured finger and wondered what stray brought those clothes with him.

Millwood was just passed the horizon, the sun setting

under a blood red sky. There was a lot to be done. The sheriff's scarred face was prominent in his mind; there was a score to be settled there. He had gunned down Sister Mejia just as he did Father Mason. It confirmed his suspicions that the sheriff was working for the mayor and Etta. He couldn't forget how easily she ordered him around when she had him release Weston from jail. He cursed himself again. How did he not see it back then? The same thing he understood so clearly now. It was right there in front of him.

He snapped Javier's reins and they moved faster. Javier whinnied. Weston's first stop when he reached the town would be the mayor. If Frank Winter really was in charge of this whole thing, he'd know where Bert was. After that, he'd settle the score with the sheriff.

CHAPTER ELEVEN

I

"He was here." It was a woman's voice, so quiet it was barely a whisper. "Take care of him."

Mejia tried to move her head to get a better look, but the pain flared in her shoulder and she had to bite her lip to keep from crying out. She felt feeble, weak.

"I'm on it." A man's voice this time, deep. He sounded impatient. "The boys are still scouring the woods. He can't have gone far." There was something familiar in his voice, but Mejia couldn't place it.

"He's a threat, sheriff. To you, to me. He must be found and killed. Do it. No more excuses." The woman's words were venom, a growl, and an order all in one. A door slammed shut and there was silence, save for the light shuffle of feet.

Mejia was kneeling on an uneven wooden floor; her knees throbbed a dull heartbeat of pain. With great effort she forced herself to look up, resting her head on her shoulder. It was a small room made of aging wood, cluttered with sparse furniture and innumerable jars that held strange and unidentifiable things. Out of the periphery of her vision Mejia could see a small, stooped form hobbling through to the other side of the room. The woman moved towards a small window that let in only enough light to illuminate the immediate centre of the room and the dust motes that floated within its beam. Mejia could tell she was in the near dark of shadows.

A soft moan startled Mejia and drew her eyes to the space next to her. Bert's arms were tied above his head, keeping him on his knees, his chin on his chest only being roused by his shallow breaths. But he was breathing. Tears welled in Mejia's eyes. The boy, the poor, poor boy. How had they found him? Guilt crushed her. A stone of would-haves and should-haves settled on her lungs and made it hard to breath. The boy had sought out protection and they couldn't give it to him. She couldn't give it to him. Still, he was alive, and that was something.

With a sigh and some renewed strength, Mejia looked to the roof. Her own arms were strung up above her, tied by a thick rope. She couldn't feel it, though it bit into her skin. Her wrists and forearms swelled, abrasions of red and purple peeking out from underneath the tied rope. She couldn't feel her arms at all aside from the throbbing pain in her shoulder. How long had they been tied here like this?

"Awake, hmm?" The woman was standing in front of a small fireplace, wisps of smoke floating around her crooked form. There was a grey shawl pulled over her shoulders and raven black hair spilled around her face. Grey and white streaks joined with the black to flow down her back covering most of the faded black dress underneath. Mejia could only see one withered hand exposed to the air, a gnarled claw that gripped a spoon to stir whatever concoction was boiling in the cast iron pot suspended over the small fire.

Mejia tried to respond but could only manage a trickle of incoherent words, garbled enough that even she didn't understand what she was trying to say.

"Yes, that is the effect valerian root and passion flower have when consumed in the amounts we had given you." Mejia could hear the smile creeping along the woman's face, a righteous pride in her misdeeds.

"Quien... who..." Mejia's tongue regained its sentience, but she was still so tired. She couldn't open her eyes fully, and her vision blurred any time she attempted it.

"Oh, I've gone by many names." The old woman chuckled and turned to face Mejia, two shrivelled hands planted on her wide hips. "Many, many names in my lifetime." Wisps of the bone-white hair fell from the hood made of the shawl. A pointed chin and one thin lip the colour of fish flesh emerged from the shadows to join the hair, though nothing else escaped to give Mejia a clearer picture of the woman.

"I suppose if you have to call me anything you can call me...by my first name. Yes, that'd be a treat for you, wouldn't it?" The old woman stroked her chin for a moment. "Ah, yes. Goody Chilton. That's what you can call me." Goody Chilton barked a harsh laugh. "Did you know it's been almost three hundred years since I was called that?" She shook her head and turned back to the fire.

Mejia swallowed. Her mouth was dry, and it hurt. "Porque somos nosotros..."

The old woman moved across the room in a blur. Mejia screamed.

"Well," the old woman whispered, "the boy there was a nosey little newsmonger, wasn't he?" Mejia could feel the heat of the old woman's foul breath. Her face was coated in the moisture of the woman's saliva. Brown, sheeplike teeth snapped close to Mejia's eye and then the old woman was across the room again, stirring the pot. "And you were always poking your nose where it didn't belong. Earned you that hole in your shoulder, and a whole lot more."

Mejia shuddered.

"Contemplating your place in things I suppose," Goody Chilton said pouring a spoonful of steaming liquid into a shallow, hand carved bowl. "Loose ends, dear." The old woman's mouth twitched into a smile, exposing her jagged yellow teeth again. "Loose ends have to be tied or burned off. Everything has to be neat and tidy."

The woman's chuckle became a cough as she hobbled closer to Mejia and Bert. The bowl sloshed a viscous green liquid onto the hand that carried it. Still steaming hot, Goody Chilton didn't seem to notice the temperature.

"It's a pity the boy had to be brought into this," the old woman said, her free hand on Bert's too-long brown hair. "He's such a handsome thing. I had one of my own you know." She stroked Bert's hair like one would pet a dog. "He's long grown, but you try to do your best for you children, try to make things easier. Wouldn't you say, sister?"

Mejia fought back the urge to scream at the other woman, to tell her to keep her filthy hands away from the boy. Fantasies of breaking from her bonds and thrashing the devilish woman flickered through her mind, but her arms were leaden and numb, her body weak. It took all of her energy to keep her eyes on Chilton as she moved and talked. Her hate seethed inside of her. "I know who you are," was all she could manage.

"Yes, you have to do what is right by your kin. All this," Goody Chilton said and gestured to the room, "*all* of this is for my son. As much as he appreciates it. I'm sure you've had arguments with your pack of strays, hmmm? Disappointments? Yes, it's something like that I suppose. But, you know, it's almost over. Loose ends. Just have to deal with the loose ends." The old woman's claw-like hand wrapped its fingers in Bert's hair and twisted his head so he was looking up at her. He moaned, his face a mask of discomfort and pain. Despite that he was still unconscious; his eyes remained closed.

Mejia, restraints forgotten, threw herself at Goody Chilton. It was a weak attempt that caused her more frustration and pain than anything else. The bullet in her shoulder seared in pain. "Leave the boy alone," she screamed, her voice the only thing that managed to return in her desperation.

The old woman only cackled, tipped Bert's head back and poured some of the thick green liquid down his throat. The boy's eyes immediately jumped open, fearful and confused. Thick and racking coughs shook him all over. His whole body seemed to tighten, and he stood, muscles straining. Mejia's tears streaked her cheeks as her screams for leniency mixed with Bert's cries of pain.

After a long moment, the boy collapsed to his knees, unconscious once more. His breathing was rapid, and his chest heaved. Mejia tried to reach for him, sobs flowing freely from her strained throat. Even her unbound legs and feet were just out of range.

"There, there," Goody Chilton said, a mischievous smile in her voice. She moved to Mejia's side and patted her head. The gnarled fingers felt like bones scratching around Mejia's scalp. She tried to pull her head away from the old woman's reach, but soon found her hair tangled in Goody Chilton's grasp. Mejia's head was pulled back to look up at the ceiling. "Easy, dear, easy. This little concoction isn't going to kill him, or you. It certainly won't be pleasant, but it won't kill. It's just meant to make you a little more... pliable." The old woman pulled on Mejia's hair hard, so hard that Mejia thought that she might rip her scalp from her skull. Still, she resisted and kept her mouth shut. She wanted no part of the drink that Chilton was trying to administer.

The old woman sneered and grabbed Mejia's chin, her sharp and jagged fingernails dug into Mejia's cheeks, threatening to pierce them if she did not open her mouth. Mejia continued to resist, clenching her teeth against the pain. The old woman's hand flashed, and Mejia's cheek felt as though it were on fire. Disoriented she hung her head, her chin resting against her chest. Drops of blood hit the floor at which she stared at in a random staccato.

"You little whore," Goody Chilton seethed, her clawed fingers flexing in front of Mejia's blurred eyes. "Just for that, I'll be sure that the boy has a long and painful death while you watch on. Now, take your medicine." The old woman grabbed Mejia's chin once more. Pain rushed to the cheek that the old woman had slashed with her nails. Whatever energy Mejia had mustered was depleted. She had no choice but to give in to the old woman's bony fingers.

Mejia immediately wanted to vomit as the thick and chunky soup started to flow through her mouth and down her throat. It was the single worst taste Mejia had ever consumed in her life, a taste that was somewhere between spoiled milk and rotten meat. Still, she choked it down, afraid of what the old woman would do if she regurgitated any of it.

An electric shock attacked her from the inside out. The potion worked as it had on Bert and tensed all of Mejia's muscles. She could feel herself scream, could feel the painful rictus that took over her face as her whole body strained against the bonds she had been placed in.

And then it was over, as quickly as it all had started. She could feel the impact as her knees crashed back down to the floor, could feel the tension release all over her body as she hunched forward. Darkness threatened her vision, and she would soon be unconscious as the boy before her. Before that though, she set her eyes on Bert. He seemed peaceful now, his features not marred by pain. If his arms weren't bound before her, Mejia might have been convinced that he was sleeping peacefully in his own bed.

The witch cackled an unnerving laugh as Mejia allowed herself to succumb to the darkness. She forced herself to look upon Bert as she faded into unconsciousness, the darkness at the edge of her eyes now complete.

II

Weston set Javier up a mile outside of town—he didn't need the extra noise or attention. For his part, the mule busied himself grazing for something to eat, happy enough. Weston expected there would be a small detachment of deputies on guard, those that could be spared in the search for him. The sheriff would want to close the circle and ensure Weston was dead. Dead was easier than capture—less questions. The monster of Millwood brought to bloody justice, the killings ended, and no one would be the wiser. The people of Millwood would be content in their ignorance as Frank Winter spread his corruption throughout the rest of the state. Frank Winter and Etta Dumond.

From a small bank about half a mile out from Millwood, Weston settled himself on his stomach and tried to get a lay of the land. The gas lamps cast a yellow haze that scraped amber fingers along the shadowed entrance into town. From the dull light, Weston could see the populace crawling through the streets, and two figures standing in partial darkness just on the outskirts of the town, rifles resting on their shoulders, muzzles to the air.

Weston cursed into the dust. The entrance into town was wide open, and there was nothing to conceal his approach save for the shadows cast by the dim light of the moon. Even so, there were no trees, walls, or even bushes to help him on his way. If the sheriff ordered his men to shoot to kill, Weston was in a bad way.

Cursing, he scuttled backwards, keeping himself low to the ground. He contemplated retrieving Javier but left the old horse to its meager meal. This was something Weston had to do on his own.

Palms itching for the feel of a gun, Weston focused his attention on scouring the ground for rocks. Three good sized stones would do, he thought, and slung the largest into one of his pockets. The others he gripped in his hands. Poor substitute for a revolver, he thought, and crept forward.

The moon worked against him, as he knew it would, its pale rays lighting the path out of town and keeping the deputies' eyes focused and clear. The odds of the pair of men being drunk were questionable, and Weston didn't think he was lucky enough for that anyway. He kept to what shadows he could.

It wasn't long before he was cozied up next to the Millwood sign, his legs burning and his back aching. He chanced another glance towards the town. The guards were chatting back and forth, their voices low and drowned out by the open air and space. They weren't looking his way.

With a sigh, Weston readied himself and tossed his first rock. It skirted along the ground, small puffs of dust billowing in its trail. The scrapping sound was quiet but loud enough. One of the deputies, a large man with a handlebar moustache and unruly brown hair, twitched at the sound. He pointed a gloved finger in the direction where the rock had come to rest — a little ways to Weston's left.

The other deputy, a smaller man with thinning blond hair, cast a lazy look over his shoulder and shook his head.

"Damn it," Weston hissed.

He tightened his grip on the second rock and threw it. This rock went a little farther, a little faster, and was a little louder. The big deputy stepped forward, grabbed the smaller man by the shoulder and shoved him in the direction of the sound. The blond deputy sneered and shuffled away with a chuckle when the bigger man made a playful kick at him. Playful or not, they were both focused on the rock. Weston took his chance.

Matching pace with the blond, Weston moved to his right, away from the rock, and toward the bigger man. He moved as quietly as he could, careful not to slide his boots over any loose gravel. His heart beat a tattoo in his chest, a thumping that sounded in his ears, and he brought out his last rock, the biggest one.

The large deputy was still focused on his partner when Weston cracked his skull. He fell to the ground like a sack of potatoes, a groan caught in his throat. Weston worked quickly. He knew that the blond would have heard the other man collapse and would be huffing it back.

Weston slipped his hands inside the coat and along the belt of the prone man then cursed. No revolvers. He reached for the man's rifle, a massive Winchester 1886.

Weston said a silent thank you that he hadn't been seen. The lever-action rifle had more than stopping power. It would have blown a hole straight through him.

The rifle was slung over his shoulder when the footsteps of the blond came thundering towards him. Weston could have waited then and there and shot the man dead. One less deputy to worry about, and an easy way to piss off the sheriff. Still, the Winchester wasn't a quiet gun. It would have brought attention down on him quickly. Weston secured it and ran into the town.

The first place on his mind was the mayor's house. The massive building near the centre of town, along with the guest house behind it, was a likely place for the mayor and just as likely for a dozen or more deputies, each man carrying his own Winchester and ready to do damage. Well, that was fine with Weston, but if he wanted to find Bert, he'd have to playthings safer, quieter. He rubbed his thighs, groaned at the thought of more creeping about, and made his way towards the Last Chance.

The boy had said that Etta and Winter were getting awfully cozy up there since the mayor's return. There was a good chance he'd be there again. Good chance that there'd be less guns in view as well. Etta would want her patrons having a good time (and paying), and nothing sours a good time like the muzzle of a gun swinging in your face. Weston wasn't stupid, though. He figured it was just as likely to run into guns in the old saloon as anywhere, but at least they'd be concealed. Well, that was the hope.

The streets were busy. Weston took to the back ways, to the alleys. He struggled through the smell of shit and piss, the burning scent of fresh vomit, the earthy smell of old puke. He crawled over trash, passed out drinkers, and lovers unburdened of modesty by whiskey and beer. No one paid him much mind; they were all night creatures, those who thrived just beyond the reach of the gas lamps.

Weston wasn't surprised, and he didn't care, but there was something off. He couldn't quite put his finger on it, but there was something besides the thick odor of the sour wine and rotten vomit. It reminded him of his first night in Millwood, the night Puddicombe and Percy had been discovered. The town had been holding a prolonged party that night as well. Did Etta have that sort of power? Raise the dead, bend them to her purpose, and befuddle an entire town to drink and forget? Or was it to conceal something else? What was she trying to conceal tonight?

The Last Chance was busy. Its patrons spilled from the entrance like blood from a hatchet wound. They laughed and sang and danced and wailed. Weston recognized some, but there were no obvious deputies waiting there with rifles under their jackets.

He was concealed in the shadows just across the street, his hands gripped tight to the rifle's sling. The gun would be no good here, not unless he intended on killing scores of townsfolk. Weston also couldn't risk exposing himself. Doing so would only leave Bert in danger; the sheriff or mayor might even take their frustrations out on the boy.

Weston made his way further down the street, the livery and Cornish's store just within sight, and crossed the road. He worked his way back to the Last Chance and slid between shadows, feeling their cool embrace as he moved. There were far fewer people around back of the saloon, though some had gathered there to inject opium or drink laudanum. Their unblinking eyes stared off into

the sky, the light, or each other. Drool crept from the corner of their idiotic grins. They wouldn't cause Weston any
trouble.

He had only been in the Last Chance once, but he had
seen the second floor and knew they were inhabited by
Etta's prostitutes. All except one room—Etta's office. A
small deck was built around the second floor, and doors
dotted the building's exterior. A little extra comfort for the
ladies on the warmer nights. There was only a window on
the farthest side. That's where Weston headed.

There wasn't a stairway, not really, but a wooden
ladder clung to the rear of the building. Weston pushed
passed the inebriates, one giggling slightly as he did, and
climbed. The shared balcony was little more than a cat-
walk, and Weston forced himself to walk gingerly, one
foot in front of the other. There were four doors in total,
and each was closed and covered. If there were anyone in
them Weston couldn't tell from the noise that arose from
the saloon itself. Good, he thought, no need to be extra
quiet, and he moved towards Etta's office.

As Weston worked his way to the final door and
opened it. He fell back, hands scrambling for the stolen
Winchester. A young woman gasped, put a hand to her
mouth, and clutched at her robe.

"Shit," Weston said and put his own hand over the
woman's hand and mouth and pushed her back into her
room. He closed the door behind him.

With his free hand he put a finger to his lips. She nodded and he slowly removed his hand from hers.

"Darlin'," the woman said, "if you wanted some lov-
ing, all you had to do was go in through the front door."
She tried to smile, but her green eyes twitched between
the rifle and Weston's clenched fists.

"No, that's not what this is..." Weston said and made himself relax. He took a deep breath and opened his hands in front of him.

"Then what *is* this?"

Weston studied the woman. Not as young as he had initially thought, her make-up was cracking and smeared around her eyes and cheeks. Her eyes were wide and intelligent behind the mop of tangled, curly brown hair. She looked tired.

"What's your name?" Weston said.

"Anita," she said backing up a step towards the bed.

"Anita, do you know Bert?" Weston said.

"Haven't seen him in a few days," Anita said and stopped mid-step. "Is he in trouble?"

"That's what I'm trying to find out."

A cheer rang out from the tavern below followed by a chorus of laughter. Anita cocked her head to the side, a half-smile on her painted lips.

"Aren't you that Weston fella, the one they say killed them people?"

"Maybe," Weston said and eyed the woman.

"Bert told me a little about you. You don't seem like a killer. Not to him anyway," Anita said and took another step forward.

Weston nodded.

"Not sure why you'd look for Bert here," Anita said. "Like I told ya, he hasn't been around for a day or two."

"I think someone here might know something about it." Weston leaned against the door frame behind him. He didn't want to hurt Anita, but he couldn't let her give him away.

"Who?"

Weston pointed a thumb towards the wall separating

Anita's room from the office.

"Etta?" she asked

"Her or the mayor. You know if either of them is in?"

Anita hesitated, her eyes fluttering around the room. Weston readied himself for a chase.

"I don't remember seeing Etta," Anita said at length, "but Mayor Winter could be here. I saw him come by last night and haven't seen him leave. I could go ask Jed, he'd know..."

"That's fine, I'd like to find out for myself," Weston said and turned toward the door. "Now, don't you run off anywhere. Best you stay in here for a few minutes, understand?"

"You're not going to get in Etta's room that way."

"What?"

"Etta nailed that window shut ages ago. Nailed it up and put a shelf in front of it. She said she didn't want no Peeping Tom's surprising her in the night. I always thought that was strange. These rooms," Anita said and looked to the floor, "well they can get pretty hot."

"Shit," Weston said, his fists clenched. He had to get in that room. Had to see the mayor. Winter would know where Bert was and might be a good bargaining chip in Bert's retrieval. Weston fingered the thick leather of the rifle's sling. A couple of shots might be enough to put a hole through the wall. Might even weaken it enough for him to push through.

Weston stepped back, faced the conjoining wall, and cocked the lever. The gun would be loud, it'd draw attention, and people would start running. Hell, it'd be so loud it might even sober up a few of those opium fiends. He'd have a lot more attention than he was hoping for, but he needed to do something. He'd be quick.

"What the hell do you think you're doing?" Anita hissed and grabbed his arm.

Weston shrugged her off. "I'm going to have a word with the mayor."

"Are you crazy? You're more likely to kill the mayor than have a word with him, and a posse of more than a dozen men would be on top of you before you could turn around."

Weston shrugged. Anita rolled her eyes.

"Don't be an idiot." A frown painted her face and she held one finger up to Weston's eyes. "Wait one minute, I'll be right back." She moved for the door.

Weston flinched. He wanted to grab her, pull her back. Before he could she was at the door, the harsh golden candlelight cutting through the dull moonlight that barely lit Anita's room. She stuck her head out the door, looked back and forth, and closed the door.

"No one's out there," she said. "The girls are preoccupied, and the bar crowd won't notice much. Save your rounds." Anita stepped away from the door, motioned toward it.

"Thanks," Weston said and slung the rifle back around his shoulder.

Anita grabbed his arm as he made his way past her. "You just make sure that Bert is okay?"

Weston nodded and slid out of the room.

The heat of gyrating bodies and their sweat-glazed skin slapped Weston in the face. He staggered back against the door, his eyes blinking away sudden tears, and tried not to process the stench that wafted up from the pulsating mass of bodies below.

Etta's door was only a few steps away, a heavy wooden door with the intricate design of a wooded area with a cabin in the middle. Something about it seemed familiar, but a shout from below pushed the thought away and Weston moved on.

He figured the door would be locked, figured that despite Anita's best efforts, he'd have to spend a few shells making his way in. Instead, the door glided open at Weston's touch to reveal the cramped room's secrets.

The blazing orange light of dozens of lit candles illuminated every inch of the room. The candles, in various stages of use, lay in puddles of white, viscous wax on every surface: books, tables, chairs, the floor. The dancing flames of several candles formed a circle in the centre of the room surrounding Frank Winter.

He was lounging back on a cream-coloured daybed, one arm resting under his head, the hand of the other sprawled across his stomach. His chest hair was thick and tangled, the remnants of paint or blood still obvious on his sallow skin. At first glance, Weston thought that the mayor might have been asleep, his chest rising and falling with a steady, relaxed rhythm, but his eyes were open and staring at the sudden intruder.

Weston closed the door behind him, and stared back into those icy blue eyes, waiting. The room took on a red hue with the rest of the bar—the rest of the world—shut off from it. The putrid scent of death lurked under burnt matches, candles, and the sweat of human bodies writhing. Weston bit the inside of his cheek and stifled the urge to gag. Still, something must have registered; the mayor cracked a smile.

"What are you doing here?" Winter's voice was low, hoarse.

"Concerned citizen," Weston said. Winter let out a wet chuckle that turned into a barking cough that forced him to sit. Weston unslung his rifle.

The mayor held out one hand. "That won't be necessary, Mr. Weston." He was younger than Weston had thought. From afar he carried himself with a confidence that exuded experience, power, mastery. Up close Weston could see the smooth features of youth. Wrinkles and scars were absent from this man, not that far removed from boy. He couldn't be much more than his mid-twenties. Ambitious, thought Weston, for a man of that age to make a bid for mayor, let alone governor. As Weston stared down upon the younger man, something familiar struck him and gave him pause.

"What can I do for you, Mr. Weston?"

"Where is he?" Weston said through gritted teeth.

"The sheriff? I can't say for sure. Here. There." Winter flung one hand around, the other ran down his face.

Weston cocked his rifle, the harsh click muted in the cluttered room. "I'm looking for the boy."

"Alberto." Winter nodded his head and stood. Weston brought his rifle up to his shoulder, but the mayor just waved him off again. "Alberto is a good boy. A good worker. Etta put him to work here when he was just another of that old nun's strays. Silly old woman, isn't she?" Winter put the daybed between him and Weston. Smart, Weston thought, but it wouldn't stop a round from the Winchester.

"She was a good woman." Weston stabbed the rifle's barrel towards the mayor.

"Was? Ah, the sheriff is out doing his job then. Good for him." Winter ran a hand over the back of the day bed. "Sister Mejia was foolish. Honour, grace, love. Admirable in their own way, I suppose, but ultimately unrealistic. The world is changing, Mr. Weston, and with it the need to be polite, honest, caring is disappearing. Take politics, for example. I say that I will do something, I get elected, and then I blame my opponents for holding back on my promises. Of course, there are things you must get done. Things that make it look like you're doing your job, but that's all it is. A means to an end. This town actually believes I'm going to make them the next New York City? Idiots!" the mayor said with a laugh.

"What are your plans then, Mr. Mayor?"

"Governor, as you know, and then... I don't know. President? I suppose I'll just have to see where this all takes me."

Weston stared at Winter. Stared into his face, all harsh lines created by the red light and the thick, black shadows. Weston couldn't reconcile with what Winter had just said, with what he intended to do. How many more would die to see that plan come to fruition? How many more people would meet their end at the hands of dead men? Afterall, Scarborough was gone, but who was to say that Etta couldn't just bring him back. Him and more.

"Where's the boy?" Weston demanded and stepped forward, rifle raised. Staring at the mayor, his calm, undisturbed features, it hit him again, something familiar. It was the thought of Scarborough that did it, of his dead, slack features. Scarborough and Frank Winter.

A gun was in the mayor's hand, a silver Colt with a pearl handle. Weston knew it immediately. It was his gun, one of the pair he'd left at Mejia's. The mayor was holding his gun. No, not just holding it, firing it.

Weston moved but pain exploded in his shoulder. With a cry he dropped the rifle, pulled open the ornate door that was now splattered with blood and launched himself out into the hallway. Another shot went off, splinters and chunks of wall rained down on him.

Anita was there, her face a pale mask of terror and shock, one hand keeping her robe closed. Weston pushed passed her into her room and out to the balcony. He cupped his shoulder in his hand, could feel the blood ooze from his wound.

"Shit," he said making his way to the alley. He wavered on the stairs, his legs wobbling under his weight, his sight blurring.

He fell amongst the inebriates, their harsh laughter searing into his mind. He tried to push on, but each time he got to his feet, he tripped and was back on his knees. He crawled, the laughing from behind him louder than before, louder than anything he'd ever heard before.

The shadows crept in, advancing from his periphery. Weston tried to push it away, tried to ignore it, but it would not be denied. He collapsed on the street, the drunken laughter ringing in his ears as he succumbed to the darkness.

III

"Bill," a faraway whisper sailed to Weston's ear. He tried to open his eyes, failed, and grunted his displeasure.

"Mr. Weston," the voice came again. It was familiar, but a sense of urgency played at its edges.

Weston rolled his head on his shoulders and faced the voice. He pulled his eyelids open. They fought and fluttered in protest, but opened all the same.

Bert sat before him, on the other side of the room, his arms tied above his head. He was kneeling but had kicked his legs out from under him. His feet flailed towards Weston.

"Trying to stand up again?" A rough voice came from behind him. He couldn't turn his head to watch its source move in on the boy and was surprised when a short, elderly woman lurched forward grabbing the boy's hair with both hands.

"I'm sorry, my legs hurt." Bert said crying and twisted his legs under him again, the witch kicking them along the way.

"That's the point, you little shit." The old crone pushed Bert's head down with a grunt and shambled away.

Weston tried to get up, but his body wouldn't respond. He looked back to Bert. The boy's tears slid down his cheek in fat globules.

They were in a small room but judging by the furniture—a dining room table, chairs, and a bed, all of which were cluttered with books or jars, and the large hearth—it seemed to be a small cabin. It was old, too, the graying boards worn with constant foot traffic over the years.

The old crone followed the grooves in the boards, her gnarled hands jutting out quickly as she passed, hoarding jars in her bonelike arms. She moved like a vulture hopping excitedly after a possible meal.

"Bert?" Mejia's voice dragged Weston's vision to just beyond the boy where the nun hung in an evil duplication. "Bert," Mejia said and tried to pull herself up, a mask of pain and tears coming over her wrinkled features. There was a deep green stain running down her chin, turning to black as the thick, dried streaks spilled onto her tunic. A hole pierced her shoulder, blood still oozing from the exposed wound.

"Sister." Bert's sobs slowed. His wet eyes blinked as

he tried to reach for the old nun, the admonitions of the crone so quickly forgotten.

Weston watched as they struggled to embrace, their arms useless to them. Instead, they reached out with their legs, their feet. Touch was all that mattered. A brief embrace that ensured that the other was there, truly there, and not just some torturous dream.

The boy cried silently; his body wracked with the power of his sobs as he suppressed any sound that might draw the ire of their captor. The sting of tears touched Weston's eyes as well, his gaze planted firmly on the nun—alive, if not well.

Strength returned to Weston's limbs and with it an awareness of the stiffness and pain that he was suffering. To his surprise, he wasn't restrained. No cold iron cut into his wrists, neither did coarse rope tie his arms above his head as was the case with Bert and Mejia. Pain was enough of a restraint though. Every shuddering attempt to move sent an excruciating bolt of suffering up his arm; his shoulder felt as though it were turning in shattered glass. Gingerly moving his head, Weston studied his ruined arm. Something was wrapped around it. By the stitching it could have been a shirt. Perhaps the mayor had spared one of his own to plug the hole he put through Weston's shoulder. Whatever it was that covered it, a deep black stain had spread through it, a near perfect circle of ugly blood that wept at the edges and crawled toward his chest and arm, like the gnarled branches and roots of the forest on the outskirts of Millwood.

Weston hissed through his teeth, his uninjured arm moving slowly to uncover the wound so he could get a better look at it. He had pushed himself into the corner of the cabin near the only door, his back pressed against the uneven wall, and attempted to inspect his arm. He was aware that Mejia and Bert's tear-soaked eyes were watching him with a fading glint of hope. He frowned.

His fingers had just managed to grip the shirt when the door opened with a loud screech of wood on wood. The door didn't fit in the frame right and the force used to open it nearly landed a blow to Weston. He flinched and plunged his thumb into the wound. A current of pain coursed through him and he was forced to clench his teeth to avoid screaming. Instead, an audible groan exploded from his throat.

Sheriff Johnson's head appeared around the door; his eyes narrowed as they fell on Weston's broken form. Beyond him, Mejia and Bert's eyes bugged, and they struggled to return to their positions directly under their restraints. The sheriff managed a smug grin around his deep scars, and turned it on the sister and the boy, tipping his hat in greeting. The mayor entered just after him, and slammed the door shut. He looked at no one.

"Ah, about time," the old crone croaked. She pulled herself away from the fire and met the men as they entered. Her wrinkled face was twisted by an evil grin as she pawed the newcomers, almost as if she were searching for something, like a child searching for a prize. Her cold blue eyes fell upon Weston and they widened with something akin to delight.

"You're awake, Mr. Weston." Her voice grated him. Unconsciously he cringed away from the approaching hag, his shoulder forgotten despite the throbbing pain that continued to flow through it.

"You're wondering about your shoulder, eh?" She bent towards him, her hand and its long, thick nails descending towards the makeshift bandage. Weston turned his head away from her and tried to flatten his body against the wall, taking advantage of every inch of space he could.

"You can thank my boy for this suffering," the old woman said untying the bandage. "He should have shot you in the head, you see." Weston could feel the heat of the witch's sneer. He cast a quick look at the mayor who stood farthest off, behind the sheriff, doing his best to not look at anything in particular. At least he had managed to get dressed since they last met, though Weston wondered how much dried blood remained on his skin. How many faded symbols lay beneath that sober exterior?

The crone had removed the shirt from his shoulder. The wet sound of the blood-soaked garment hitting the ground brought Weston's gaze around to look at his shoulder. The wound was open, oozing. He couldn't tell for sure, as blood, both fresh and old, coated the area, but it looked as though the bullet had torn through the centre of the thick purple scars that had been there before. It would have severed the scars in several places.

"Interesting," the old woman said, her wreck of a face inching closer to Weston's shoulder. Her tongue descended from her mouth as though she were about to taste the gore that was his shoulder. "That is a nasty scar you have there. What made it?" She made a claw like motion at his shoulder. Her yellow nails nearly touching his arm made him flinch. The witch turned her face to him, the heat of her stagnant breath crawling on his cheek. A wide smile split her wrinkled face revealing jagged, brown teeth. She gripped his shoulder with her cold and dry hand. Her thumb pushed into his flesh and she wiped away blood, bouncing over the ridges of his elder scars. Pain scraped Weston's nerve endings. They fired through his entire body and rocked him back into the wall. A jagged scream filled the small space and pierced his ear drums.

Weston was surprised to find that it hadn't come from him.

The old witch had recoiled to the centre of the room. Her mouth was agape, and she was gripping her hand in front of her. Mayor Winter had stepped forward and held her in his arms. The commotion had broken his brooding.

"What did that?" The crone growled as she shook her hand in front of her. She shrugged off the mayor's hands and grabbed Weston's face in her claw like fingers.

"What did it?" she whispered, her face now close to Weston's ear. "It must've been something very old. Tell me, what was it?" Her free hand made to touch Weston's shoulder again, but it wavered as it got closer and shook, hovering over the wound.

The witch pushed his face away and hissed in frustration. "It matters not. You'll be dead soon enough." She pointed at the sheriff. "Make sure to scoop out some of his shoulder after it's done. I could use it." The sheriff nodded.

"It was older than Scarborough." Weston's voice cracked through dry lips.

The witch turned on him, a smirk on her face. "Oh yes, no doubt. A man-eater?"

Weston nodded. "They were both punished though, Scarborough and the creature, punished for their wrongs."

The witch faced him now, blue eyes glowing. "Yes, in a manner I suppose. Scarborough played a hard role in Millwood. Entertaining while he was around but unnecessary after a point. The man-eater enjoyed a much more insidious sin." Her smile had grown and displayed her teeth yet again. They seemed sharper now. Animalistic.

"Unnecessary after he knocked up Amelia Hart you mean." Weston studied the witch's face, but it was the mayor's face who cracked some. His voluminous eyebrows raised, his eyes turned to the witch.

"Was the mayor aware that you were using the corpse of his father to kill all those folks?" Weston asked.

The sheriff started to say something, but the witch silenced him with a look.

"It doesn't matter. It's the only thing he ever did to help his son, and it was the most important thing. He got rid of all those who stood in the way of his destiny." The witch turned towards the mayor some as she said this, her hand caressing his arm. "Until you had to go and get rid of him for good."

Weston could feel a strained smile pulling at his lips. "Apple doesn't fall too far from the tree though." He nodded to the mayor and the gun belt that sat around his hips. Winter refused to meet his eyes.

"The boy needed to get his hands dirty. Can't be in politics without a little blood under your fingernails," the crone cooed, still caressing the mayor even though he looked away from her. "If only he had the stomach for it, I wouldn't be here talking to you right now." A sneer clouded her face. "You know, Mr. Weston, if I had known what a pain in the ass you would have become, I never would have freed you from prison. I would have let you rot in there. Or, I would have listened to Port here and had him kill you in your cell."

For a moment, as Weston watched, the old woman seemed to shimmer. A rainbow of colours passed over her as if oil had been spilled in water, and the old woman disappeared, leaving behind the form of Etta Dumond. The witch's sneer was all that remained, but that too faded under ghostly blue eyes.

Bert screamed, bringing the room's attention to him and the nun. He twisted away from the witch, mumbling under his breath and pulling at his restraints to no effect. Mejia sat very still. Her face clenched, she darted her eyes towards Weston.

"If you'd left town like I said," the witch moved in a blur and gripped Bert's mousy, brown hair, "none of this would've been necessary."

Bert tried to pull away from the old woman, tufts of his hair left behind in the witch's grasp. His screams mingled with Etta's cackling laughter.

"Enough!" the mayor's voice boomed in the small space, his eyes a balefire blue as he studied each person under his gaze. "Do what you need to do, but I won't sit by for any more of this foolishness."

Etta Dumond pouted, and her hand caressed the mayor's face. "My boy has always been impatient." She placed a finger on her chin and her stare alternated between Weston and Mejia.

"Kill the nun," she sighed, eyes rolling toward the sheriff. "Make him watch," she pointed in the general direction of Weston. "Then kill Mr. Weston. Drain their blood, it'll work as well even after they're dead."

Etta looked towards Bert, rubbing her chin, a smile crossing her face. "Leave the boy. His blood is more valuable fresh." She bent forward and kissed Bert on the forehead. He didn't move, but he shook in place, his eyes still on Weston.

The sheriff pulled his gun. He motioned with it to get Weston standing and closed in on him. The witch, still smiling, moved to Mejia.

"Get up." The sheriff kicked Weston's legs, his gun still steady on Weston's head. "Ms. Dumond doesn't mind a bit of blood, but she'd rather not mop the floor if she can help it."

Weston made the attempt, but the pain drew him back to the ground. "I can't."

The sheriff aimed a vicious kick at his stomach, sinking his boot deep into Weston's flesh, driving the breath from his body. Weston coughed, the urge to vomit on the precipice of his stomach as his lungs struggled to suck in air.

"I said get up." The sheriff grabbed one of Weston's arms and started to drag him to standing. Weston grabbed the gun with both hands, his teeth clenched to ignore the pain.

"What the hell?" the sheriff said, his free hand flailing and trying to find purchase on Weston's head or back.

Weston twisted the gun out of the sheriff's hand and shot him three times in the stomach and chest. The sheriff dropped to the floor and Weston followed him.

The shack echoed with the gunshots. A dull ringing sound assailed Weston's ears, and he dug at them with his free hand though he knew it would do very little. He had managed to fall into his former place leaning against the wall, the gun trained on the middle of the room to keep Etta and the mayor in his sights.

"Let the woman and boy go," Weston said through clenched teeth. The mayor and Etta cast dark looks his way. The mayor had moved his jacket back but hadn't the time to grab a gun from his belt. The witch still held Mejia's arms, the nun partially untied.

"Let them go." Weston tried to control his shaking hand, but it was no use. The witch and the mayor refused to move.

Weston kept the gun trained on them and crawled to Bert, his legs flailing to gain purchase on the worn floorboards. He untied him, the boy's arms falling to his side. Bert muttered a quiet groan as he feebly moved his trembling arms from the floor to his lap.

"Get out of here." Weston winced as he grabbed Bert by the collar and pushed him towards the door. "Now," he said to Winter, "cut her loose."

The mayor settled back on his heels, and crossed his arms, as if suddenly uninterested in what was taking place. The witch, on the other hand, squeezed tighter to Mejia's arms, her talon-like fingernails drawing small droplets of blood to run down Mejia's brown skin.

Behind him the door jiggled in its frame, the boy's grunts of effort followed and finally a sob. Weston peeked at Bert from the corner of his eye. The boy was struggling with the ill-fitting door, his still weakened hands unable to grasp the door knob. Tears streamed down his face.

"Don't move." Weston pointed the gun at Etta and the mayor and crawled closer to the door. "It's okay, Bert, I'll give you a hand."

It took only a moment. He turned just enough to grip the door and pull on it, tugging it open for the boy to squeeze through. It was just a moment, but as he turned back to the room everything had changed. The witch had conjured a knife from somewhere and now held it to Mejia's neck, the tip of which was imbedded in the soft flesh just beneath her jaw. Weston pointed the gun at her, his hand wavering more than ever.

"Don't," Chilton said, her voice a strained whisper. She jiggled the knife a little. "Your hands are so shaky you may hit this little old bitch."

Mejia gritted her teeth and pulled at Etta's grip.

"I won't miss," Weston said holding the gun in two hands to steady himself, but the pain that emanated from his shoulder produced the opposite effect.

"Even so," Etta Dumond smiled and spared a quick glance at the mayor. "Can you be sure a bullet will kill something like me. How did your guns fair against the maneater?"

Weston could feel the sweat running over his fore-head. The strain put on his arms to stay upright was almost too much, but he pushed himself despite the tremors that made him waver and the sharp pain that exploded with every breath he took. Etta was right, he thought. Bullets didn't kill the beast in the forest. They hurt it though, gave it pause.

"Decisions, decisions," Etta cooed. "Perhaps I can help. I do so enjoy helping people." She gripped the knife harder. A horrendous smile cracked her face and exposed horrible wolf like teeth.

Weston felt his finger caress the trigger. He poured all his will into his aim. With his arm steadied, if only for the moment, he fired. The recoil echoed all the way to his open wound, and he could feel the gun drop as soon as he had shot it. But his aim had been true.

The witch's head was flung backwards with the impact, a spurt of blood stretched into the air, and Etta fell backwards in the desperate finality of everyone who's been shot in the head. The knife dropped to the floor with a dull thud.

Mejia collapsed at the same time. Her arms were still hanging above her head, but as she dropped, they loosened some; the witch's fiddling had not been forgotten by the knots that held the nun bound. A new round of painful moans escaped her straining throat.

Weston's left arm was dead. He couldn't command it anymore, and it wouldn't respond if he did. He accepted it as easily as he'd accepted the death of his horse in the time before he'd met Mejia. Without further thought about it, he picked up the gun he had dropped, and pointed it at the mayor.

"Untie her." Weston clicked back the hammer of the gun.

The mayor was standing transfixed on the fallen body of Etta Dumond. His eyes were wide, and he was breathing in long, slow breaths.

"She's dead," he said, a small quiver in his powerful orator's voice. The mayor loosed a shuddering sigh and narrowed his eyes at Weston. "You killed her." The silence was thick in the shack, an undercurrent of what had just occurred and what was about to happen.

Weston motioned to Mejia with the gun. The mayor moved to the woman, his thick fingers scraping along the coarse rope as he untied her.

Mejia's arms collapsed as Bert's had done before her. Her breathing was stilted but quiet as she attempted to move, frantic as she was to get away from the body of Etta Dumond.

"B...b...blood," Mejia said pushing herself away with her feet and legs. The mayor stood back, a grimace engraved into his face.

"The guns," Weston said. The mayor raised his eyebrows and pushed his jacket away from his hips.

"Keep it real slow," Weston said, his gun still tracking the mayor. His hand and arm were getting tired. A pain preceded by a dull numbness started to crawl through them.

The mayor nodded.

"Bill," Mejia said sitting beside him, letting her face edge close to his ear. "The blood, Bill. The blood."

The mayor slid the guns and their belt towards Weston; they stopped just out of reach. The mayor shrugged, a grin curling the corners of his mouth, and he crossed his arms.

"I know," Weston said to Mejia, but his eyes were locked on the mayor, and his feet were reaching out to hook around the gun belt. "My shoulder's a mess."

Mejia pulled his face to hers. Her fingers dug into his cheeks and chin, trembling some, but sure and with purpose.

"There's no blood," she said and pointed to Etta's body.

The shack went dark.

CHAPTER TWELVE

I

The grass was cold. Wet. Bert could feel the dew push its way through his shirt, soaking his back and shoulders. It soothed his aches and pains.

It was dark outside the small cabin; twisted old trees reached to the sky and blocked it out with their thick branches and leaves. Only some light managed to fight its way through, little pin pricks of a pale light that could have been from the sun or moon.

Bert looked around. He'd never been in these woods before, was never allowed to play there. Father Mason had said that it was easy to get lost within them and warned him away. He had always wanted to play within them, to take his father's knife and run through the trees pretending to hunt down bank robbers or monsters. Now that he was finally in amongst the trees, he wanted nothing more than to leave.

He couldn't remember being brought here. Couldn't remember anything that had happened since the church, since the sheriff had taken him. There were no trails that he could see, just trees surrounding him on all sides. Bert squinted into the darkness and it frightened him.

The trees made strange shapes in the low light, and they made subtle movements like they were caught in a gust of wind, but there was no sound. No animals or birds, no echoes of life, not even of the town just beyond the treeline. The movement though, it was there. Bert could see it in the darkness, the shapes by the trees. They were there but they made no sound.

Then Bert heard it, the squelching of boots in mud, and his eyes were drawn to her. A young woman—not much younger than the girls who worked for Etta—pushed through the branches in her too big boots on a trail that had appeared out of nowhere. She wore a large poncho, but even with that flowing around her Bert could tell she was pregnant.

She had her hands pressed into her large stomach, teeth clenched together, and she floundered in the mud. It gripped at her boots, sucked them down deeper as she attempted to pull herself away, threatening to claim the boots as its own. She fell to a knee instead, drenching her dress skirts, and screamed and cursed. Bert tried to move towards her, to help her, but he couldn't. He was frozen, watching her struggle to pull herself free with rage and frustration painting her efforts.

"Come on, Amelia," she growled. "The old women's house is close. You can do this."

The mud climbed out between her fingers as Amelia pushed herself up and got herself moving again, only losing one boot in the process. Another practiced curse fell from her mouth as she clutched her bulbous stomach and stumbled forward. A grimace came over her face as she ran her hands over her guts until she flinched and pulled her hands away as if she were bitten. *The baby is kicking*, Bert thought. *It's kicking and she doesn't like it.*

"Fuck Deneen, the old woman is your only chance now," Amelia said into her chest and Bert held his breath.

She's not seeking help from Etta Dumond, not now. She can't be. He turned back to the cabin, but it was farther away than he remembered. Did he move after all?

Amelia fell against a tree, gasping. She sighed, and a relieved smile came over her red painted lips. She could see the cabin as well and pushed toward it, her eyes on the lamplight that extended from the lone window that stood on its face. Bert tried to free himself from his invisible bonds, tried to scream, to warn Amelia that the old woman was a witch. That the old woman only meant harm. It was useless. He could do nothing but watch.

She shook her head, flicking drops of water from her hair and nose. "You did what the old crone said, you drank that awful cotton root tea. You ate raspberry leaf and basil. Now she needs to live up to her end of the bargain."

Amelia shivered as she ambled forward, her eyes darting back and forth. A shadow darted in front of her. Bert saw it too, large and misshapen. She wailed with fright and fell backwards.

"Ow, ow, ow," she said, a pout took over her face as she rubbed at her bootless foot and ankle. A heavy rain set in. The whole forest was moving now, its noises drowned out by the downpour and splashing that followed. Amelia sighed and let herself laugh. The laugh surprised her, but it also lightened her. Bert could see her face clear some, could see her relax. She needed it. Amelia sat there, letting herself laugh until she cried, rubbing her eyes with the back of her mud-covered -hands.

A rustling in the trees behind her forced her to stop mid-cry. She jumped to her feet only to fall to the ground once more, biting her lip in pain and the urge to remain quiet. She looked to the old woman's house.

A branch snapped behind her, Amelia refused to look

in its direction and forced herself to crawl to the door. Her hands, like claws, pulled her forward, an excruciatingly slow pace that brought more tears to her eyes. Bert could see nothing besides the young woman. His heart beat against his chest, his breath shallow and rapid. Something was after her.

Her scream pierced the night and rain, and echoed through the trees.

"Hush child," a shaky, high-pitched voice said bringing Amelia and Bert's eyes back toward the trees. The old woman was bent over her, hooded cloak wrapped around her. A gnarled hand reached out toward her. Etta Dumond was here.

Tears flowed from Amelia's reddened eyes. "I did everything you asked. I did it, I did it."

"Good. That's good," Etta Dumond said and helped Amelia to her feet. She wrapped Amelia's arms around her curved back and helped her into the house. The scent of decomposition hit Bert as soon as they broke through the threshold and he stifled a gag. He was in the house with them now, back in the cabin that he had just escaped. Mr. Weston and Mejia weren't there. It was empty.

The old woman grunted and sat Amelia in a rocking chair next to the fireplace. "Here, drink this," she said and pushed a cup of honey-coloured liquid into Amelia's hand.

"What... what is this?" Amelia bent her nose to the small cup. "It smells like honey."

"Drink. It's good. It will help with the pain." The old woman had thrown off her cloak and was scurrying around the room, filling her arms with glass jars as she went.

This Etta Dumond was a squat woman, bent with age

and a hard life. Her dirty gray hair hung over her lined face, but it didn't seem to hinder her machinations any. Bert wondered at the speed of the woman, her aged legs working without stop as she ran between the fire and the kitchen on the opposite side of the small shack. He wondered at her strength, for that matter. The old woman was able to carry Amelia into the cabin with little effort. Her ancient face was split with a small smile and she hummed a tune that Bert wasn't familiar with. Despite her form, Etta Dumond was powerful. He tried once more to warn Amelia but nothing worked. Except, for a moment, did Etta look at him? Did her old head twitch in his direction. He held his breath, averted his eyes. He couldn't bare her eyes on him.

Amelia sighed, and took a long draught from the cup she had been handed. She gasped, clutching her breast, and dropped the ceramic mug to the ground where it smashed.

"There, there," the crone smiled a yellow-toothed grin down on Amelia. "It'll all be over soon."

Amelia screamed and clawed at her stomach. "Get it out, get it out!"

The old lady smoothed down Amelia's mousy brown hair, her claw-like hand caressing the swollen belly. "It's coming dear, it's coming."

Amelia's eyes went wide. "You said you'd get rid of it. You said you'd kill it!"

The old woman gave her a knowing stare and moved to her legs.

"No, no, no!" Amelia screamed. "No, it can't."

"Here it comes, dear," the old crone's watery voice broke through her mind.

A new scream broke the air, a cry and wailing that

filled the room.

"It'll be so nice to have company again."

Bert sat up with a start, his breath was coming in hard gulps. The grass was cool on his back and hands, but it brought him no comfort. He stared at the door; it was still ajar. A sliver of light peeked around the opening but didn't extend far enough to help him see what was happening inside or out. He saw movement out of the corner of his eye, and he wanted to run to the cabin, but he remembered the witch and he stopped himself.

"He'll come out soon," Bert told himself in a hoarse whisper, "him and the sister. They'll come out and then we'll leave. We'll leave and go home." He nodded, rocking back and forth in the grass.

Bert couldn't hear anything from the cabin, but the light was on and that's all that mattered. He refused to look around him any longer, refused to face those shapes in the darkness. It was the light he looked at, the bouncing orange light of a candle or a lantern that called to him, bid him to enter. He wouldn't though. He sat and watched the light.

Until the light went out.

Bert rubbed at his eyes; the light had been there one second and the next it was gone. It was as if he had blinked and it died. He blinked and it left him. He failed.

A twig exploded behind him with a harsh snap. He jumped to his feet and twirled in a circle. Shapes. Dark shadows in the trees, but no more sounds. The image of the dark, misshapen shadow stirred in his mind.

He turned back to the shack, still no light. His breath was heavy, rapid.

"Mejia," Bert whispered, his eyes twitching at their periphery. "Weston."

Snap

He ran to the cabin and pushed open its lopsided door. Bert was back inside.

II

Weston fired into the shadows and dropped the gun with a curse. His arm gratefully gave up the extra weight, and he almost sighed in relief, but he didn't have the time.

The mayor had rushed toward him; the clomping of his large feet on the creaking wooden boards gave him away. He lunged atop of Weston, flailing in an uneducated flurry of fists and curses of his own. Beside them both Mejia groaned.

With only one arm, Weston avoided blows as much as he could. The mayor was the larger man, and though he had probably never been in an honest fight in his life, he was strong and rested and uninjured.

Weston brought his knee up between the two men and used the space to kick the mayor away. He tried to make it to his knees, to give himself a better chance, but the mayor was atop of him again in an instant. Weston continued to block most of the mayor's barrage until a stray fist landed on his shoulder's open wound. The world spun and he let out a small cry of pain and shock that only bolstered the mayor to continue to pound away on him.

Consumed by pain, Weston was willing to let the mayor beat him. His vision was blurred with explosions of every colour, and he felt that if he died right there it would at least end his suffering. Numbness took over, and all the blows he was suffering seemed to be just distant echoes of pain, pale in comparison to his shoulder.

The door swung open just enough to let Bert through and then he slammed it shut. The mayor paused and looked at the boy, a growl rising in his thick neck. Weston's mind cleared some at the sight of Bert breathing heavy and braced against the door ensuring it was shut. With a quick twist of his hips Weston shot out his good elbow and struck the mayor on the temple and just above his eye. Winter grunted and fell to the ground, his hands covering the blood that began to flow from his forehead.

"Sister," the boy said and threw his arms about the nun's shoulders. Mejia did her best to wrap her own arms around his back.

"You should've left," Weston managed between swollen lips, as he rolled himself to his stomach and made for his gun belt once again.

"I... I couldn't," the boy said. "There was no path to follow, and it was so dark. And there were things..."

"Hush, nino," Mejia said and smoothed his hair.

The mayor held his eye and slapped around on the floor, looking for the dropped gun.

"Stop," Weston said. The smooth sound of metal on worn leather as he pulled his gun from its old and cracked leather holster was like an elixir for his wounds. A genuine smile parted his swollen lips as he felt the cool iron and how its grip fit his hand.

The mayor stopped, blood masking his face. A smile was there too, his teeth glowing like the death grin of the skull in the darkness.

"I ought to shoot you right here," Weston heard himself say. He was surprised at how steady his hand had become. Just a few minutes ago he couldn't hold the sheriff's gun for more than a few seconds before his strength wavered. Now he held the weapon straight and true.

"You won't," Winter replied, his grin growing, a laugh on his breath.

It was just a moment of thought, a moment when Weston tried to understand the smirk that met the point of his gun. It was a moment too long.

A high-pitched wail came from beside him, and before he could look he was launched into the far wall with a thud, more pain prickling at his shoulder, back, and head.

In the dark room he could see the figure of the witch, her sharp taloned hands before her. Gone was the guise of Etta Dumond. In its place was the old crone with her withered cheeks and dead eyes.

"I told you," the witch cooed. "You can't kill me, Mr. Weston. You haven't the tools nor the ability."

Weston groaned. Gun still in hand he pointed the barrel at the hunched over carcass of Etta Dumond.

"Not a fast learner are you, Mr. Weston?" the witch cackled, and with the snap of her fingers the candles in the cabin ignited with streams of flame. The room glowed a harsh orange and red.

In a blur she scurried to Weston's side. One hand grabbed his wrist, the other twisted the front of his shirt and picked him up off the ground, her maniacal laughter exploding from her sharp toothed mouth.

A sudden change came over her face as she dangled Weston in the air. A look of shock and pain replaced her malevolent smile, and a shriek of pain replaced her laughter. Weston was tossed atop the body of the dead sheriff.

"What is it?" The mayor stood, a handkerchief covering his wounded forehead. The witch just screamed in response—anger and pain in equal measure—as she studied her hand.

Weston felt the heat from the chain that hung around his neck and pushed himself to sitting. He felt around for his gun. Patting the sheriff's body, he picked it up, but it was caught on something in the sheriff's belt. The boy's knife.

He took the knife in his hand, studied it, but was soon flung back against the wall again, the witch atop of him and the blade skittering off into the darkness.

"Your bitch of a nun gave you this?" Etta Dumond spit as she tore open his shirt exposing the silver crucifix and chain. It glowed, the dim light glinting off it. "Or was it the bumbling Father Mason?" A twisted grimace grew on her face, a curl in her withered lips that may have been a smile. "Either way, it won't keep you safe." She straddled him and ran her long claws down his chest and stomach, caressing his scars. She licked his face, her slug-like tongue scraping over his heavy stubble. The smell of rot and death made Weston cough.

"Mother," Winter said. "Perhaps we can hurry this up." He grabbed a handful of Mejia's hair and pulled her along the ground toward the fire in the hearth.

"He's right, you know," Etta said with a pout and began to drag Weston in the same direction. "Don't go anywhere child." She turned toward Bert. "We'll be back for you." But Bert wasn't in the mood to wait his turn.

The boy ran toward the witch, his face clenched tight like a fist of anger and fear. In his hand he brandished his father's knife, the blade orange in the reflected lamplight.

Weston could hear the knife sink into the old crone's leathery flesh. She sang out with surprise pain and grasped at her side. Black ooze dripped from the corners of her mouth, which seemed to sizzle as it hit the floor.

She tossed the boy aside and dropped Weston, his head bouncing on the old boards. All he wanted to do was rest, to take time to get his energy back, to heal his arm. He couldn't though. The boy was up again and ready to fight. Weston wouldn't let him do that on his own.

The witch still flailed with the pain, her hands trying to grip the knife to remove it. She drew the attention of the mayor who had dropped the sister by the hearth and was coming back.

"Bill!" The boy's voice was frantic as he kicked Weston's gun belt over to him.

Weston pulled the gun free and fired two shots in quick succession. *Bang bang.* The mayor went down with a cry, his knee shattered by Weston's bullets.

Dislodging the knife from her side, the witch roared and threw it to the ground. She'd seen Winter go down and had begun to stalk Weston with her claws and teeth bared.

Bang bang bang bang. Four more shots filled the air. The acrid smell of gunpowder nearly overpowered the rest of the cabin. The bullets hit home, two in the witch's chest, one scratching her cheek, and the fourth in her right shoulder. The witch cackled.

"Your manmade weapons can't kill me, Weston." She picked the bullet out of her shoulder and held it in front of her face. Black ichor was slathered all over it. "Did you really think something as simple as this could kill me?"

"It was worth a try," Weston said getting to his knees. He let his hand and gun fall to his side, empty, useless. His vision had begun to blur; streaks of white light crossed in front of him, a hazy rainbow at his periphery.

"And what now, Mr. Weston? Did you think you aimed with silver bullets, that a holy light would guide your weapon true? God doesn't live here anymore, Mr. Weston." Etta Dumond laughed, tossing the bullet to the floor.

"I had hoped..." Weston said rocking back and falling to his ass. "I had hoped...."

The witch tittered a high-pitched laugh. "What did you hope, Mr. Weston?"

"I had hoped that I could distract you." Weston's eyes felt heavy now.

"Oh, you've been quite a distraction, Mr. Weston. But enough of —"

Weston waved off the witch and pointed just over the witch's shoulder. As she turned the butt-end of a flaming junk of wood struck her on the forehead and threw her to the floor. Mejia stood behind the piece of firewood and continued to beat upon the former tavern owner with all the rage and fear and hate she could muster. The old witch's greasy, grey hair and ancient robes caught quickly, but only in spots. Mejia was tiring, but she was still landing blows on the old crone.

"Quick, boy!" Weston pointed to an old oil lamp that lay on a table nearby.

Bert ran to the table, picked up the lamp and threw it at the flailing witch. The glass smashed on the floor next to Etta Dumond's feet and the fuel splashed on her robes and skin. The old woman instantly ignited in a shroud of fire, her screams filling the shack.

"Mother!" Frank Winter cried and crawled away from the flaming witch.

Weston could feel Bert's hands gripping under his arms. He was vaguely aware that he was being pulled toward the door.

"Sister!" Bert's voice called, "Mejia come on!"

The nun was holding her shoulder, her face pale around a tired smile. "Go on, child, get him to safety."

"No," Weston started to say. The fire was catching. With each movement, the witch would start a new fire that would join the existing flames. The cabin was sweltering. Board was cracking and turning brown even without the presence of the growing flames. Etta's collection of specimen jars exploded in the heat, their contents spilling to the floor and sizzling in the fire.

"Está bien," Mejia nodded her head. "You go. I'll keep them here. Trust me."

Weston's eyes were nothing but slits as he was dragged to the door. Smoke and heat didn't help his heavy eyelids, and he could feel himself drifting, but in that moment, he thought he saw Etta Dumond's fire engulfed hand reach out for the mayor as well. Then Mejia slammed the door shut.

The sound of a gunshot echoed around him. He didn't feel the impact, but he fell, the cool ground nice on his aching muscles. It wasn't until he felt the warm, sticky sensation of blood oozing behind him did he realize something was very wrong.

CHAPTER THIRTEEN

A bright light pulled at the corners of his eyes. It disturbed the darkness he had found there and had become accustomed to. Weston's eyes fluttered open, the light exploding now from the open window. Curtains lifted in the cold breeze.

He was aware of someone stalking through the house. He heard the squeak of shoes on boarded floor, the swish of someone running past the open window. Laughter — foreign to him, alien.

The bed was sufficient. The sheets were crumpled at the foot, kicked off during his rest. Weston's exposed skin prickled in the breeze; gooseflesh spread across his chest and he shivered despite the too-hot room.

It had been weeks since the fire, Weston had been told, though he remembered very little. It was Anita who had arranged his rescue. Having seen the mayor and sheriff carry him off into the dark forest, she managed to wrangle one of her suitors to follow along. Ezra Hames was the young fellow's name, a thick-limbed logger's son who only had eyes for the eldest painted lady at the Last Chance Saloon. They were engaged since.

Anita said he had been in a coma. Not that they could risk bringing Doctor Sutherland to the young lad's home, but the eldest Hames had some experience in medicine from the war. He bound up Weston, kept him alive. He could do nothing for Bert.

Weston remembered the coma.

He dreamed of his life before, of a life with Mary, a home; he dreamed of a modicum of happiness gone too soon. He also dreamed of death, and dismay, of words left unsaid. He dreamed of blood and loss and hatred. He dreamed of monsters.

The boy had been buried before Weston woke from his slumber. A nondescript grave just outside Sister Mejia's old place. Weston hadn't seen it yet, but Anita assured that she put some fresh daisies there for him.

Weston sat up, minding the twinge that echoed from his still bandaged shoulder. The elder Hames said it would almost certainly work as well as before, or close enough to. He said it would probably give him the fits into his old age, but it would do the trick for now.

Once dressed, he headed for the kitchen, the smell of brewed coffee drawing him like a moth to flame. Bacon and eggs were waiting for him on the stove, and he poured himself up a mug of coffee. The Hames' residence was suitable enough for the brood of seven that lived there—eight with Anita, nine with Weston. All wooden and handmade, even the furniture had the elder Hames' touch to it. None were in the house right now; chores to do. Weston felt at home in the loneliness, alone with his thoughts and plans.

He had just taken a sip of his coffee when Anita backed in through the door, a gentle laugh in her throat, a smile on her quartz-coloured lips. It disappeared when she saw Weston standing there. Her whole body closed, her head and eyes moved to the floor and she did her best not to look his way. Weston could hear Ezra laughing to himself in the field, an echo of what he had just shared with Anita.

"I didn't expect to see you there," she said around a nervous laugh and made herself busy cleaning up the kitchen. "How did you sleep?"

"Just fine." Weston tried a smile and took another sip of his coffee. They stayed in silence, hearing the sounds of work from outside echo in the family cottage, the muffled noises of Anita playing at tidying.

"I think today is the day." Weston broke the silence and drained the last of his coffee.

Anita raised her blue eyes to him. A smile battered her scarred lips. "You sure? Your arm still ain't healed, Papa Hames says so." she sat across from him, scrunching up a cloth.

"I'm sure," Weston said. "I've been putting it off for too long."

Anita nodded. "You know, you don't have to. Millwood isn't perfect, but it... but there are some good people in it." She said and put one small fist on a jutted-out hip. "Say, do you remember the night that... the night that you came to my room. Of course you do. I'm not—er, I wasn't, the type of whore to give some fool free range. I made my money, and I wasn't going to be swindled. I bet you didn't know that I had a six shooter right there next to the bed. Someone like you ever barged in on me and I would've put some holes in 'em. But I didn't do that with you, never even crossed my mind. I think there was something I could see in you then, a light. Lights like that, we shouldn't ever let them go out. They're like the dying embers of a fire, we can stoke them up again. You don't have to do what you are about to do. Stay, here. Or go—

live your life. Find those embers before they're gone for good."

She was right, of course. Weston didn't have to, but he was going to; he had to. Anita saw this in the line of his jaw, the slight downturn of his head.

"Is there anything you need?" Anita said, a sigh hitching her voice.

Weston reined in the big draft horse and peered through the brass spyglass, the eye socket cool on his cheek. Millwood was alight, its people crowding the streets. Etta Dumond's demise did little to slow down the flow of booze and opium consumed; the Last Chance Saloon was open for business.

Guards, the sheriff's men, were few and far between. According to Anita they hadn't gotten around to replacing Port Johnson just yet. That was good for Weston.

He let himself linger on the mayor's house. The lights were out, but he knew someone would be home. He'd get to him soon enough. In truth, it was equal parts genius and stupid in what Winter had done. He'd wanted gas lines run through the town, so he put the means in his own backyard. Just another way to make himself look good to the townsfolk while robbing them blind. It reminded Weston of the magicians he saw once in Denver. Pick a card, any card. Swindlers that used sleight of hand to mimic magic. He saw a fellow once, the Amazing Bartini, make a ball disappear by and palming it. That was the mayor too—distract you with one hand, while the other does his dirty work.

Weston had been around gas lighting before. Knew the basics of the process. It was all about coal. He knew that if you heated coal in an oven, making sure that it was sealed tight enough to keep any oxygen out, you could use the gas created to pipe to houses, businesses, lights. Normally, a factory or some facility would ensure that the coal gas was purified and filtered, but Weston doubted the mayor cared that much. He only focused on the lamp lights and his home, of course.

Smart and stupid.

Weston wouldn't have pegged Frank Winter as the survivor type. Would have figured him to give up when it got rough—say a shattered kneecap, and burns all over his body. He didn't give up though. The terrible will of his father and adopted mother must of rubbed off some. Didn't matter, that was all going to end. Weston would make sure of that.

"C'mon, Atlas," Weston said and urged the large horse toward the town. It was time to finish it.

The people of the Millwood shuffled through the streets. Their slow and stifled movements bogged up the walkways and irritated the draft horse as Weston guided it through the town. From far off, Weston may have thought that they were drunk, under the influence of their preferred vice, but that wasn't it. The folk looked confused, unsure. Many stood as if rooted to the ground, stroking their chins and blinking at their surroundings. Some people pushed their way through the others, giving wary side glances as they passed to go about their business, and Weston saw at least one building boarded up.

The Last Chance drew the masses with each stumbling townsperson making their way to its doorstep. It was lit up, the fiery glow of candle and lamp light casting weird shadows in the growing darkness. Weston studied it as he went passed, Atlas whinnying and twitching as people floated in front of him. It was the same, the building intact with nothing added or removed from the surface. All the same, it didn't hold the prominence as it once did. It waned in the background, melding with the shadow of the buildings surrounding it. It was fading.

Weston urged Atlas onward. There was nothing left to see.

The mayor's home was as washed out as the old saloon. The splendor and majesty of the welcome home party was all but gone, with nothing left behind but the cracks in its bricks, now obvious. Weston passed the front gate, his hat pulled low over his face. Two guards, neither looking their best. One was slumped over a double-barrel shotgun, his eyes rimmed red with one large hand rubbing absently over his stubbled chin. The other guard sat cross-legged on the ground, his guns in his lap. Weston moved around back.

It might have been smarter to use the old crone's shack as a makeshift gas distillery, at least add on to some of that prime land no one was using. Then again, Weston supposed, Etta Dumond was likely particular on the matters of her home and business. No, it was always going to be this way, with the mayor building it too close to his own home, a too big shed in his backyard. That's the only place it could be, every other building had been spoken for. Not that it really could be called a shed, more like a guest home with all the innards ripped out and pipes and ovens put back in. In his own way, the mayor was following in his adopted mommy's foot steps. No old magic, but the new stuff—science, that's what he was playing with.

No guards. Weston hitched Atlas nearby and hopped the fence. His shoulder pained him some in doing so, but he managed. The guest house wasn't quite as big as the main house, but it was close enough. Weston peeked in one of the front windows. There was little light, and not much he could make out of the shadows that made up the inside of the makeshift factory. Glints of light bounced off some metal contraptions that lined the walls and sat on tables. The type of thing Weston might have seen an old moonshiner use to ply his trade. Even so, the similarity to Dumond's lair and Winter's gas distillery hit him hard.

"Raised him right," Weston muttered and shook his head. Not that this was a part of their great scheme. No, the addition of gas lighting to the town of Millwood was a ruse. Just something to make other towns jealous and keep Millwood loyal to Winter. Loyalty meant more support when Winter climbed that political ladder. Pick a card, pick any card.

Weston slid off the towering workhorse, rummaged through the saddlebags. The Hames brood provided him with more than a horse after all.

The mayor didn't wake with a start, but with a slow stirring into consciousness. It was disappointing—Weston had hoped to put some real fear into that son-of-a-bitch. That'd have to come later.

No, the mayor didn't seem to care that Weston sat next to his bed, smoking a loosely rolled cigarette and dashing the ashes on the once crisp, white sheets of his bed. Nor did the mayor seem all too surprised by Weston's visit.

"Weston," he said with a stiff nod from his pillow.

Frank Winter was in slings, literally. The knee Weston had shattered with a well-placed bullet was propped up on a sheet hanging from the ceiling. Fire and heat did the rest—sizzled the skin, made it pop like too tight leather.

"Mr. Mayor."

"I figured you'd be back around these parts sooner or later," Winter said and pushed a heavily bandaged hand over his moustache, straightening it.

"That so?" Weston threw his smoke to the floor and ground it out with his heel. "I suppose you'd like me to congratulate you on your foresight?"

The mayor grunted, looked away.

"Besides," Weston edged on. "I doubt you'd planned on me arriving with you in such a…position." Weston cast a glance towards the mayor's leg.

"Perhaps. What brings you back to my town, Weston?"

"Not many guards around, I guess you should thank me for that. No sheriff, no loyalty. Not that it would do you much good. Tell me, have you seen the state of your fair town, of its townsfolk?"

The mayor grunted. "They're in a state of withdrawal, or something very close to it. My mother, like her or not, *did* provide a service around here—it just wasn't what people had thought it was. Now, we all feel those after effects. In a way it's a kind of grieving." The mayor nodded to himself, pleased with the analogy.

"That'll be none of your worry soon," Weston stood and smiled. "Time to go."

"I'm surprised one of Sister Mejia's disciples would stoop to killing someone in cold blood," Winter said, his voice trembling under the bravado of attempting to keep himself steady.

"As you say, your mother had quite an impression." Weston pulled the mayor from bed. Amid the screams of agony and appeals for mercy, Weston got him standing, a cane gripped tightly in one hand.

"W-where are you taking me?"

"A man of your disposition could use some fresh air," Weston answered with a tightened grip on Winter's bicep and a violent wrench that pulled him toward the door.

Weston managed to get the whining mayor to his horse, a dappled grey thoroughbred named Celeste, settled him in the saddle, and got him riding out of town. Weston followed on Atlas; a gun pointed at Frank Winter's back for persuasion.

They came up against no resistance. The guards at the mayor's door gave them a slack-jawed stare and continued to busy themselves with confused thoughts that matched their muddled expressions. Winter did all he could to gain their attention, to sic them on Weston, but all of his thunderous throat-clearing and violent head-nodding were for nought. Weston thumbed back the hammer of his revolver; the click meant to save the mayor from further embarrassing himself.

They rode out of town, the mayor refusing to take in the sight of his town's people fumbling through the motions of their previous normal. He remained as oblivious to it as he remained silent, which was just fine with Weston. Winter could keep his trap shut the entire time for all Weston cared, as long as he kept his eyes open.

They passed through the town and into the barren plain, the mayor risking a final look over his shoulder. Weston imagined that he wanted to call out for help, maybe ask where they were going, but he held it in, his mouth drawn down into a scowl under his thick moustache.

"Just up here," Weston said after a few minutes. They pulled up along the sparse rocks that he hid behind the night of the fire. "That's far enough."

Winter reined in his horse and brought it around to

face Weston and his gun.

"C'mon, we'll get you on your feet." Weston slipped from his own saddle with a grunt.

"What is the point of this performance?" Winter demanded as Weston managed to get him off his horse and arranged with his cane.

"Millwood looks downright pretty from up here," Weston said in return and nodded toward the town. "In the dark, it almost looks like a real city with all them lights."

Winter sighed and leaned heavily on his cane, giving a dismissive shake of his head.

"That wasn't a bad idea, Mr. Mayor—installing those gas lamps. Of course, the bigger cities are already moving on to electric lights. You'd know that though. Your fellow townsfolk? Well, maybe not."

"Again," Winter said and turned towards Weston, "I must ask what the point of this performance is?"

"Keep an eye on the town," Weston said and backed out of sight. "Don't look at me, look at the town." Winter heard the click of the revolver's hammer. "You'll see."

Frank Winter could feel a cold shiver run up his spine, an electric current that made him shake in place. He held on tight to his cane, both hands flexed on the small pommel. Millwood stood before him, the town he'd grown up in, the town that had been his since he'd been born. "Is this what you want, Weston, do you want me to look upon Millwood, to see it for one last time, before you put a bullet in me? Fitting, I suppose, to look at my town, the town my mother had made for me. Oh yes, it's mine, if it's anyone's. There's no one else around that could stake that claim anymore. Del Cornish, that old buzzard, is dead. The priest and that infuriating nun—dead. Even those newcomers, those would-be usurpers—the livery owner, Dermot, and his rich buddy Puddicombe—killed. Even the god damned governor is out of the picture. I made sure of all of that. This is *my* town, and it will be great as long as I'm here to guide it. So that's your choice now, Mr. Weston. You kill me and you damn those people. You let me live and they'll have some sort of purpose. That's your choice."

"I was thinking of something a little quicker," Weston said.

Winter heard the click and before he had a chance to look behind him the town exploded into flames. It was a cascading blast that moved through the whole town in just a few seconds, but in those seconds, there was enough time to for him to see the progress of explosions that soon covered the whole of Millwood.

He turned on Weston, his eyes wide and mouth agape. "What... what..."

"You've been a naughty boy, Frank," Weston said, a smirk touching the corner of his mouth. "I figured I'd just take all your toys away." Weston slipped his gun into its holster, still eyeing the confused look on Frank Winter's pale face. "You said it yourself, it was *your* town."

Weston had barely taken his hand from the gun's handle before Winter launched his attack. Hopping on one foot he lashed out with his cane, catching Weston in the temple and sending him sprawling to the ground. Then the mayor was on top of him, spit hanging from his teeth, and his big hands fumbling for Weston's neck.

He flailed under the mayor's weight, his hands reaching for those that surged toward his throat. Weston's vision wavered, the world moved in and out of shadows, colours dancing at the periphery. He fought to stay conscious, but in the end he blacked out—it was inevitable.

Weston's shoulder throbbed, but the pain soothed him. It brought the world back into a crisp and vibrant reality. The night was brighter, the pale rays of the moon and stars bled into the darkness, tearing it open for him, laying it bare.

Frank Winter sat a short distance away with one gore-encrusted hand held tight to his chest. His face was a mixture of terror and pain. "Stay away from me," he whispered, scuttling backwards.

Weston stood, he felt something slick on his chin, cool on his face. Panicked, he ran a hand over his chin and drew it into his line of sight. Blood. It stained his hand, the metallic scent of it filled his nostrils. Blood.

"What… what happened?" he asked, but he knew. Maybe not the complete picture, but he knew. He had bitten Winter, had taken a chunk out of him by his reaction to it. His shoulder throbbed, not in pain this time, but in satisfaction.

The former mayor continued to move away from Weston, moving toward his horse as best he could with one hand and one good leg. Weston frowned.

"None of that," he said and fired from the hip. The bullet blew through the horse's neck in a gout of blood. The strangled whinny of the animal pierced the night before it stumbled and fell. "I'm going to give you as fair a chance as I had," Weston said. "I came to this town without a horse, left for dead in the barren no-man's-land you see around you. If it weren't for that 'infuriating nun' I'd have been out of your hair before I was in it. Who knows, maybe a Good Samaritan will come along and help you out, but I doubt it. Those wounds you got there, the blood you're leaking? I don't like your chances. If you survive, look me up. We'll finish this."

Frank Winter watched in silent fury as Weston walked away in search of Atlas. He never said a word.

Atlas wasn't too far off, attempting to graze but having no real luck with it. Weston patted the horse down, made sure he was calm, and went to work cleaning himself up. He used his scuffed-up shirt to get rid of most of the blood and tossed it to the ground, replacing it with an extra shirt the Hames' were nice enough to give him. Atlas waited patiently, though he snuffed from time to time and pawed at the ground with one big hoof, kicking up dust in hopes of finding something to chew on.

"Not much left here is there, boy?" Weston said and pulled himself into the saddle. His blood was still on fire. Exhilaration shot through his body, and it took some effort to keep it in check, to keep himself from jittering off the saddle. A happy side effect was that the pain in his shoulder had subsided, though he had no doubt it would be back in due time. He counted on it.

"Only one more thing to do," he whispered into the horse's twitching ear and kicked him into action.

There was something missing from Mejia's place; the warmth was gone out of it. A thin layer of dust crept over the old clapboards, the windows. The charm and pleasantries were as vacant as the shell it had now become. An empty husk, a corpse.

Weston toyed with the idea of going inside, of taking one last look around—take in the scent of it for the final time, and maybe regain some of those feelings that Mejia had instilled in him. But he couldn't bring himself to touch the doorknob under the scrutinizing stare of St. Jude.

There were two new additions to the property. Two graves marked with barebones crosses, little more than two stickers tied together. Anita had directed the Hames boys to put the graves next to Mejia's garden. Good girl, Weston thought. Mejia may have been a nun under the church, but the garden had been her place of worship. It was as fitting a resting place as any for the old nun, for Bert too.

Javier was no where to be found, probably sold by Anita or gifted to the Hames family. Either way, Weston filled up the trough and scattered out some hay and oats — just in case.

Weston stepped back and took in the sight of the old cabin one last time. He spent precious little time there, but it was a time he'd look back upon. Something told him that he'd need the good memories to outweigh the bad.

He inhaled one more time, trying to take what little was left of the old place into him. The sweet smell of the garden, the musky odour of hay in the barn, the latent scent of warm meals that precipitated good conversations. It was all there, all of it, but there was something else too. An undercurrent of blood and death.

Weston hastened to Atlas, mounted the horse, and spurred it on into the vast remainder of Colorado. He knew the smell, but it didn't belong with Mejia or Bert. So he left, fearing that the blood and death he'd smelled came with him.

The End

ACKNOWLEDGEMENTS

I once thought that writing would be a perfect career for me, I'm an introvert, after all, with a side of antisocial tendencies for good measure. Writing, it turns out, and no matter how much it attempts to protest the fact, is not a solitary endeavour. It took a lot more than me hunched over at my computer, punching keys, to produce this book you hold in your hands. A lot of people have had their hands on this book in its various forms and I wouldn't have it any other way.

First, I would like to thank my family. My wife, Ashlee, and the kids have been as supportive as I could ask for, even when writing time bites into family time.

I'd like to thank Steve Power for being a great beta reader, and a supportive brother. Not to be outdone, Kevin Woolridge is a bright spot of childish enthusiasm who tries to read everything I throw at him, but is always supportive.

Jon Mercer, brother, you did a fantastic job on the cover. Thank you. Now, get out there and do more, it's definitely your jam.

Thanks to Write Club, you wild and crazy bunch of talented miscreants. I miss our meetings in this time of COVID.

Thanks to Matt LeDrew, his writing classes, and those

that took part for helping me look at this old book in new ways.

Thanks to Engen Books who continue you to take a chance on my strange brand of writing.

And thanks to Brad Dunne for editing this book into fighting shape.

Finally, thanks to you. I hope you enjoyed the book.

Did you enjoy Bill Weston?
Read his continuing adventures -- as well as other short fiction
from author Jon Dobbin -- in Chillers from the Rock and
Dystopia from the Rock, on sale now from Engen Books.

The From the Rock series features short stories written by a
diverse mix of the best authors in Canada, including award-
winning veterans of their craft, and brand new talent.

Featuring the work of Ali House (The Segment Delta
Archives), Matthew LeDrew (Coral Beach Casefiles, The
Xander Drew series), Jon Dobbin (The Starving), and more!

Edited by Erin Vance and Ellen Curtis, these collections
showcases the talent, imagination, and prestige that Canada
has to offer. From stories of censorship gone awry to sentient
buses, global warming to corporate-branded culture, this
collection has it all!

THE XANDER DREW SERIES

COMING SOON FROM ENGEN BOOKS:

FATE'S SHADOW

A violent past case is reopened as Xander must contend with
Detective Thomas Horton, the vigilante Shadow Flame, and
a returning figure from his youth in Coral Beach -- all while
trying to prevent a murderer from running free. Can Xander
stay the course even as his world crashes in around him?

The early years of **Xander Drew** as he struggles with the evils of his small rural hometown of Coral Beach, Maine. Cursed with the heart of the Womb and the gift of seeing the world around him for what it really is, Xander must learn the hard lessons about the nature of humanity to traverse the minefield of criminals, gangs, and abusers that stand between him and ultimate happiness -- but most of all that **sometimes it takes a monster, to catch a monster.**

"THE WRITING OF ITS GENERATION- - VISUAL, TO-THE-POINT AND IN-THE-MOMENT."

- The Northeast Avalon Times

The Coral Beach Casefiles series by Matthew LeDrew:

For more information, please visit

www.engenbooks.com

ABOUT THE
AUTHOR

Jon Dobbin is an award winning author living in the St. John's, Newfoundland metro region.

He is a father of three, the husband to an amazing wife, an educator, and a tattoo and beard enthusiast.

Dobbin's work has appeared in the *Terror Nova, Chillers from the Rock, Dystopia from the Rock, Pulp Science-Fiction from the Rock, From the Rock Stars,* and, *Kit Sora: The Artobiography* collections. In 2019 he released his first novel, *The Starving*. In 2020 he released the fantasy adventure novel *The Broken Spire*.

The Risen is his third novel.